VAMPED

"*Vamped* is a total delight! Diver delivers a delightful cast of undead characters and a fresh, fast take on the vampire mythos. Next installment, please!"

—Rachel Caine, *New York Times* bestselling author of the Morganville Vampires series

"I really sunk my teeth into Lucienne Diver's *Vamped*. A fun, frothy, teenage romp with lots of action, a little shopping, and a cute vampire guy. Who could ask for more?"

—Marley Gibson, author of *Ghost Huntress: The Awakening*

"This book rollicked along, full of humor, romance, and action. Gina is a smart-aleck heroine worth reading about, a sort of teenage Besty Taylor *(Undead and Unwed)* with a lot of Cher Horowitz *(Clueless)* thrown in. Fans of Katie Maxwell will devour *Vamped*."

—Rosemary Clement-Moore, author of *Prom Dates from Hell*

"Move over Buffy! Lucienne Diver transfuses some fresh blood into the vampire genre. Feisty, fashionable, and fun—*Vamped* is a story readers will sink their teeth into and finish thirsty for more."

—Mari Mancusi, author of the Blood Coven Vampires series

"Those who enjoy a good giggle will respond eagerly to this brassy, campy romp."

"Teenagers will likely bite at the fun premise of Diver's YA debut, first in a planned series."

—*Publishers Weekly*

"A lighthearted, action-packed, vampire romance story following in the vein of Julie Kenner's Good Ghouls (Berkley), Marlene Perez's Dead (Harcourt), and Rachel Caine's The Morganville Vampires (Signet) series."

—*School Library Journal*

"Diver uses wit and adventure to hook readers with this teen vampire story, and the novel gives teen girls plenty of romance."

—*VOYA*

"*Vamped* is a delightful escape into the world of a rebellious teenage vampire. Readers will not only enjoy Gina, they'll want to be her."

—*Examiner.com*

ReVamped

"This is a witty vampire romance/adventure with plenty of heart and action. Diver has written a supernatural sequel to *Vamped* that will attract even reluctant readers. It is filled with wry twists, as well as all the typical agonies of being young and trying to fit in."

—*VOYA*

"Thoroughly enjoyable, this sequel is a light, fizzy read. Listening in on Gina's thoughts and quick-witted dialogue is what makes this such a treat."

—*Kirkus Reviews*

FANGTASTIC

"Gina never fails to please, as she strides down the runway of afterlife with just the right mix of humor, make-up advice, youthful lust that never crosses the line, and a kung-fu style all her own. *[Fangtastic]* doesn't miss a beat."
—*Kirkus Reviews*

"Gina has a biting, sarcastic voice that makes the *Vamped* books quick and entertaining reads."
—*VOYA*

"Diver spins an action-packed story that is filled with humor. Gina is a sassy heroine who tackles issues and challenges with proper vampire style."
—*School Library Journal*

"A welcome lighthearted departure from gloomy vampire romance."
—*Booklist*

To all of my drama club friends—
for friendship, belonging, and continued fabulosity.

LUCIENNE DIVER

fangtabulous

flux
™
Woodbury, Minnesota

First Edition
First Printing, 2013

Book format by Bob Gaul
Cover design by Lisa Novak
Cover art: Christ Church burial ground © iStockphoto.com/Les Byerley
        Girl © iStockphoto.com/M. Eric Honeycutt
        Woman © MIXA/PunchStock

Flux, an imprint of Llewellyn Worldwide Ltd.

Library of Congress Cataloging-in-Publication Data
Diver, Lucienne, 1971–
   Fangtabulous/Lucienne Diver.—1st ed.
      p. cm.—(Vamped; #4)
   Summary: Salem, Massachusetts seems like a great place for Gina Covello and her supernatural gang to hide, but they find the town crawling with ghosts, including the spirit of George Corwin, the infamous sheriff from the witch trial days.
   ISBN 978-0-7387-3150-6
[1. Supernatural—Fiction. 2. Vampires—Fiction. 3. Spies—Fiction. 4. Witches—Fiction. 5. Ghosts—Fiction. 6. Corwin, George, 1610–1684 or 5—Fiction. 7. Salem (Mass.)—Fiction.] I. Title.
   PZ7.D6314Fak 2013
   [Fic]—dc23
                                                    2012030547

Flux
Llewellyn Worldwide Ltd.
2143 Wooddale Drive
Woodbury, MN 55125-2989
www.fluxnow.com

Printed in the United States of America

Acknowledgments

I first have to thank my wonderful family, especially my husband Peter and my son Ty, who endured lots of "I can't do XYZ until the book is in!" You're all so supportive, and I love you.

Next and very especially, I have to thank Don "Vlad" Deich, who does a great Gothic Magic Show like the one featured here, for showing me around Salem and introducing me to the behind-the-scenes reality. (BTW, you should totally check out more about him at www.gothicmagic.com.) I want to thank Deborah Blake for her invaluable input and equally invaluable friendship, and so, so many other people for being my readers, friends, and cheerleaders over the years: Amy Christine Parker, Lynn Flewelling, Su Minamide, Faith Hunter, Martha Ramirez, Joshua Kane, and Abby Feder-Kane. I also want to fall at the feet of Rachel Caine, Rosemary Clement-Moore, Marley Gibson, and Mari Mancusi, who gave me great quotes to kickstart the series and who are lovely people and writers to watch. And my fans! OMG, you keep me going with your letters and emails. Please keep them coming. I love to hear from you!

Some of the many places I visited in Salem that you might want to check out include Count Orlok's Nightmare Gallery, the Witch Dungeon Museum, the House of the Seven Gables, the Witch House, and the Old Burying Point cemetery. Also, if you're a goth (or a closet goth, as we begin to suspect Marcy might be), you might want to visit Fool's Mansion and Life and Death in Salem, which may have inspired the Morbid Gift Shop in *Fangtabulous* a teensy bit. Enjoy!

A Brief and Bloody, or Fair and Fabulous, or Short and Stylish … History of Salem, Massachusetts

Everyone knows that Salem, Massachusetts, was if not founded then at least overrun by a sect of colorblind cultists* who had never seen a single episode of *Project Runway* or *What Not to Wear*. And that a batch of bad bread or boredom led to some young girls cavorting around like they were in the throes of Bieber-mania and blaming it on women (mostly) who they claimed consorted with the devil. Really, these women had the audacity to be different or to tick off one of the girls. One was even, wait for it, known to *wear red*.** That's right, the Salem witch trials claim fame for one of the first true fashion victims. By the time the ghoulish girls finally accused just the wrong person and lost their approval rating, twenty people had been put to death on their say-so alone, and almost that many more had died or gone mad in prison.

Oh, yeah, a lot of other historical stuff went on in and around Salem too, like international trade on the tall ships, which led to America's first millionaire long before anyone thought to ask who wanted to marry one and to televise the answer. And like Nathaniel Hawthorne, who you reader-types might know for stuff like *The Scarlet Letter* and "Young Goodman Brown," but who I remember best for a horrifying story we had to read back in the eighth grade where a woman's psycho husband performs surgery to remove her one imperfection and ends up killing her instead. Like perfection and woman couldn't survive together on this earth or some sexist thing. ("The Birthmark," in case you're wondering.)

But now? Modern-day Salem? One of the most haunted places in America and somewhere, we hoped, where a few vampires, a mad scientist, and a reformed Fed with a touch of magical mojo could blend in without drawing too much attention. As it turns out, we were wrong. But it wasn't our fault. Really...

Bobby's notes:

*The Puritans were not colorblind, but were—how should I say it?—ascetics. (Gina's giving me a *huh* look, so let me try again...If it looked good or felt good, it was probably a sin.)

**This was Bridget Bishop, first person put to death in the trials. Not only did she have red hair and clothing, she was said to drink and was known to play that morally bankrupt game of shuffleboard, still beloved by the seaworthy over-sixty set.

1

Did you know that Nathaniel Hawthorne added the *w* to his last name to distance himself from his ancestor, Judge John Hathorne, who participated in the Salem witch trials?" Bobby asked—the world at large, I guessed, since no one in the van was actually listening. He'd had his head buried in a visitor's guide—damn vampire night vision—since he'd picked it up at the last rest stop and kept spouting these pearls of wisdom. "When asked what it stood for, he answered *wicked*."

Marcy gave me a look that practically begged me to get my guy under control.

"And did you know that—"

"Stop!" she said finally. "You're giving me a history headache. Just because you're dating my BFF doesn't mean I won't end you."

That got Bobby's attention. He popped his head out of the book and looked around the van at the rest of us—Eric, the mad scientist of the group and our getaway driver; Nelson, his nephew who'd been body-swapped with a vampire twice his height and was still getting used to his new body; my gal pal Marcy, who put the *vamp* in vampire; her boyfriend Brent, telemetric and former Fed; and last but so not least, *me*, Gina Covello, fashionista of the fanged.

"You going to let her talk to me like that?" Bobby asked me.

"Well, someone had to. Besides, I'm giving you credit. I figure that if it comes to a cage match, you can take her."

Brent snorted and Marcy protested. "Hey!"

"*Children*," Eric said through gritted teeth, "don't make me pull this van over."

"And what?" Marcy challenged. "Spank us?"

We all looked at Eric.

"Well, I hadn't really thought that far ahead," he answered, sparing a glance from the road to all of us. "But I suppose I could start with an impromptu lecture on the very painful and public ways they used to deal with fighting in the Middle Ages..."

We all groaned, and Eric turned back to the road with a smirk.

I smacked Bobby. "See what you started? Is that what you're going to be like when you're older, because I have to say, totally not attractive."

"Gee, thanks," Eric said dryly.

Bobby looked at me with those big blue puppy-dog eyes, the ones that had made me throw caution to the wind back at our after-prom party, where I'd ended up necking with him in the broom closet ... a make-out session that led to some eerily eternal consequences. Giving in to Bobby's magical mojo had lost me my old life and set me up in a new one, as a super-spy/slave to the Feds. Until I'd bought a clue. It turned out I really didn't want to be part of any club that would have me as a member, especially when we discovered they performed experiments on my kind for fun and profit. So we'd destroyed one of their torture chambers and were now on the run, public enemies #1-6. Yeah, giving in to those baby blues hadn't exactly done wonders for my social life so far.

On the plus side, I finally had minions.

"Oh, stop with the eyes already. You know I lo—adore you," I said testily, turning to look out the window. Some days I was convinced that while men might be from Mars, geek-boys were from farther off, like a galaxy far, far away. The fact that I'd even made a reference like that—a *Star Wars* reference, for goodness sake—meant that maybe we'd been spending a little too much time together. Maybe the true test of a relationship was whether you could spend two days cooped up together in a van and not kill each other. The jury was still out on that one.

"So, Eric, I just gotta ask—are we there yet?" I crouched at the console between the driver's and passenger's seats, staring at him hopefully. Nelson was playing copilot as the rest of us banged around in the seatless area at the back of the van.

"Almost."

"How 'bout now?" Marcy added.

Eric growled and she grinned, tension diffused.

Bobby read the visitor's guide silently after that, and I continued to squat oh-so-ladylike at the console, watching road signs and trying to get the lay of the land. I hadn't learned much in super spy club training beyond lock-picking, a certain amount of stealth, and the punishment for giving my fatigues a miracle makeover, but I'd always known how to pay attention. Except maybe in history class. Or physics. Or...anyway, I'd never been to New England before. I'd always thought of it as a place where squinty-eyed fishermen smoked pipes, wore cable-knit sweaters, and talked like Captain Ahab or Popeye the Sailor. But, of course, none of them were materializing out of the midnight mist draped in seaweed and babbling in gibberish about the one that got away. Nope, the ride was not nearly so interesting. We were on a road like any other. Signs and signals, uninspired waystations, and the occasional billboard. The most exciting thing I saw was the sign that announced

Salem 10
Danvers 13

Miles, I presumed, and not some kind of grudge match scoreboard.

"Salem can't be very big then," I said to Eric, nodding toward the sign.

"It isn't. Not that I recall," he answered.

Danger signs flashed before my eyes. "*You've been there?*"

The whole idea of running off to Salem was for anonymity. It was supposed to be a place where no one would think to look for us. Not the Feds and not the vampire council that, I admit, had plenty of good reason to want us dead and out of their fanged fraternity.

"As a kid," he said. "Don't worry. It was a family road trip and we were just passing through. There's nothing to connect me and no one to remember."

I relaxed and watched as we turned off, finally, onto a smaller street that slowly gave way from diner/gas station combos to New England–type houses, mostly one or two stories with sharply sloped roofs to encourage the snow to slide off. Maybe it was just the darkness, but the town color palette appeared to be grim and grimmer-er. Grays, browns, and brick.

The streets were narrow and seemed to change names inexplicably—from town to town?—without a turn or any other sort of indicator. Eric just kept following the signs for Salem Center.

"Nelson, you have the directions?" he asked.

His nephew reached into a pocket and pulled out a folded piece of paper. Loose-leaf, covered in scrawl. So retro. "Got 'em."

"Good."

Bobby came up and settled beside me as Nelson read out twists and turns. We watched silently as we passed signs for the Witch House, the Witch Dungeon, the Old Burying Point cemetery, the Witch History Museum. I was sensing a theme.

Bobby put a hand to my neck, gently sliding his fingers through my hair and caressing my nape. I tingled everywhere he touched. He had that effect on me. There was magic in those hands. And lips. And ... well, everything. It was just that sometimes I was reminded that we were from two different worlds. I could debate the finer points of style, while his fashion IQ stopped at admiration of Princess Leia's bronze bikini. Gah, two *Star Wars* references in one car ride. It was like the road trip from hell. But still, those hands ... I moved away from them before I could start purring and totally embarrass myself.

"What did your guy say about our contact in Salem?" Bobby asked, reluctantly letting me go.

"I have an address, a name, and the fact that he runs the Gothic Magic Show. There really wasn't time for anything else."

"What with the biting and all," Bobby said, avoiding eye contact.

I stared at him until he looked at me again. "Are we back to that?" I asked. "The whole kiss-of-death thing was the price of admission. You know that."

"Yeah, I also know how well that worked out for you last time."

Okay, looking back, the first time I'd bestowed the kiss eternal had been a mistake. Rick-the-rat, one of our former classmates, had gone over to the dark side—aligned with the council vamps, who thought humans should be beaten and eaten without even the benefit of fava beans and a nice chianti. But Hunter, one of the Tampa-area vampire lifestylers—also known in medical circles as Charles Orl-off, DDS—was different. I hoped. And anyway, when you turned against two really powerful groups like the fangs and Feds, you weren't left with a huge pool of potential allies. Hunter had been willing to help us ... for a price.

"Sure, rub that in," I huffed. "Anyway, since you turned me, and I turned Rick, he's kind of your grandbaby, so don't come crying to me about the way he turned out."

"By your logic, I'm macking on my own daughter," Bobby said, licking his lips at me.

"Okay, ewww." I pushed him, and he tumbled over onto his butt. "Let's just call me a self-made vamp."

"Agreed." He reached out a hand for me to pull him up, but when I grabbed it, he yanked, and I went sprawling down beside him. "Ha, gotcha!"

"Oh, you think so?" I knew all his ticklish spots, and I wasn't afraid to use them. Oh yes, vamps can giggle. Fear us.

"Children," Eric barked out.

"What?" Bobby asked, gasping for breath. "She started it."

"We're there."

Bobby sat up, suddenly no longer ticklish. When I pouted,

he raised my fingertips to his lips and kissed them. I got all warm and tingly in the general vicinity of my heart.

I looked around. We were in a parking garage like you'd see in any big city, which was weird. Even weirder, it was almost to capacity, even at the midnight hour. We were on the top level before we found a parking spot. But like in any civilized city on the planet, there was a sign on the wall saying *This Way to the Mall*, so it was easy enough to find our path.

"Mall!" Marcy and I said together.

"Holla!" she added, and we clapped in an explosive high-five.

"His friend does a magic show in a *mall*?" Bobby asked.

"You have something against the mall?" I asked, giving him the evil eye. "Not highbrow enough for you?"

It was so much fun to watch his face contort as he tried to come up with an answer that I had to laugh. "Nevermind, let's go shopping!"

"Down, girl," Nelson said, like he was as old as the body he wore. "Contact first. Besides, we're not exactly rolling in dough right now."

"Rolling—dough—I get it," said Marcy dryly. "Really, you're a laugh riot."

"*Children*," Eric said again.

"Okay." Brent's voice cut across the banter like a lash. "Everybody move out. Go, go, go. Nelson, you take point. I'll bring up the rear." He opened the back panels of the van and waved us through.

We all looked at each other, shrugged, and followed orders, although Bobby whispered in Brent's ear on the way past.

"Fine," he barked. "You bring up the rear then. Everyone else, move out."

Made sense. Brent was, after all, human, and thus vulnerable, while Bobby was, if not bulletproof, then at least bullet-resistant. He had some really major mojo and could stop stuff in its tracks if he knew it was coming, and he could also influence and cloud men's minds like some comic-book super hero. Plus, if anything *did* get through to him, he'd heal, as long as it didn't decapitate him or pierce his heart with wood. Of course, that healing part was something all of us vamps had in common, which was probably why Nelson took the lead. Marcy and I would have done just as well, only we were at least half a head shorter than Nelson's hulking husk. The vamp that Nelson's body used to belong to was named Xander; Nelson's own body, piloted by Xander's consciousness, had gone on a little killing spree and was now enjoying downtime in some Federal facility. As far as we knew.

"What kind of mall *is* this?" Marcy asked.

"A tourist-town mall," Bobby answered reasonably. "At the shore you get seashells and beachwear. In Salem you get witches and pentagrams."

"Oh, *that* Salem," Marcy said. "I was thinking about the place where they make the cigarettes."

Brent coughed, and we all immediately looked to see if he'd covered the smile quickly enough or if he was about to get whapped ... or both. Marcy didn't seem to have caught the smile, but she pounded on Brent's back to help him over his cough. From the way he winced, I figured she'd forgotten about her vamp strength.

"I think that's Winston-Salem," Bobby said. "North Carolina."

I covered my own smile and looked around. I saw what Marcy meant. The mall consisted of a Thai restaurant, T-shirt and souvenir shops, and some kiosks of bling and things, but everything else was Halloween-themed, even though we were only at the tail end of September. It was like Christmas carols blasted before Thanksgiving or Easter bunnies in August. The goth gang from my first-ever mission would have loved it. I felt a little pang of loss. Somehow, they'd gotten under my skin, like a sentimental splinter.

"There it is," I called, spotting the place Hunter had told us about. The Morbid Gift Shop. Inside it was dark, but not so dark that we couldn't see the old-fashioned punishment cage with a full skeleton inside, an arm hanging through the bars as though it had died begging for a hand-out.

"Cool!" Nelson said. "Let's go in."

We pushed through the door, and the humans among us let their eyes adjust. Nelson looked right past the browsing customers and made for the display of skulls and potions on the far wall. I had to remind myself he'd been a teenaged vampire lifestyler before he became a Cro-Magnon vamp dude with an overabundance of jawline and a body like someone had merged a linebacker with Lurch from *The Addams Family*.

In addition to the cage, the gift shop's collection of the macabre included a life-sized coffin set atop a wooden cart displayed in the window catty-corner to where we'd entered. Brent accidentally brushed up against it when he moved out of the way of a bevy of browsers squeezing past him toward the door. He flinched as he made contact, which was totally weird. Sure, Brent could read the histories of things with a bare touch, but *bare* was the operative word. He knew better. Except for his face, he had everything covered: dark-wash jeans, navy pea coat, gloves, and watch cap.

Marcy took him in hand, and since he was her boyfriend, thus her problem, I let myself get distracted by a display of bling, which on closer examination turned out to be shrunken heads, bats, and sparkly spiders. The fashionista in me did a little recoil. In my mind, the line should be drawn at bejeweled bugs. More intriguing were the black velvet chokers the next rack over with garnet drops (or pretty good imitations thereof) cascading from the side, as though to simulate the blood dripping from vampire bites. As if we'd be so wasteful. Still, they were pretty, and I thought *what better way to hide being a vamp than to go around looking like a victim?* Maybe I could convince the others to part with some funds in the name of blending in.

"May I help you?" asked a voice, nearly in my ear. I jumped, like a half inch, just enough to play girly, because, really, I'd totally seen him coming.

I put a hand to my heart and looked up at him through long, dark, perfectly natural lashes. It was a stunner not to have to look up too far. At five foot nothin', I was used to four-inch heels or a permanent crick in the neck.

"Yes, thank you." I answered, returning a choker to the rack. "We're looking for Donato."

The guy who'd snuck up eyed me with heavily kohl-lined eyes. He wasn't just under-tall, he was celery-stalk thin on top of it. His pants were black, baggy, and overly pocketed. A chain dangled from a belt loop to his back pocket, probably linked up to a wallet, making me wonder how painful it must be for him to sit. His T-shirt had a graphic of a dove-gray skull with a diamondback snake weaving in and out of the eye sockets, providing the only spot of color in an otherwise monochromatic ensemble. In short, his outfit was consistent with what all the cool goth guys were wearing this season.

I was in stealth hottie mode myself, which is to say I'd had to leave all my couture behind when we went on the run. I was currently rocking a girly version of a sports tee—a pale blue scoop-neck with white piping around the neck and down the sleeves and the number eighty-eight emblazoned across my chest. I had no idea what it stood for, but the shirt clung to me in all the right places. My mother would have needed a Valium if she'd ever learned I'd shopped off the rack . . . at a rest stop, no less . . . but beggars/choosers and all that jazz.

"You're friends with Donato?" he asked, like he doubted it.

"More like family, really."

He cocked an eyebrow, spiky piercing rising all the way to his hairline.

"Hunter sent us," I added.

"You're going to have to be more specific."

"From Tampa." Geez, you wouldn't think the name "Hunter" would be so hot with pretend vampires, although I supposed it beat "Slayer."

"Well then." He smiled, and that "Schizophrenic Psycho" song from the radio went through my head. If we were here on one of our super-spy missions, he'd be at the very top of my watch list. "Follow me."

We all followed him to the curtained archway at the back of the store that I'd been too distracted by bling to attend to before. Psycho had probably come straight through that curtain when he'd snuck up on me. Okay, maybe it was unfair of me to think of him that way. I didn't actually *know* he was a psycho. Vamps didn't have an app for that.

"I didn't catch your name," I said as he pushed aside a heavy black curtain. It had to be sound-muffling or surely we'd have twigged to the fact that there was a whole performance, audience and all, going on in the back.

"Chip," he whispered, so as not to disrupt the show.

"Chip—really?" I asked, just as quietly.

"Yeah, like the one on your shoulder," he answered. "Now, shhh."

Oh, sure, *I* was the one with a chip on my shoulder.

But I hushed, mostly because I wanted to catch what was happening on stage. I moved aside so the others could get in, and we ended up lining the wall between the theater area and the gift shop. If our entrance disrupted the show, we couldn't tell. On stage—well, at floor-level in front of the rows of filled seats—was a tall man dressed all in black but for a white poet shirt complete with ruffles. His jacket was an old-timey cut, like something out of *A Christmas Carol*. His black hair was long and framed a vampire-pale face. Ice-blue eyes too cool for reality challenged the audience to see through the illusion that he was performing. The *probable* illusion—we'd seen enough real magic to know that it existed. But could books really bleed? Color me skeptical. I sniffed. Well, if they did bleed, it was stage blood. My fangs stayed sheathed. Anyway, I preferred practical magic, like the kind that zapped zits on contact.

My gaze wandered, but only got as far as the assistant striding to center stage to remove the bleeding book. There was something familiar about the assistant, which was not at all a comforting thought. If Donato looked like something out of Charles Dickens, his partner was a character out of *Oliver Twist*. Wait, was that still Dickens? Anyway, he had those scruffy fingerless gloves on, a shabby coat, a cap pulled low at a jaunty angle, and a half-mask, like on all the posters I'd ever seen for *The Phantom of the Opera*. I couldn't see enough for him to remind me of anyone, so why was I so sure... something in his walk? He was cocky and confident, tall but not freakishly so. I felt a weird flutter in the pit of my stomach.

I was so taken with the mystery man that I missed what triggered all the applause, but suddenly the audience was in a frenzy of appreciation, and Donato was bowing his thanks. I'd missed the finale, whatever it was.

Marcy had to nudge me with her elbow to move me away from the wall so that we could let the audience out past us.

Donato and his assistant remained on stage, greeting a few friends and admirers who'd hung behind. I and my minions stepped behind the stragglers, not calling attention to ourselves, but I felt the assistant's stare on me anyway. If this wasn't one of those lust-at-first-sight moments when you catch a stranger's eye across a crowded room, we had a problem. If he had any connection to the fangs or Feds who were after us, we'd be in big, big trouble. Possibly even fatal.

Marcy looked from the masked man to me and back. "You know him?" she whispered.

There was something about the way those eyes sparked and glinted, something about the quirk to the one side of his lips that I could see... "Maybe," I whispered back.

"Introduce me?"

I nudged her with my hip. "You're taken."

"So are you," she pointed out, not wrongly.

I tore my gaze away just as the last of the stragglers let out a hearty laugh and moved on. As the exit/entryway curtain closed behind them, Donato turned his ice-blue eyes on us. His assistant reached up to remove his hat with one hand and his mask with the other, and flipped his hair back to reveal a truly breathtaking sight—Ulric, my goth guy from New York. Nosy. Insufferable. Blood like mulled cider. Here, in the flesh.

2

Donato stirred his coffee, apparently perfectly okay with being out in public in full costume. Except for those who greeted him as he entered, no one in the well-filled café gave him a second glance. The woman at the coffee counter had known his order without even asking. It arrived in a cup the size of a swimming pool and had some kind of mystic spiral swirled into the foam. Ulric and Eric had opted for plain black coffee, and the rest of us, except for Brent, who still looked oddly shaky and alert, went drinkless. I wasn't thirsty ... for coffee. Not that I could drink it anyway. But if bleeding books didn't do it for me, Ulric certainly did, and my fangs had been at half-mast ever since he'd ripped off his mask. I'd tasted him once back on that very first mission. I'd needed the blood so very badly, and he was there. And willing. And, okay, hot. But even though we were bloodsuckers, and Bobby *should* understand—hell, he'd made me that way—I knew he wouldn't.

Ulric had taken care to arrange things so that he'd sit beside me. I made sure not to look at him, for fear something would show on my face. Then I feared the lack of eye contact would be telling and glanced up when I thought I'd felt his attention shift. I was wrong. Immediately our eyes met, aventurine green (mine) to topaz (his).

Ulric leaned toward me. "I knew you couldn't stay away."

"Oh yeah, like I knew you'd be here. If anything, you're a total liability for me. Maybe I should just take you out."

"I'm free tonight," he said, eyes twinkling, just as they'd done right through the mask.

"Not in the fun way," I hissed, exasperated.

He gave me a slow, intimate grin, and I had to look away . . . straight into Bobby's frowny face. I debated sticking my tongue out at him, because I was totally my own person and he had no say in it if every once in a while I got my head a little turned by some stone-cold hottie. I wasn't dead . . . well, except maybe in the technical sense. To stake his claim, Bobby blew me a kiss across the table.

Ulric couldn't help but notice. Yet, undeterred, he leaned in close, his mouth right up next to my ear to ask, "You're here because of that girl, aren't you?"

It wasn't exactly the sweet nothing I'd been expecting, which meant the intimacy part was completely for Bobby's benefit.

I pulled away from him. "What girl?"

"The one who was murdered last night," Ulric answered, watching me with those deep amber eyes to see if I was playing him with my ignorance. I half-wondered if he was some kind of human lie-detector. I'd met one before, and Ulric *had* nearly blown my cover back in New York when he'd figured me out.

"We're not here about any girl," I said honestly.

"Ah, then it must be my wolfish charm. I knew it!"

I punched him in the arm, but that only got me a grin as wolfish as previously advertised.

Bobby wasn't the only one watching us. Brent looked like he'd tried to eat a lemon whole. I knew it was bad that I'd been recognized, but I didn't see what I could do about it at the moment. Maybe we'd decide we had to move on. Maybe we wouldn't. After all, Ulric hadn't given me away the last time. He'd even helped me on my mission. His leer said that he might be willing to do so again.

A hand reached across me into Ulric's line of vision, flashing long, shapely nails in Plum Passion. "Since Gina's too rude to introduce us, I'll have to do it for myself," Marcy purred. "I'm Marcy, her BFF."

Real names? Was she crazy? Second thought, silly question.

"*Marley*," I said with emphasis.

Ulric took her hand, and instead of shaking, pressed his lips to it. "Enchanted," he said, staring deeply into her eyes and then sliding a glance toward me, as if to see whether I was jealous. So not.

"I can't believe *Gia* didn't tell me *all* about you," Marcy said, emphasizing right back for good measure.

Apparently, the only people who weren't fascinated by Ulric were Eric and Nelson, who were deep in conversation with Donato about his act. Eric, who had a very special gift for gadgetry, was trying to wheedle out of Donato some of the tricks of the trade, and Donato was staying mysteriously mum. I didn't think Eric would appreciate me wrecking the flow of his interrogation, but it was getting late and we needed to figure out a place to stay, if indeed we were staying and my reunion with Ulric hadn't compromised us all.

Even if it had ... Bobby could probably find a way to fade Ulric's memories of me or something. We didn't have many more options. Being on the run meant that we couldn't access our bank accounts or credit cards without leading our pursuers right to us. We only had the funds that'd been on us when we bolted, which meant we were bottoming out on cash. New identities would cost us an arm and a leg, and while the vamps among us might be super healers, I wasn't totally sure whether our bodies would regrow the appendages or just smooth over the stumps. And I was totally not willing to experiment.

"You all right?" Ulric asked, no doubt catching the odd look on my face. Also, no doubt deciding it had something to do with him. Gah, *men*.

"Yeah, just ... it's late. We still don't have a place to stay. Plus, you weren't supposed to be here. You can absolutely not, *on penalty of death*, tell any of the old gang that we're here. Or let anyone know that you knew me ... before."

"I'm pretty sure Donato's figured it out," Ulric said helpfully.

Hearing his name, Donato finally looked up from his conversation and I was able to catch Eric's eye. I didn't have my boy Bobby's mental messaging system, but Eric nodded anyway like he totally got it.

"So, Donato," Eric began, "Hunter said you'd find us a place to stay and help us get established?"

Donato seemed to size us all up before turning those frosty eyes back on Eric. "Hunter also said you might not mind a bargain?"

Eric didn't look a bit sure about that, but he nodded.

"Then I've got just the place for you."

• • •

We drove a little way down the road, to the nearby town of Danvers, and were now standing in front of an old brick building with arched windows on the first floor and smallish barred windows the rest of the way up. It looked like it had once been an institutional building of some sort—governmental, maybe, the kind of place where an office party meant that you took the cake back to your cubicle to eat. But the sign outside said Ravenswood Apartments.

"Wow, this is ... grim," Brent said, eying the place as we waited for Donato to open the outer doors.

Ulric, thankfully, had been sent back to clean up at the shop and get everything ready for the next day's show, but he'd left with a wink and a promise that we'd meet again. Bobby bristled. He and I held hands now as we stood in the cold, the breeze blowing my dark hair across my face, nearly blinding me. I tucked it behind an ear, but it insisted on escape.

"Well, just wait," Donato insisted. "The place used to be a psychiatric facility, way back when. Actually, it only closed in the 1970s when certain, um, problems came to light. It was shut down for a while, but a few years ago a developer got ahold of it and turned it into apartments. It's been completely revamped and refurbished. Very modern."

"So what's the catch?" Eric asked. "You don't rent out brand new apartments at discount prices."

"They've had a little trouble filling one or two of the basement units—not enough natural light and all." He had the outer doors open and hurried on with his spiel as if to discourage more questions. "The lobby door is always locked. Residents have to buzz visitors in. It's very secure."

The lobby *was* well-lit and lined with marble ... or faux marble. I was no expert. At least not as far as nonwearable rocks, but give me precious or semi-precious stones any day of the week ... seriously. Not just an expression.

He led us down a set of stairs toward the basement, still talking, but I'd lost track and anyway, it was clear he wasn't getting to the heart of things. "Uh huh," I cut in. "What aren't you telling us?"

Donato looked back at me and then away again with a shrug. "The place *might* be haunted. If you believe in that sort of thing."

"Says the guy who makes books bleed," I muttered. "What else? For some people, a haunting might just add a little thrill."

"Guess we haven't found the right kind of people." With a flourish, he whipped open the door we'd come to and flicked on the lights. We all pushed in to see a spacious unit. There were almost-immediate steps down to a sunken living room, complete with couch, coffee table, and empty entertainment center.

"It's mostly furnished," Donato said unnecessarily.

"It came furnished or the last tenants abandoned it, stuff and all?" I asked.

"Does it matter?"

I'd have given him a *hells yeah* but Brent got there first. "This doesn't feel right," he said, a funny sound to his voice, almost like he was speaking through a long tube, even though he was right there beside us. He'd been funny ever since we'd first gotten into town. Or at least since we'd first exited the van and entered the mall. Marcy raised a hand to rub his back and he actually flinched.

"Hence the cheap," Donato answered, unconcerned. "My friend at the management company has agreed to a short-term lease. If you decide to stay, well, the rent is negotiable. I've, ah, got another friend who does ritual cleansings if you need one."

"What about exorcisms?" Brent muttered.

"Who are you helping?" Bobby asked, pure steel in his voice. "Your friend or us?"

"Hopefully both," Donato answered, meeting his gaze without so much as a blink. "Real estate is at a premium around here, close to Boston and Salem. On short notice, with no references or credit check, this is the best I can do for you. Take it or leave it."

Bobby and I both looked at Brent and back to each other. We weren't too afraid of whatever else might go bump in the night. After all, we'd mostly be up and about, sleeping during the day when any spirits from the asylum would most likely be off-duty. But the non hemo-sapiens, they were another matter, and it looked like Brent was going to bear the brunt of things. Unfortunately, Donato had a point about our options, which were going on nil.

"Ulric mentioned a murdered girl," I said into the sudden silence. "It didn't happen here, did it?"

I watched Donato extra closely this time, waiting to see if he'd give anything away, but, if anything, he actually seemed to relax. "No. That was back in Salem by the Old Jail. One of only a handful of murders in Salem in the past hundred years."

"How did she die?" Marcy asked.

"Strangled with her own necklace," he answered.

Marcy's hand went to her neck as though with sympathy pains. "Did they catch the guy?"

"Not yet."

This time the look that got passed around was a little more all-inclusive, but Brent settled it with a shrug. We'd give things a try. What choice did we have?

"Any chance you can hook us up with new IDs?" he asked Donato.

"I'm not a magician."

Brent cocked a brow at him.

"Not that kind anyway. I don't think I'm going to be much help to you there, but I'll put out feelers. I'll be subtle." Said the man in the poufy shirt.

We left Eric to talk terms, and the rest of us went to explore the other rooms. There was one off to the right— an eat-in kitchen, as bare as Mother Hubbard's cupboard— and three to the left—two bedrooms and a bath, all painted builder's white, which was dull enough to scare anyone off, ghosts or no. Brent poked his head back out into the living room.

"It gets worse," he announced to Eric. "There's only two bedrooms. No beds, but there's a mattress up against one wall."

"We'll give that to the girls," he answered. "The boys'll have to bunk down in the other room.

I was about to lodge a protest when Bobby piped up. "Gina and I will take the couch."

"Dibs on the mattress!" Marcy called, ducking back into that room and pulling Brent in with her.

I socked Bobby in the arm for not thinking of it first.

3

Besides the haunted apartment, Donato had one more trick up his sleeve—some potential job leads. I always thought I'd be walking a runway or, given my lack of stature, a hand or foot model at the very least ... or neck. I had a pretty, swanlike neck, especially for someone my size. It was probably why Bobby'd felt the need to gnaw on it at that fatal after-prom party. Tour Guide of the Damned had never even popped up on my radar as a job prospect. But Ulric moonlighted at a place called Haunts in History, and apparently there were positions available.

The next night, when Bobby and I presented ourselves to Kari-with-a-K at Haunts, she instantly proclaimed that we'd do, handed us each a garment bag from a rack in her shop, and sent us off toward the changing area. Haunts was located in the same mall as the Morbid Gift Shop and specialized in old-timey photographs by day and ghost tours by night. Bobby and I had to wait out the last of the picture-taking tourists already occupying the dressing rooms to get all retro. If the costumes fit and we could look the parts, I guess we were hired.

My eyes grew wide as the first tourist emerged from behind the privacy curtain, and I turned to Bobby in whispered horror. "Oh no, I am *not* going around looking like the Sun-Maid Raisin girl!"

My voice must have risen at the end, because Bobby slapped a hand over my mouth, which did nothing to ease my panic. He let me go as the tourists cleared the area, shooting us none-too-certain glances like we might just possibly bite. Which, of course, we might.

"The Sun-Maid Raisin girl?" he asked quietly as they left. "I don't know what you're talking about. I think she's supposed to be a Quaker."

"Yeah, and—?"

"And Salem was settled by Puritans."

"The difference would be?"

"As far as I know, the Quakers never hung anyone for witchcraft."

I blinked. So we were expected to be not only stylistically challenged but murderous as well. Go us!

"Come on, Gina, you've worn worse," Bobby cajoled.

I had, actually—specifically, a black vinyl dress that had melted into my body on our last mission for the Feds. It had nearly become one with my skin. I shuddered. "Not helping,"

I told him. But I ducked inside the dressing room all the same. Maybe I could find a way to work it. I mean, guys seemed to have a thing about librarians and Catholic school girls. Could Puritans really be that far off?

I pulled up the plastic wrap on my costume. Oh yeah, worlds apart.

Beneath the garment cover was a white granny gown under a dirt-brown skirt and bodice. Oh, with a matching white bonnet. That made *all* the difference. I scowled at the costume and I swear it scowled right back.

"How's it coming?" came an overly cheery voice from outside. Kari-with-a-K.

"Almost there," I called back.

I peeked out to see Bobby already in his pilgrim suit or whatever. He had a yuck-brown shirt with a wide white collar, short-pants with a buckle just below the knee, and hose covering his calves. Somehow, all that brown made his eyes look even bluer. Or maybe it was something about the lighting.

"Hey, no fair you getting to show more leg than me," I said.

Bobby caught my curtain and pulled it back for a look. "No fair that you're not already stripped down and getting into your Sunday best."

"Make up your mind. Which way do you want me— stripped down or suited up?" I started to unzip my jeans and shimmy them down my hips while he watched.

"Is that even a question?" Bobby's eyes and even nostrils flared.

I started to pull my shirt over my head, and Bobby backed out before . . . well, before things could get crazy. Most guys would have stayed for the show. I liked to think he was afraid of being overcome with lust in a public place at the very sight of me. Probably, though, it was his own Puritanical streak and thoughts about appropriate behavior and other such humbug.

When I stepped out, he was swinging a little half cape over one shoulder and finishing off the look with a wide-brimmed hat.

"You're about the sexiest thing since Harrison Ford in *Witness*," I told him.

"I think they were Amish."

I stuck my tongue out at him. I knew he couldn't help himself, but *sheesh*.

Kari swooped in on us without warning. "Let's take a look!"

Her eyes went cartoonishly wide at the sight of us, and she actually clapped her hands together like a little girl who believed in fairies. "Perfect! You look almost like the real Mary Warren, though she could never have let all that gorgeous hair flow free. With you it would be almost a crime to contain it," she said, tucking a few stray locks of jet hair up under my bonnet, though the rest tumbled down my back to my waist. "And *you*!" She studied Bobby like she wanted to eat him all up. "Gorgeous, even if you are kind of the villain . . . the dreaded Sheriff Corwin."

Bobby looked as sick as I felt. "But . . . really? Couldn't I be Giles Corey or one of the good guys?"

"Few enough of them," Kari said, the light in her eyes dimming. "No one in Salem wanted to stand against the accusing girls. The few who dared suggest they might be lying wanted to beat the truth out of them. Besides," she said, her smile creeping back, "Old Giles Corey was eighty when he was accused. You're hardly that, m'dear. Come on, there's a tour about to start. Ulric can show you the ropes. No, no, don't change. You're perfect the way you are."

Bobby was such a white knight, I could tell the Sheriff Corwin thing weighed on him.

"Don't worry about being a baddy," I whispered. "I'd let you interrogate me any time." I had to stand on my tippy toes to reach his ears. He was kind of magnificently tall, like six-foot. My old friend Becca back home had always complained that short girls got all the tall guys. I preferred the word "petite" to "short," but as far as I was concerned, all the best things came in small packages . . . diamonds, charm bracelets, rings and things.

Bobby smiled and kissed my upturned nose, stroking a hand down my free-flowing hair. I shivered—because he was Bobby and it felt good, *not* because he was playing a hanging judge and I had the sudden sense of someone walking over my grave. I wasn't in it, anyway.

We stepped with Kari into the midst of the tour group that had formed while we were getting all ridiculously retro. The folks at the back turned to look at us, and Bobby and I nodded, but they quickly faced forward again as Ulric called them to order, except for one woman who raised a camera. I quickly pulled Bobby to me, as if I had a secret to tell him, averting our faces. I wondered whether our costumes would show up in the photo without us, or if the whole shot would go wonky, or what.

"Hear ye, hear ye," Ulric was saying. "The seven p.m. Haunts in History tour is about to begin." He must have been standing on a soapbox or something, because he towered above everybody else, and his voice carried back to us. "Your guide, Philip English, at your service." Ulric gave a theatrical bow, and I thought I heard a sigh from somewhere in the tour group. "I'm here to take you through the trials and tribulations—natural and, most especially, unnatural—that befell Salem and its surroundings in its darkest days. The year was 1692..."

I looked over at Bobby, thinking to ask him who Philip English might be, but he shushed me, concentrating on Ulric's speech, probably already memorizing it word for word. I was going to need CliffsNotes, and maybe even a cheat sheet, but it was a pretty good spiel. And Ulric had just the right voice for it, smooth and rich like dark chocolate, but sliding right over you like silk. For a standard-issue human, he definitely knew how to weave a spell.

"Follow me, if you dare," he continued, "to some of the historical hot spots of the most haunted town in America. But keep your wits close and your loved ones closer."

He leapt off his soapbox to a collective gasp from some of the girls up front. His half-cloak flapped and settled dramatically about him. Oh, Ulric had it all right. Stage presence, sex appeal, *it*. I caught Bobby checking me out for my reaction and so crossed my eyes and stuck my tongue out at him. *His* eyes crinkled cutely at the corners before he turned to follow the crowd. It was like Ulric was the pied piper and we were all his rats. No, wait, I didn't like that analogy *at all*.

He led us out through the back doors of the mall and off to the right, and then left, where we stopped in front of a bunch of buildings that had been, I deduced from Ulric's talk, lifted from various places about town and plunked down together to form the Peabody Essex Museum complex. I tried not to snort when he got to the part in his spiel about how people should aim their cameras here or there, where paranormal activity had been spotted. Still, Ulric managed to catch my gaze across the crowd, as if he read my mind. He shot me a wink, and I could feel Bobby bristle beside me.

"When you check your pictures," Ulric continued, "you might spot what we call orbs. Look for floating lights where there are no light sources. These orbs are the spectral energies left behind, particularly in the cases of traumatic or sudden death."

"Like that girl who died the other night?" someone called. "Has she been spotted?"

At the interruption, Ulric looked like *he'd* like to trigger a traumatic event on the spot, but he gave the man a smile halfway between charming and predatory and said, "It often takes such spirits time to pull themselves together. But once they do, they seem unwilling to disperse again. I have some examples here"—he held up a flexible binder I'd only just noticed he was carrying—"of orbs that have been captured on film." He flipped to the first page and held the book over his head for everyone to see. "In some cases, you can begin to make out faces in the enlarged orbs." He flipped to another page to demonstrate his point.

I could see pretty well from where I stood, given my super-enhanced vampire vision, but it took a better imagination than I had to make out features within the glowing ball in the picture. Or, wait, was that a girl?

"I think my mind's playing tricks on me," I whispered to Bobby, low enough to be sure that no normal human could hear.

"Hey, we're vampires," he whispered back. "Who's to say what's possible? Donato certainly seemed to believe there was something haunting our apartment, and Brent was spooked."

I gave him a look, but didn't say anything else because we were moving on, down a walkway just past the museum and over to the Witch Trials Memorial and the Old Burying Point cemetery.

"I bet Brent would pick something up here," I said when we stopped again.

Ulric was talking about how the various stones of the memorial represented people who'd been killed in the witch trials—nineteen people hanged, one pressed to death, and over a hundred accused and imprisoned, the youngest being little Dorcas Good, who was only four, but the daughter of an accused witch and seen to carry a small snake in her pocket, a sure sign of conspiring with the devil. He went on about the historical figures buried in the cemetery and more about orbs.

This time, his spiel was interrupted by a gasp up front—a teenaged girl swore she'd captured a picture of one of the orbs. An older friend with her swore that *her* camera had gone dead, refusing even to open though she'd charged the battery earlier that day.

Bobby wandered around, looking at the various stones and avoiding the cameras, until we got started again. It was another quarter hour before we came to the piece de resistance—or one of them, because Ulric promised that *yes*, we would get as close as was allowed to the location of the recent murder. We were at Hale House, the site where the remains of the infamous Sheriff George Corwin were buried after his corpse had been stolen by Ulric's current alter-ego, Philip English. English had held the body hostage against Corwin's estate, insisting he be paid back for the property that was seized when he was accused of witchcraft.

"This," Ulric said, making eye contact with the girls up front who were hanging on his every word, "is one of the primary places people have reported encounters with the deadly sheriff. People describe a cold, dark weight compressing their chests and squeezing their hearts, or ghostly hands around their throats, or tugging at their feet as if to end their death dance on the gallows."

Oh, he was good. I nearly felt it myself. I didn't have to breathe, so no worries there, but the pressing on my chest … the feeling of being watched and studied. I couldn't help but look over my shoulder for … something. I didn't find it. Not that I expected any different. Still, the creepy feeling just wouldn't go away.

"This place always gives me the creeps," Ulric said, echoing my thoughts. "It's as if Old Sheriff Corwin is still out looking for rowdies and rule-breakers."

"Have you ever experienced anything yourself?" a man asked. It seemed to be the same one who'd spoken up earlier about the murdered girl. Now that the group had shifted over the course of the walk, I could see him—deeply weathered skin, a dark close-cut beard, baseball cap, navy blue wool jacket with brown leather sleeves, and a matching navy ball cap pulled low with a fighting turtle logo front and center.

He could have been anyone, but he wasn't. He was someone specific…someone I recognized. I just didn't know who. I half-hoped he'd look straight at me and half-hoped that he wouldn't, in case I was just as familiar to him.

Who's that? I mind-spoke to Bobby, afraid that even a whisper might draw the man's attention.

Bobby looked quickly over to me and back. *Why? Who do you think he is?*

I huffed. *Do you recognize him or not?*

Not.

I relaxed. It was probably just one of those cases where someone reminds you of someone else, like an actor or your Uncle John. And then it hit. I knew where I'd seen this guy before. The weight on my chest was probably dread. He was from that ghostbuster-type reality show, *Ghouligans.*

Crap. We weren't in danger of exposure from recognition.

We were in danger of a lot worse. *If* he noticed us. He didn't have a camera or crew with him, so maybe he was just scouting things out, like for some future episode. No instruments meant he'd have no way to tell we weren't your garden-variety tour guides. By the time *Ghouligans* got around to filming, we'd be long gone. Probably. Maybe. Hopefully?

Ulric was winding up, and I tapped Bobby's arm to pull him into the shadows with me as I mentally gave him the bad news.

Never seen the show, he told me. *Do they ever find anything? Like hard evidence?*

My old friend Becca had been the *Ghouligans* addict, but the couple of times she'd convinced me to watch with her, their sightings had been pretty sketchy, I thought. Heat signatures and noises you could just barely make out if they were magnified, like, a thousand times and slowed down or sped up or filtered for effect, but if you were a true believer you'd find it totally convincing. Becca had. I told him as much.

Nothing to worry about then, he replied. He sounded soothing, which so had the opposite effect on me.

He was right, though, right? Why was I so on edge? Maybe Brent had nailed it and there was just something about Salem. Or maybe Ulric's tour of terror was psyching me out.

We hit a few more landmarks—the Witch House, the Witch Dungeon, witch, witch, whatever ... and then the Old Jail. The way Ulric said it, each word got its own capital letter, probably even in some big fancy font called Thriller or Chiller or just Boo.

"The Old Salem Jail," he repeated. "This is as close as we're allowed to get to the site of the murder. You'll note the crime scene tape." Ulric pointed off into the distance. "Years ago, the Old Jail was turned into upscale housing. They, of course, tore out the old cells, and in doing so found an old passage underneath and the skeleton of a prisoner who'd tried and failed to escape. It was said that he'd fallen down a shaft and broken half his bones. He died trying to crawl to freedom. But it's not *his* ghost you have to be afraid of. Remember Sheriff Corwin? Well, behind the jail, an old man named Giles Corey was pressed to death during the witch hysteria. If you were accused back then, the officials could seize all of your worldly goods, as they did with mine." Oh right, he was supposed to be Philip English, wronged man and corpse-kidnapper.

"But, you see, Giles was a smart man," Ulric continued. "He found a loophole in the law that said his property, which he wanted to preserve for his heirs, couldn't be forfeit until he entered a plea. Thus, he refused to enter one. Sheriff Corwin, not to be thwarted, ordered Mr. Corey staked out in the courtyard and weight to be piled atop him until he should rethink his decision. Three days he lay baking in the sun. Nothing to eat or drink, his ribs and lungs collapsing under the stones heaped upon him. Corwin came out to check on Corey's progress and had to poke the near-dead man's tongue back into his mouth with his cane in order to ask again for his plea, to which Corey, a tough old bird, responded only 'More weight.' He died very shortly thereafter, pressed to death."

The hair on the back of my neck and all along my arms actually stood on end.

"It's said that Sheriff Corwin, whose rest I, Philip English, so gleefully disturbed, wanders here, looking for innocent victims, unsatisfied with his inability to break old man Corey. People have reported necklaces and scarves twisted up about their necks, the air being choked out of them just as it was pressed out of Giles Corey."

"And the girl who died?" the aptly named Ghouligan asked.

"Strangled with her own golden chain," Ulric admitted. I liked him for sounding more sad than dramatic at this.

"Do you think—?" the man started to ask.

"What I think," Ulric cut in, "is that, sadly, our time together has come to an end. It's an easy trek back to the mall, and if you'd like, you're all welcome to walk back with me. If you need directions to somewhere else, I will happily supply them. Otherwise, I bid you a fair and pleasant evening." He swept his hat from his head as he said it, and I felt chill, ghostly hands at my throat.

4

Instinctively, panic welled up in me. I didn't have to breathe, but the idea that I *couldn't*... it hadn't been so long since I'd been human. Not long enough to forget vulnerability.

I kicked and hit nothing. The awful costume's collar twisted up around my neck as I struggled. The hands continued to tighten.

A woman toward the back of the group shrieked at my obvious distress, and the reaction rippled through the crowd as the sound made everyone else turn.

Bobby rushed to me and tried to get his hands up under the ghostly grasp choking the afterlife out of me, but it was no good. The shrieking woman recovered and dashed in to help. A gold crucifix swung from her neck, and for a minute I forgot the hands in the face of true terror. I still wasn't sure whether Bobby and I were actually damned, like fiction suggested, but I wasn't eager to find out. I didn't recoil in instinctive revulsion, which was a point in our favor, but my gaze stayed riveted on that cross as the woman leaned in, trying to loosen the collar she could see twisted up like a tourniquet around my neck.

As she leaned, the crucifix swung toward me. I flinched as it brushed across my hair. Did I smell something burning? I couldn't be sure without a deep breath, which I had no opportunity to take. Fear threatened to restart my heart, which by human reckoning should be *pounding*, but even the adrenaline jolt of sheer terror couldn't quite raise the dead.

But it did make it hard to think. How long had it been since I'd been seen to draw a breath? If I were still alive, would I even be conscious after so long? Just in case, I let my hands flop uselessly to my sides and let my knees soften, as if I were about to pass out. Bobby still clawed uselessly at my neck.

The tourist lady got in closer, trying for a better angle on the problem, and this time her crucifix struck with a sizzle like meat hitting a hot grill. A howl sounded in my ear, unearthly with rage and pain, and then the hands were gone and nothing separated me from the crucifix. Sudden searing pain rolled my eyes back into my head. There was no air left in my lungs to scream and no strength left in my legs. They went out from under me.

The world tilted and I crumpled, past looks of horror, fear, and fascination. It was no act, no graceful fall for the tourists. I was a rag doll in a fiery inferno.

The last thing I saw before my light extinguished was a pair of glowing eyes—eyes I recognized but was too far gone to place.

·   ·   ·

I came to on an honest-to-God fainting couch, with four walls and retro family photos surrounding me. Bobby hovered anxiously and Kari-with-a-K flitted across my vision, asking herself where she'd put the damned first aid kit.

Ulric sat at my feet, which I noticed were bare. He was rubbing them, but since I'd been in no condition to appreciate it, I'd have bet money it was more for Bobby's benefit than mine. I almost wished one of them would just plant a flag in me and be done with it.

"She's awake," Bobby announced needlessly.

"Aha!" Kari said, from somewhere out of sight. She rushed back holding a big red case with a large white cross on the front. It was all I could do not to flinch. I had to remind myself that the lady's crucifix hadn't hurt me until it touched flesh, and that this cross was more a medicinal than religious symbol, but still … did the fact that the cross hadn't burned me on sight mean that I was only slightly damned? Was that like being only *slightly* preggers?

I gingerly touched a hand to the still-searing pain on my neck, but even that hurt so badly I snatched my hand away before I could test out the wound. I prayed it wouldn't leave a permanent mark. I didn't want to try accessorizing a scar, and there was no way I was going all Daphne from *Scooby-Doo*. Seriously, whoever had costumed those cartoons needed a fashion intervention. An orange scarf with a purple dress … as if! And the others—ascots, page boy haircuts … *knee socks*!

I knew I was thinking crazy to avoid *going* crazy.

"Let's see," Kari was saying. "I know I have burn cream in here somewhere. How did you say it happened again?"

Bobby and I made eye contact, but he looked as lost as I felt. How exactly did you explain being branded by a crucifix without throwing in talk of eternal damnation? And Salem was just the kind of place where someone might take us seriously on that point.

"Friction," Ulric piped up.

We all looked at him.

"Huh?" Bobby asked.

"The ghost of Sheriff Corwin—sadistic bastard—was throttling the life out of Gia here," Ulric said, remembering to use my fake name. "Benjy and the customer rushed in to help. It was a freak thing—the friction of playing tug of war with a ghost and trying to untwist Gia's collar heated up the customer's cross pendant to where it was, like, scalding."

We all continued to stare.

Finally, Kari said, "*Really?*" Bobby and I real-held our pretend-breaths as we waited to see if she'd buy the ridiculous explanation. "The ghost of Sheriff Corwin? You *saw* it?"

She sounded way too excited by the concept.

"Did anyone get pictures?" she continued. "This could be great for business."

Bobby cleared his throat. "Uh, Kari, you do realize that he almost *killed* Gia, right? Something tried to, anyway. I'm not so sold on it being a ghost."

"But what else could it be?" she asked. "Anyway, 'almost' is the key word. She's still here, and now we know the ghost is allergic to crucifixes. All we have to do is get all our tour guides to wear them."

"Shanti's Jewish," Ulric cut in.

"Religious symbols, then," Kari said with a huff, as though it should have been understood. "Stars of David, sacred circles, whatever."

"Um," I started, not really sure where I was going. I couldn't point out that religious symbols weren't really an option for Bobby and me. Of course, neither was suffocation. If the ghost twigged to that and started throwing around stakes ... well, we'd be in a world of trouble. "Maybe we should avoid Corwin's haunts altogether? You know, until someone performs an exorcism or something."

Kari was already shaking her head ... vehemently. "Not an option. Those are prime spots. Every single tour in town is going to hit them. If we don't, people will just go elsewhere. Besides, Bryson Seacroft wants to do a special segment on us. He talked to me before he left. *Bryson Seacroft.* We'll be famous! The tour to beat all tours. In your face, Gaslit Ghosts!"

I looked at Ulric in panic, hoping he could pull another crazy explanation out of his butt.

"Oh, and the best part!" Kari added, looking at me like I was some kind of Lady Gaga, Beyoncé, and Britney all rolled into one. "He wants you to recreate your experience for the camera. Isn't that great? You'll be famous!"

I nearly wept blood. All my natural life I'd dreamed of fame, walking the runways or red carpets. Now ... *now* that it was so close I could taste it, I had to turn away. Vamps didn't show up on film, or even in mirrors. I was doomed to an eternity of avoiding sun and stage lights, of living in the shadows. Basically, I was nothing more than a good-looking corpse.

The devastation must have shown on my face.

"What?" Kari asked. "Don't you want to be famous?"

"Stage fright," Bobby said, rubbing my shoulders. "Gia's okay in groups, but put her on a stage or in front of a camera and she freezes."

"Oh." Kari looked completely crestfallen for all of a second. "I know—I'll just get one of the other girls to play you. Problem solved!"

Good to see I was so easily replaceable, I thought with a twinge. That was too close a call.

With at least one of the Ghouligans in town poking into the paranormal, and Ulric already able to blow my cover if he wanted to, I didn't see how we could stay in Salem. On the other hand, with a supernatural strangler running loose, I didn't see how we could go.

• • •

Bobby and I caught a ride back to the apartment with one of the other Haunts in History guides. We were the first ones home, and made really good use of the couch before the others arrived. My boy could kiss, and he'd totally mastered running his fingers over sensitive spots with a feather-light touch that left me wanting... so much more.

If it wasn't for Bobby pulling my shirt quickly into place as the doorknob turned the first time, I might have treated everyone to a show.

Marcy and Brent came in, apparently having gotten a ride of their own. Marcy practically glowed in skin-tight jeans and a black scoop-necked shirt that said "Salem Stout" in screaming red letters. She looked smokin'.

"No fair," I said immediately. "You get to wear a cute little T-shirt and I have to dress up like something from *Little House on the Prairie*."

Bobby opened his mouth, probably to correct me, but Brent shut it with, "Dude, your fly's open."

Bobby blushed right up and fixed it in a flash.

"You like it?" Marcy asked, modeling—left side, right side and straight on, chest out, stomach in. "Salem Stout's their trademark draft. Brent and I got jobs at the brew pub."

"I do like it. Totally beats the heinous garb Bobby and I have to wear for the ghost tours. You'll never believe—"

"What's that on your neck?" Marcy asked, dashing to sit beside me on the couch, edging Bobby out of the way. "Hickey?"

She brushed the hair aside and drew back in horror. "Gina, you've been branded! What happened to you? Tell me everything."

"Maybe we should save the updates until everyone's back," Bobby cut in.

Annoyed, I stuck my tongue out at him. He stuck his out right back, which made me think of what we'd been doing right before Brent and Marcy walked in. A burst of heat raced through me and Bobby picked up on it, his gaze promising that as soon as the opportunity presented itself, we'd pick up where we'd left off.

"Okay, you two—cold shower. Seriously. You're making *me* blush," Brent said.

"Oh, right, like you have any shame after your liplock back in the van," I countered.

"Fine," Marcy said, giving me a *let's get the guys under control* look. "We can all agree to no more public displays of affection."

"Easy for you to say," Bobby grumbled. "*You* have a room."

"You two boys fight it out then. Gina and I need to talk concealer." Marcy pulled me off toward the bathroom and our limited cosmetic supplies to see what could be done with my crucifix-shaped scar. But it turned out to be too tender yet for any kind of cover-up. The slightest touch brought back the burn. Marcy had to settle for interrogating me on how I got it.

It was about an hour before Eric and Nelson rolled in,

clutching two large paper bags full of groceries. Brent abandoned us to help put the food away and came back with a raspberry yogurt, already half-eaten. Curse him and his human digestion. The thing I missed most—after the ability to feel the sun on my face and see myself in the mirror—was flavor. Blood just didn't cut it, especially not when we'd only had time since our flight from the Feds to nip and run. There'd been no time to savor, no lingering until we were flush with new blood racing through our veins. And even the best blood didn't tantalize the taste buds like, say, chocolate. The variations were subtle, without the tang of Tabasco or the melt-in-your-mouth of a meringue.

I didn't mean to, but I glared.

"What?" Brent asked. "Want some?"

"Now that's just mean."

Marcy kicked at him, but he caught the foot before it connected, and anyway, she hadn't really been trying. "Play nice," she ordered.

He stroked the foot he'd caught. "Always do," he said.

I snorted.

Luckily, he had to abandon the foot in order to eat his yogurt.

Eric was more substantially armed, with a twelve-inch sub and a soda. The former I didn't miss so much—all those carbs!—but the latter... I was a Cherry Coke fiend all the way.

"I'm almost embarrassed, the way you're eying that soda," Nelson said.

"How am I eying it?"

"Like you want to be alone together."

I shrugged. "It wouldn't last five minutes with me."

"I believe that," he said with a smile.

It was hard to remember that he was my age. The body he sported now was, like, Neander-tall. He looked like a star basketball player, with his muscley limbs. His russet hair, close-shaven on top, led into narrow sideburns and a chin-strap beard that skirted a square jaw. Deep brown eyes stared out of a nicely featured face. The only things not hard about the whole body were those eyes. Yup, he'd gotten the better end of his bodyswap with the vamp ... except for the whole light-allergy thing and the all-liquid diet. Of course, considering the fact that he'd been a lifestyler before the exchange, playing vamp in the club scene of Tampa, Florida, maybe he didn't mind the reality all that much.

"Anyway," Eric was saying around a mouthful of sandwich, "we need to talk. Clearly, we can't stay here."

"What? But you've just loaded up the pantry," Brent protested.

"And one of the things I bought was a cooler, so we can just take it all with us. We'll leave tomorrow night."

"The hell we will," Marcy said, pouting. "I like it here. I make good tips." She contorted in order to pull a wad of bills out of her skin-tight jeans, to show us.

"Good, that'll replace the money we spent on groceries. We should have enough gas left to get away."

"I'm not going anywhere," Marcy said, tucking the bills away where Eric couldn't get at them. "We have to stop somewhere. Here's as good a place as any."

Eric swept us with a look. "So it's decided? You talked it all out while we were gone?"

"Well, I don't think Bobby and Gina were doing much talking at all," Brent said, waggling his brows.

I stuck my tongue out at him. "Anyway, how did you find out we had a problem?" I asked Eric.

"I was helping Donato out with some technical aspects of a new illusion he was playing with when Ulric came in. He mentioned you'd nearly been choked to death by the ghost of Sheriff Corwin."

I wondered what Donato would think when he found out that whatever Eric had rigged for his illusions wouldn't work without Eric around. It was sort of his superpower... gadget whisperer. Thankfully, it did *not* come with tights.

"Donato also said some film guy had witnessed the whole thing."

Marcy's eyes huge. "You held out on me? What TV guy? Tell me it wasn't the hottie from that new show. If you got close to him and I didn't, I might have to throttle you myself."

"Hey!" Brent protested.

"Oh relax, he's on my freebie list."

"Your what?"

"You know, the list of five celebs you could go out with if you ever got the chance and your SO would have to understand."

"But I wouldn't—" Brent started.

"Yeah, like if you had the chance to get with Megan Fox you'd be all like, *but I'm taken*. I don't think so."

"*Children*, can we focus?" Eric asked, voice rising in frustration.

"Not if you're going to call us 'children,'" Marcy answered.

"Agreed," I said.

She put her fist out and I bumped it, apparently forgiven for potentially meeting her new fantasy crush, which I *hadn't*.

"As I said, we clearly can't stay. It's too dangerous," Eric continued.

"There's no *clearly* about it," I said. "I mean yes, for *our* safety we should leave. But something's going on in this town, and it's just the kind of thing we're trained to handle. How can we just leave, knowing some ghost is out there killing people? If it hadn't been *me* tonight, and I hadn't been a vampire, someone else would have died already."

I met everyone's eyes, willing them to see things my way. I'd died in terror—in a car crash rather than a murder, but still—and I didn't want anyone else going through that if it was in my power to prevent it. Sure, I'd risen from the dead, but most people wouldn't get that lucky.

"If any town is equipped to handle a supernatural threat, it would be Salem, don't you think?" Eric asked. "I saw four or five witchcraft stores just on our way through town. Besides, I swore after what happened to Nelson that I'd keep him safe. I can't do that here."

Marcy looked Nelson up and up and up, then back down to Eric. "You seriously think some supernatural stranger is going to choose *him* to mess with? Unless the ghost or whatever is, like, seven feet tall, he'll never even be able to reach around that bull neck. Plus, *hello*, vamp. I'd say he's the safest of us all."

"And what if that TV guy tries to get any of you on film?" Eric asked, desperate. "You'll be found out when none of you show up, and Brent and I will be discovered when we do. We *are* wanted by the Feds, remember."

"As if we could forget," I answered. "We just have to be careful, and what we can't prevent, we fix." He opened his mouth to continue the protest, but I headed him off. "All in favor of staying and putting the ghost to rest?"

Marcy's hand went up right away, and she nudged Brent's along as well. Bobby's was slower to rise. If I knew him, he was playing out every possible scenario in his mind, all the way to its conclusion. I could imagine that took time.

Nelson looked apologetically at his uncle before raising his hand as well.

Five to one.

The motion carried.

"Fine," Eric said, with really bad grace. "Just fine. Throw yourselves into danger again. What do I care?"

Nelson shot his uncle a look that was both fond and exasperated. "So where do we start?" he asked the rest of us.

"The Morbid Gift Shop," Brent said, surprising us all. "I

felt something there last night. I don't know if it's related to everything else going on, but I think we should check it out."

"And after that," Bobby added, "the spot where Gina got attacked near the Old Jail."

"The nights are getting longer, but they're still not *that* long," Eric grumbled.

"Don't worry, we'll be back before sun-up," Bobby promised.

Brent went to gather his coat and hat. "You'll need me to read the place. I'll need Bobby to tumble the locks and get us in."

"And me to … mist inside or something if the locks stick," I insisted, not about to be left behind. After seventeen human years of making sure that I was the center of attention, I'd found that my super-vamp power was being able to go invisible and unnoticed if I chose. Yup, fate had a way of laughing in your face.

"And you'll need me to"—Marcy floundered—"play look-out."

Even though she'd been vamped by the same vixen vampiress as Bobby and me, Marcy didn't seem to have any kind of special power beyond the super-speed, strength, and senses that came with the territory. Yet. Of course, she'd never needed one to get her way before.

"I'll drive," Eric said.

"No!" Marcy and I chorused.

"Uh, if something goes wrong, we'll need you and Nelson to bail or break us out," I improvised. "Best you stay behind."

"Sure, and we'll ride to the rescue in what?" Eric asked. "You'll have the van."

"You'd find a way," Bobby said. "We have faith."

"Great. That and a crucifix could get you killed."

"Four less for you to worry about, then."

Strangely, Eric didn't look comforted.

5

Brent insisted on driving, since he was the only one who'd actually show up to any traffic cameras we might pass. I'd never even thought about that in the past, but then, cover-up had been the Feds' problem. Now that we were on our own, it was all on us. Not that we had to worry about anyone *reviewing* those traffic tapes, at least not where the van was concerned. Brent obeyed the speed limit precisely—stopping on red, going on green, and even slowing down for yellow rather than speeding up to make it through an intersection.

"Boy Scout," I accused.

"All the way to Eagle," Brent answered, sounding proud of it.

It was so late the parking garage was closed, but with the

commercial part of town shut down for the night, we were easily able to find parking not far from the mall.

We walked the streets in silence. A brisk wind had blown up and Brent huddled in his coat, pulling his watch cap a little lower to cover his ears, but the rest of us carried the chill of the grave with us, I guess, thus the chill outside wasn't any big thing. I could hear Brent's teeth chattering as we reached the outer mall doors.

"Could you stop that?" Bobby asked mildly, as he closed his eyes to concentrate his mental mojo on the locks and alarm system.

Brent clenched his teeth together to keep them from chattering and wrapped his arms around himself. Marcy added hers and huddled against him for warmth, but since she didn't generate any of her own, I doubted she was good for more than a windbreak.

The door popped open in Bobby's hand.

"Quickly," he said, holding it aside for us. "I gave the alarm system a burst, which should blank it temporarily. If we're lucky, it'll look like a natural power surge."

We hurried through, and Bobby yanked the door shut behind us, making sure it was firmly locked again so that we'd be the only people who didn't belong skulking around the place.

"Okay, guys, just in case the security company sends someone to check things out, we want to get in and get out.

No dawdling," Brent commanded, like he was still one of our handlers back at spook central.

"Sir, yes, sir," I said, giving him a mock salute.

Marcy, maybe to prove she was her own person, paused in front of a window display that held an incredible cobalt-blue kimono-style dress with golden dragonflies taking flight across it and a matching gold sash. She came with us when I tugged her away, but reluctantly, like she was already planning how to spend her tips—and not on gas and food. Not that I blamed her.

Bobby tumbled the locks of the Morbid Gift Shop with his mental mojo, and we all ducked inside. There was plenty to gawk at here too, of course, especially if you were in touch with your inner goth, but I think we all felt Brent's sudden tension in some way. It infected us with an unnatural seriousness.

Gravely, Brent removed his gloves and tucked them into his jacket pocket. He removed his cap, too, as if it might stop him from getting some kind of signal. Or maybe it was just about not overheating, now that we were out of the wind and into a store that still retained its heat even if it had been shut off for the night.

"Quiet," Brent warned us, though no one had spoken.

I looked at Marcy, who made a funny face behind Brent's back. I tried not to laugh, which would definitely break the quiet. Instead, I watched, curious. I'd never really seen Brent work before. Not up close and personal. Spying from a distance, before I was sure we were on the same side, hadn't given me a really good feel for what he could do.

Brent approached the coffin on the cart that made up the front window display. The look on his face was something between determined and... scared? Nervous, anyway. I wondered what he thought he'd find.

Marcy, Bobby, and I hung back, Marcy apparently taking seriously her offer to play look-out, because she kept glancing back and forth between the window and Brent, keeping an eye on both.

I watched as Brent closed his eyes, took a few deep breaths as if psyching himself up for what he was about to do, and reached out to touch the coffin. Even with his eyes shut, I could see them roll up into the back of his head. His whole body tensed and began to shake. Then his mouth fell open with a low moan. It was eerie. Goose bumps started on my arms and flowed right on up to the back of my neck, standing my hairs on end. Brent's shakes started to give way to more violent twitching, almost convulsions.

Marcy let out a gasp and moved toward him, but Bobby got there first. He reached for the hand connecting Brent to the coffin, and as soon as he made contact with it, images burst into my head—like Bobby's mind-reading was being overloaded and broadcasting on all frequencies.

Inside the coffin, someone thrashed... or once had. I *knew* that terror. I'd awakened in a coffin myself and had to claw my way out, but this guy—and I knew it was a guy from the dark, wiry hair on the back of the hands beating at the sides of his prison—didn't have super-vamp strength. He was purely human and running out of air, his lungs working hard to inflate in the absence of oxygen. He was dying, using the last of the stale air in a desperate attempt to batter his way out of the grave. His hand slipped and slid off the sides of his cheap coffin as the rough wood tore them to shreds and coated the walls with his blood. I felt the grave close in, his vision flicker and fade, panic give way to hopelessness, defeat. The movement slowed nearly to nothing. Brent started to sag.

Bobby broke Brent's hand away from the coffin, and we all stood gasping in the middle of the Morbid Gift Shop as if we needed the air, as if breathing for the man who'd been buried alive.

"*That* is no prop coffin," Bobby said, proving his mastery of the obvious.

"No," Brent agreed.

"But where's the body?"

Because it wasn't still in there. The wood had retained the marks, the terror, the blood, sweat, and tears, but not the body.

Brent looked around. His gaze caught on the skeleton in the cage with one hand outstretched, the one I'd noted last night.

It was too horrible to contemplate, a whole different and terrible kind of immortality than the one we vamps lived through. Key word: *lived*.

"No," Marcy gasped, echoing my thoughts.

Brent stepped toward the cage, arm outstretched, and Bobby slapped it away. "Dude, you can't. If just the *coffin* had that effect on you, the body could drag you right into the grave. Have you ever touched a dead guy before?"

Brent turned haunted eyes on Bobby. "I need to know," he said.

"Is it worth your life?"

"Don't be so dramatic," Brent answered, but his words were slurring with exhaustion. Clearly, the coffin had taken a lot out of him.

"Don't do it," Marcy said. It was more like an order than a request. We all knew it. She wrapped her arms around Brent to be sure he kept himself to himself … or maybe to her. But I saw her pause first, a millisecond hesitation, as if touching him might offer up some residual terror. The pause was probably too brief for a human to notice, but I saw and understood.

Brent was rigid in her arms, as if touch was something he could barely tolerate at that moment. But then, maybe he *had* seen Marcy's reaction and knew the hug was costing her as well. I wondered … could he read *her*? She was a living thing … mostly … depending on your definition. Did that bring them closer, or …

Not my business.

The look Brent gave Marcy was so full of pain and love, it was like they were the same emotion.

"*I have to,*" he said, holding the intimate eye contact as if willing her to understand.

She stepped back, but not far, ready to pull him away herself this time, with no Bobby in the way to channel the horror.

Brent reached out just two fingers and touched the skeleton's hand. His body instantly seized up and he dropped like a stone, falling away from the contact. His head hit the floor hard enough to rattle brains.

Another rattle sounded right at that moment. I was so focused on Brent—we all were—that it took me a second to realize that it was coming from outside the store. Marcy dashed to the window, looked out, and dropped down into a squat so she was below window level, behind the coffin cart and hidden from a casual glance.

"Get down," she hissed at Bobby and me.

We each grabbed one of Brent's arms and dragged him out of the line of sight, behind a bookshelf that held old herbals and hex books, just as a piercing light flashed through the window. Only our vamp reflexes had gotten us out of the way in time to avoid being seen.

Brent started to moan, and Bobby put a hand over his mouth as the bright flashlight panned back and forth over the interior of the store. The beam cut to the side, and we all heard the door rattle as the security guard or police officer or whoever it was behind that blinding light tried the door to make sure it was still locked up tight. Nobody moved. Nobody except Brent breathed. Finally, the guard moved on, rattling other doors and flashing his big light stick.

Bobby removed his hand and muttered. "Sorry."

"No problem," Brent answered softly, sounding all but done in.

Marcy duck-walked over to us, carrying Brent's jacket and hat. "You okay?" she whispered. "What did you see?"

"At least you asked the important question first," he answered with a weak grin.

She shrugged. "Well, I'm not quite finished with you yet."

"I'm touched."

"Maybe later," she agreed.

Brent's smile gained a little strength at that and as they looked at each other, it was like the rest of us, the coffin, the body, and the security guard all ceased to exist.

Bobby cleared his throat.

"Right," Brent said. It took him time to refocus, though. This second vision had pretty much done him in. "That's definitely the body. And he didn't die easily."

"So how did he end up buried alive? And how did he get here? I mean, he's got to be historical, right? If he'd been embalmed, he'd have been in no condition to scratch up that coffin," Bobby said.

"More likely, too poor for embalming," I said. "Did you check out the pine box he was buried in?"

Everybody stared at me. "What? I know quality. That's not it." I flung a hand toward the coffin.

Bobby grinned. "That's my girl. What about it, Brent?"

"I don't know. Definitely old, but how old? There've got to be some records around here somewhere about where this came from. You know, provenance—though I can't imagine they know what they have here."

Bobby had been studying the coffin and cart and said suddenly, "Uh, guys, I think they do know, at least part of it. Check out the plaque beneath the coffin."

It was facing the mall window, which was how we'd all missed it originally. Bobby read it aloud for us. "*Coffin, circa late 1800s, with evidence that the inhabitant was buried alive. It was a fear so prevalent at the time that the safety coffin was invented, complete with a bell and pulley system to let grave-yard attendants know if the recently 'deceased' required rescue. Such rescues are the origin of the expression 'saved by the bell.'*"

"Wow," I said.

"Yeah."

"Look at that price tag," Marcy added.

"Ten thousand dollars—you've got to be kidding! Who'd want this gross old thing?" I asked.

"A collector," Brent answered. "Especially if it's authentic."

"Which we know it is," Bobby said. "But how did they get it? Is it even legal to buy and sell stuff like this?"

"All good questions. And here's another one," Brent said. "Is there any connection with the Salem Strangler? If this guy was buried alive, he'd have suffocated to death. If there was a woman involved—"

"There's always a woman involved," Bobby interrupted. I swatted him.

"—it could explain why he's throttling them, cutting

off their air," Brent continued. "But then, the same goes for Sheriff Corwin and his punishments—hanging, pressing—or any number of ghosts who were killed that way and are hanging around righteously upset about it."

"We've got to get at those purchase records," Bobby said.

A light strobed through the window, and we all dropped to the ground again.

Bobby crawled over behind the counter and started tumbling locks and opening drawers, as quietly as possible. He quickly reclosed the bottom cabinets.

"Inventory," he announced, then sorted through various receipts. But they were old and unorganized. No convenient data storage or computer in sight, though there was a hand-held scanner locked away in one of the drawers.

"Looks like they're changing over to a paperless office," Bobby said with a sigh. "Good for the environment, bad for us. Probably Chip or whoever keeps everything on a laptop and takes it with him when he leaves."

"I bet they use off-site backup for their records, then. I would," Brent offered.

"But those things are like Fort Knox. We'll never get in."

"Then we have to get that laptop. Tomorrow, when everyone's in the theater watching the Gothic Magic Show. Eric's a genius hacker; he ought to be able to find a back door into the system. Gina, you think you can get Ulric to help with distraction so that no one notices when Eric goes for the computer?"

Everybody looked at me. Again.

"Piece of cake."

By the time we were certain the security guard had gone, dawn was too close for comfort. The Old Jail would have to wait until tomorrow night. We raced the sun back to Danvers, and made it with just moments to spare.

6

The Gothic Magic Show didn't start until midnight, after the Haunts in History tours ended, so the first order of business the next night was keeping our cover. I was in the midst of getting costumed for my first tour when Ulric pulled aside the dressing room curtain and poked his head in.

"Damn, I was hoping to catch you in some form of *dishabille*."

"Dish-what?"

"Undressed."

I looked for something to throw at him, but I didn't really think lobbing my panties would have the desired effect.

"Sorry to disappoint," I answered dryly.

Luckily, I was more or less dressed, except for the oh-so-sexy bonnet.

"Oh, you don't," he answered, a gleam in his eye that despite *Bobby* and *taken* gave me a little jolt of excitement.

I stepped out of the dressing room, and Ulric moved—barely—to let me pass.

"When I told Kari I wanted to talk to you, I didn't mean BC," I said.

"BC?"

"Before clothes."

He laughed and looked at me like he was wishing for a superpower of his own, like X-ray vision.

I sighed. Ulric was a force of nature. Or nature's evil twin, anyway. There was no point in trying to convince him he'd done anything wrong. He'd never buy it.

"Tonight at the Gothic Magic Show, we need your help," I told him.

"Go on."

"Can you arrange it so everybody is distracted, focused on you?"

"For how long?"

I thought about it. "For as long as it takes."

"Why?"

"That's on a need-to-know basis."

Ulric didn't roll his eyes. In fact, their intensity continued to bore into me. I licked my lips and nearly nicked my tongue on my fangs, which had extended and locked into place at his nearness. It had been days since I'd fed—not since we'd hit the road in our flight from the Feds. It didn't help that I *knew* the taste of Ulric's blood … a flavor like heat and spice, adrenaline and youth. Liquid life. I nearly moaned just at the thought of it.

Bobby stepped out of his dressing room, swinging his cape around his shoulders and catching Ulric in the face with it. Ulric flinched back and the spell was broken.

"Did I interrupt something?" Bobby asked, staring at Ulric for an answer. I somehow didn't think the cape had been an accident.

"Yes," Ulric said, at the same time I answered, "No."

Exasperated, I huffed, hands on both my hips now. "No," I repeated.

Ulric looked from me to Bobby and back. "I'll help on one condition."

"What?" I asked, dreading the answer.

"A date."

Bobby answered for me. "Nevermind, we'll handle it ourselves."

"Oh, I'm sure you will," Ulric responded.

"Okay, *seriously*? Down boys. Ulric, *I'm taken*. Bobby, dial it back before you come down with testosterone poisoning."

They both stared at me, then Ulric's lips quirked up in amusement. "It was worth a shot. Sure, I'll help."

Bobby didn't look so sure the help was worth letting Ulric off without a punch in the nose, but that wasn't really his style. In the end, he smiled back.

"Thanks," he said.

"I'm not doing it for you," Ulric answered.

"I never thought you were."

Men. Can't live with them, can't stake 'em.

As the three of us walked together toward the front of the shop, I noted Kari talking with a stunning redhead. Exactly the kind of girl I'd always hated—model-tall, runway sleek, legs that probably went on for miles. Thank goodness they were currently covered up, along with everything else, by her Pilgrim suit. Sorry, *Puritan*. Only *her* dress was red. My signature color. All my secret insecurities rose to the surface. So I was short—no way around that. But I'd always fought frumpy and overlooked, tooth and nail, even before said weapons became instruments of crass destruction.

Kari's eyes lit up when she saw me. The redhead's eyes skimmed over Ulric, saw and dismissed me, and moved straight on to Bobby, where her gaze caught and held. Bobby seemed equally gobsmacked, to the point where I had to nudge him in the ribs—*hard*—to get him to blink.

"I'm so glad you're all here. Gia, this is Rebecca. Rebecca, Gia. The boys will take the first two groups. Rebecca, Gia's going to take you out and show you where it all happened so you can get in some practice before the filming tomorrow." As always, Kari was way too cheerful about everything. At some point, I'd apparently gotten in touch with my inner goth, to the point where perky was now painful. Or maybe it just came with the whole creature-of-the-night gig.

"I am?" I asked.

Rebecca's gaze slid toward me, as if now that she realized I was important she had to size up the competition.

"Hi," she said, doing a halfway convincing impression of friendly.

She held a hand out to shake, and I'd love to say that it was clawlike with hangnails, calluses, and critically cracked skin, but it was perfect, just like the rest of her. She had the kind of hands they used in lotion commercials. Her fingernails were all buffed, shaped, and shined but without color, probably in keeping with her Puritanical role. When I looked from that hand to her face, she was just painfully pretty. Her skin could survive cosmetics commercial close-ups. Her uptilted green eyes were almost as bright as mine.

But I had two things on her. *My* glittering green eyes were framed by long black lashes most women would kill to possess, and while she might be a long stretch of highway you could handle full throttle, I was a cool, curvaceous road, like San Francisco's Lombard Street, that needed serious time and attention to navigate.

"Sure," Kari said, oblivious to any undertones. "You said you got stage fright, so Rebecca offered to step in."

"I'm a drama major at Boston College."

"Of course you are," I mumbled.

"What was that?" Kari asked.

"I said, 'Bet you go far.'"

Rebecca gave a million-kilowatt grin. "Thanks."

"Don't mention it." *I mean, like, ever.* "Come on, I'll show you what happened."

"Don't be long," Kari said. "I need you to lead the nine o'clock tours."

"Will do." I'd have her back by eight.

We were barely out of earshot when Rebecca asked, "So, what's the story on the new guy?"

"He's taken," I said, shortly.

"Taken?" Rebecca's steps slowed and she turned to me, eyes wide. "You mean, you and him?" She looked me up and down, which didn't take long considering my height.

"Yeah, is there a problem with that?" I asked. I hadn't meant to seem so defensive, but somehow, tall and leggy (at least I presumed there were legs and not, say, a serpent's tail under that costume) drama majors brought out the worst in me.

"Oh, no," she answered, but not with conviction. "I just … didn't realize."

Moving right along. "Kari gave you the lowdown? You're wearing a cross or some type of protection? A crucifix saved me yesterday." And today my hair was arranged so that no one could see that it had also scarred me for life.

"Yeah. I've got protection." She patted her chest, which I took to mean she had a pendant hidden under her costume.

"I'm not sure hiding it away is gonna help. The crucifix didn't do anything until it touched whatever attacked me."

Rebecca looked vaguely uncomfortable, which was interesting. "I'm pretty sure my religious symbol doesn't go with the costume. Kari would probably have my head."

Definitely interesting.

"We're not on a tour right now," I argued.

We were already outside, heading toward the Old Jail. It

was just the two of us, but still, it was a no-go. In fact, she put a hand over her chest—over the pendant—as if I might see it right through her shirt.

Curiouser and curiouser.

"Come on," I wheedled. "What's the big secret? This town was founded on the idea of religious freedom, right?"

"If you mean the right to practice one *particular* religion, then yes. Anyway, I'm sorry, but how is my belief any of your business?" she asked.

Fair point. It wasn't … *technically*. Not unless she was some kind of witch and could actually work magic. Even then, I guess it wasn't my business unless she'd used that magic to create the kind of supernatural incident that would bring the Ghouligans to town so that she could act out a little drama and get herself discovered. But even as I thought it, I knew it was more jealousy than logic speaking. If Rebecca wanted to find fame and fortune, there were far more direct paths on which no one had to die.

"It isn't," I admitted with a shrug.

She relaxed, her hand slipping away from her pendant. "Anyway, I'm supposed to be playing *you*, so I need to get into your head, not the other way around. Tell me all about yourself."

My favorite topic.

Of course, I skipped right over my death and resurrection and started with going to work for Haunts. I took her through my near-death-due-to-strangulation, the feel of the chill hands on my neck, my collar twisted tight across my throat like a gallows rope ...

When we hit the approximate spot where the attack had happened, I acted it out for her six or eight times, then watched her go through it herself, critiquing her performance, suggesting improvements. I had to admit that she was good, totally better than I'd be at taking direction. But giving it—that was a whole 'nother matter. Maybe my dreams of stardom hadn't completely gone up in smoke with my death ... maybe I just had to wrap my mind around working on the other end of the camera. *Directing*—now that was something I could sink my teeth into.

By the time we were done, I was almost having fun. Rebecca's eyes were shining, and I was just glad Bobby couldn't see her like that, because as knock-out as she was standing still, animated she was powerful. She made a better me than me.

"Nailed it," I told her, and she came in for a high-five. I met her part way.

"You must have been terrified," she said, not for the first time. "I almost wish I felt something here. It's so hard to *imagine* that kind of thing ... ghostly hands around your neck." She shuddered.

Strangely, I was no longer compelled to throttle her myself so she could get the experience first-hand.

"Just be glad you only *have* to imagine. Remember, the last girl was killed. I only escaped by the skin of my teeth."

The light in Rebecca's eyes dimmed. "Sorry, I wasn't thinking."

I shrugged. "That happens to me all the time. Or so Bobby would tell you."

"I bet he wouldn't."

It was sweet of her to say, but I suspected she wasn't the kind to go around offering praise without an ulterior motive.

"So, is he The One?" she added casually.

"The one what?"

"*You know.*"

"You mean, like, forever, until death do us part?" Or... not, in our case.

It was a terrifying thought. I loved Bobby, but eternity was a lot longer for us than for most people. I didn't exactly have commitment issues, but I'd thumbed through the fashion spreads before placing the magazine back in the rack.

"Whoa, sorry, it wasn't meant to be a tough question. You look like you've seen a ghost."

I smiled feebly at that and suggested we head back. Rebecca touched her chest again, as if to be sure the pendant was still locked and loaded before leaving, but I stopped her as I spotted something in the distance, which looked suspiciously like a lantern bobbing and weaving all on its own.

"What's that?" I asked, forgetting her eyesight wouldn't be as good as mine.

"Where?"

I pointed it out for her.

"Past the Old Jail? That's the Howard Street Cemetery. It's right by the site where Giles Corey was pressed to death. Didn't you listen to the tour?"

"Not *that*," I said, as if she hadn't just scored a point. "*That*." I directed her toward the light.

"Oh." She laughed. "That has to be Tommy Haskins. He's the caretaker. He's a real throwback. Says electricity riles up the dead. I heard that Haunts used to lead tours through the cemetery, but then there were some incidents, and the people in the new condos at the Old Jail didn't like it. Now no one's allowed."

"So it's closed to the public?"

"Except by special arrangement."

"What kind of incidents closed it down?"

"Ulric's tour didn't cover that part?"

"Um, maybe? It probably went straight out of my head when the Ghost of Murderers Past decided to put in an appearance."

"Oh, right." Her face crinkled, and even her embarrassment looked stupid-cute on her.

Note to self: keep your friends close and your rivals closer.

"Well," she continued, "it was small stuff at first—women claiming their skirts had been blown up by freak winds on totally calm nights, tripping over invisible things poking up out of the ground, saying that hands had grabbed at their ankles, men reporting trouble breathing, a weight on their chests, seeing ghosts. Also, graves were disturbed, either from people tripping around in panic or from vandalism. Kids would dare each other to spend the night and come out with some real horror stories—or be chased out when Tommy caught them. That kind of thing."

I had her go into the specifics with me on the way back—anything I might have missed on Ulric's tour. As a guide myself, I should commit it all to memory. *And* come up with a really good reason why my tours could take pics of anything but me.

•   •   •

By the time my tours ended that night, I was stunningly thankful for my bonnet. Every time I caught a camera aimed my way, I found something fascinating on the ground or far off to one side or another. I also did my best to stay in perpetual motion, so that any blurs on camera would be easily explained. But it was exhausting being always on guard, and I was more than ready to get down to straightforward stealth.

We decided to divide and conquer. Eric and Nelson were already at the Morbid Gift Shop, helping Donato prep for his show. Eric was acting as a consultant (for free, at least for now), and Nelson ... well, I wasn't really sure exactly what Nelson was up to. He was definitely fascinated by the illusions and interested in picking up as many tips as he could. I suspected that he might be planning an act of his own for when we moved on. With the vamp thing going for him, he'd be a natural—water escapes, rising from the dead and all that jazz. But it wasn't so smart a pursuit for a vampire in hiding. I'd have to have a talk with him.

Anyway, Bobby and I planned to meet up with them later. First, we had a little recon to do at the Old Jail and the Howard Street Cemetery. Those were the spots so far where the disturbances seemed to be centered. Maybe we could figure out why.

We ditched our costumes for street clothes and moved out. I'd never been so grateful for skinny jeans in my entire life. And if my T-shirt didn't have my signature bling, at least it was form-fitting and scoop-necked and a stunning green to match my eyes, not Puritanical poop-brown.

Bobby took my hand, and we walked out into the night like we were just two teenagers looking for someplace to be alone. It was nice. No one was trying to kill or capture us. The moon hung low—a Spielberg moon, where a boy might sit and fish for stars.

We sauntered through several streets, and a few twists and turns, over to the condos that had once been the Old Jail. We stopped in the exact spot where I'd been attacked the night before and waited to feel a ghostly presence. Unlike Rebecca earlier, we were completely sans religious symbols. Completely defenseless.

Nothing. Not a tingle or a tweak, a sizzle or a strangle.

"Anything?" I asked Bobby, knowing the answer.

"Nada."

"Think you can get us inside the Old Jail?"

"I don't even need my mojo for that. Push enough buzzers, someone's bound to let us in."

Second note to self: never buzz someone into a building without knowing exactly who they are. They might be some fearsome, fanged creatures of the night up to no good. Not in our case, of course, but you never know when someone might bust into your place to feng shui your furniture or rearrange your internal organs. Caution is just common sense.

"Well then, let's go," I answered.

We strolled right up to the front doors and, as it turned out, didn't even have to wait to get buzzed in, because a guy—weaving a little, possibly from a trip to Brent and Marcy's brew pub—held the door open for us when he let himself in. We thanked him. He nodded like a dashboard Elvis and went on his merry way, leaving us in the foyer to look around.

It looked more like an high-class hotel than a former prison. The only thing that gave it away was the tasteful sign back on the walkway talking about how the building fit into Salem's history. No mention of the conditions folks had found within or anyone who might have died there, of course.

I wondered what Brent would make of the place, but with history as alive as it seemed to be in Salem, I wasn't sure we dared find out.

"Let's go deeper," Bobby suggested. We took a set of stairs down to the basement level, and found nothing but a laundry and a lounge. Still, my hair seemed to literally stand on end.

"Static electricity?" I asked Bobby.

"I don't think so. Hush for a second," he said, though I'd already stopped talking.

Bobby closed his eyes and stood in absolute stillness. With no one else around, neither of us even pretended to breathe, so the only noise, the only motion, came from the single dryer still going in a corner, miraculously quiet for an industrial-grade machine.

"Stop thinking so loudly," Bobby whispered.

"What? I wasn't—"

Okay, so he was in receiver-mode, listening with all his mental mojo. I did my best to blank my mind.

Think nothing at all, nothing at all. Damn, he looks hot in those jeans; nothing at all. I wonder how soon someone's coming back for those clothes in the dryer. There's a nice couch in the lounge. Nothing at all, nothing at all.

"Gah."

"Did you get anything?" I asked.

"Nothing at all," he answered.

"Wanna move onto the couch?" I asked.

Bobby grinned at me. "I thought we agreed with Brent and Marcy on no more public displays of affection."

"They're not here."

Bobby closed in on me, his grin getting wickeder and wilder by the second. Those amazing blue eyes looked into mine with so much love, so much feeling, that I got happily lost in them, forgetting ghost hunts and other ghastliness.

He backed me right into the dryer, which was humming along, until it vibrated against my back. Then he pulled himself to me, hands first spanning my waist, then moving down to hold my hips while he swooped in to kiss me. His lips closed on mine, firm and wonderful, and his tongue slipped into my mouth. I let mine duel with his, startling an intake of breath out of him. He was breathing in my air, but I didn't need it. Anyway, I was too distracted by the press of those jeans I so admired. The motion of the dryer rocked me into him, but it might have had a little help.

Then something went *thump!* It was like a sneaker being

tumbled dry, suddenly thrown against the side of the machine. It threw me forward, and I almost bit Bobby's tongue. He drew back, startled, and the dryer gave another double-thump and seemed to shuffle toward us.

I admit it, I shrieked. Totally girly. It was a *machine*. But it seemed possessed.

Ba-da-bump. Bum-bum-bum-BUMP!

All of the sudden, the machine, which had gone airborne with the violence of its shaking, came down with a crash and opened, spewing clothes at us like someone had hit the eject button.

It was just at that moment, of course, that a girl walked in, an empty basket in hand, probably to collect the clothes that were all over the floor.

"Hey, what are you doing?" she yelled.

"We didn't—" I started, at the same time Bobby said, "The machine's possessed."

"Possessed?" the girl asked, eyes about bugging out. "Bull crap. I'm calling security."

Bobby and I looked at each other, had a whole conversation in a glance, and dashed for the door. Past the stunned late-night launderer, up the stairs, and out the front door.

The sillies struck me along with the night air, and I burst into uncontrolled laughter. "*It's possessed?*" I breathed, the words barely intelligible through my giggles.

"You have a better explanation?" Bobby asked, indignant.

"No, but the look on that girl's face—"

"Priceless," Bobby finished for me.

A few more gasps and I managed to get the laughter more or less under control.

"Well, that was a bust," I said.

"Not entirely. We found out the Old Jail has a demonic dryer. Makes our haunted apartment seem positively tame. What do you think we'll come across in the graveyard?" Bobby asked.

"I say we go find out."

Bobby offered me his arm, and with one final giggle, I took it and we were off to the Howard Street Cemetery.

"I take you to all the best places," Bobby commented.

I squeezed his arm. "You sure do."

We followed a long, tall, wrought-iron fence around and around, looking for a gate, even knowing it would be locked. It seemed better to play with the locks than try to climb the sheer vertical struts. We finally came across the gate and looked around to make totally certain the coast was clear.

If I were on my own, I would have just misted through the bars. But I couldn't leave Bobby behind, so I waited and played look-out while he used his mental mojo to pick the locks.

With a small *snick*, the lock fell open, and the cemetery gate swung inward a touch. Bobby pushed it farther, and the gate creaked every bit as much as I'd expect it to. I think, actually, I'd have been disappointed if it hadn't—like getting a fab dress home and discovering it was a whole different color than it had looked in the store.

I went to step inside, but Bobby dashed a hand to my

arm to hold me back. "It's just occurred to me—what if we can't enter because of hallowed ground?"

"Won't know until we try." And I really, really wanted to try. Getting nearly strangled made this whole thing awfully personal for me.

Before Bobby could react, I stuck a toe in. Nothing happened. He relaxed his hold on my arm and I shifted to allow my entire foot to come down inside. I looked up at the sky. No lightning streaked down to strike me dead. No angels appeared before me with flaming swords barring my way.

"I think we're good," I said, surprised.

"Weird," Bobby answered.

We stepped all the way in and Bobby closed the gate behind us, so that the cemetery would still looked locked up to anyone passing. As soon as it shut, the biting wind that had made Brent's teeth chatter stopped, as if the iron bars were some kind of solid barrier against the elements. It was freaky . . . and this from a fanged fashionista on the run from the Feds.

"Stay together or fan out?" Bobby asked quietly.

"Fan out, I think, but stay close." I didn't know why. The breath-stealing ghost—Sheriff Corwin, as rumor had it—couldn't hurt me, at least not that way. Yet something about this place made all my hair stand on end. By the time we left Salem, I'd look like the Bride of Frankenstein . . . and that so wasn't the movie monster I wanted to be associated with. Elvira, Mistress of the Dark, maybe, though with a totally more modern hairstyle and a little more sense of decorum. Always best, I'd found, to leave more up to the imagination.

"I'll go right," Bobby whispered.

I nodded again, heading left, glancing at inscriptions as I went.

Sarah Jenkins
3 years old
Rest in Peace

James T. Essex
Lost at sea
1823 –1841

Faith Godsey
died of consumption
Age 34 years
God Rest her Soul

My eyes started to burn, and I realized there were blood tears forming at the corners, the only kind I was able to cry since being vamped. Hadn't anyone lived to a ripe old age? Ah, there, I found one.

Charles Timmons
called home 1849
Age 65 years

But I wasn't here for the dead—at least, not the ones who'd truly been called home. The cemetery was neatly cared for, the grass trim, if a little extra long right around the grave-stones and monuments. No gnarly tree roots or skeletal hands rose up to trip me. All was quiet.

Yet I couldn't actually say it was peaceful. The stillness had the feeling of a held breath of someone waiting in the shadows...an intruder, or someone hiding in fear of one.

"Hello?" I said tentatively into the night.

No answer. I reassured myself that Bobby was still not all that far to my right and moved forward another few steps, to a new row of graves. Something stopped me.

Jenny Coggs
1821-1827
An Angel called to Heaven

Six years old. Cripes.

One of the blood tears got loose of my lashes and started to fall, tickling its way down my cheek. As I raised a hand to brush it away, something tiny and cool, like a puff of fresh air, seemed to brush my fingertips and then to rest on my hand, as if to offer comfort.

I froze. I'd never believed in all those John Edward, *Crossing Over* type shows, but if I was right, the dead had now reached out to me...twice. Three times, if that dryer had been trying to get my attention.

"Hello?" I said again, even quieter, because I was afraid Bobby would hear and call out to see who I was talking to, thus breaking the spell.

Slowly, I squatted down, so as not to spook the spirit—

if that's what I was really feeling and not just the power of my own imagination.

The cold touch retreated, but I stayed in position, low and still, as I would with a timid animal I wanted to pet. "I won't hurt you," I whispered for good measure.

I waited. Then I dove deep. I didn't have Brent's powers of telemetry; I couldn't touch grave dirt or headstones and know everything there was to know. I couldn't read minds or manipulate objects like Bobby. What I *could* do was mist. "Ghost," in a sense. I didn't actually have sight in that form, not having physical eyes and all, but it gave me a special awareness of things—places of disturbance in the atmosphere, for lack of a better way to describe it. A sense of densities and patterns.

I focused on going insubstantial ... or maybe *unfocused* would be more like it ...

Then I felt it. Just ahead of me, there was movement. Something darted around Jenny Coggs's headstone and seemed to huddle there. The something was small ... child-sized and radiating freezy-cold fear.

I solidified again, because all I had were my words, and no way to use them when I was in mist form.

"Can you hear me?" I whispered toward the huddling form. "Knock once for yes."

I was hoping that since she'd been solid enough for me to feel her touch, she could do this as well. I listened hard, straining my ears to hear, and was rewarded by a small knock.

"Are you afraid of something? Is it me?"

A knock, and then, in a second, two more. Oh, right, that had been two questions. Okay then—afraid, but not of me.

"I wish you could tell me what's going on. I want to help."

The wind stirred a little then, enough to ruffle my hair. I thought it carried with it the words "don't let him get me," but I couldn't be sure.

Him? Sheriff Corwin's ghost? Someone else?

"Gina," Bobby hissed.

I felt the cold patch that was, I was now certain, the spirit of a young girl, retreat even farther from me and then wink out. It left an imprint in the night like the images on old TV screens that lingered a second after they were shut off.

My head snapped around toward Bobby, ready to give him a piece of my mind, even though he couldn't have any idea what he'd interrupted, when I saw the light. The same light I'd asked Rebecca about earlier—the caretaker, Tommy Haskins, headed our way.

"We'd better get," Bobby said.

I was debating the slower but stealthier crouch and slink toward the exit versus the faster and flashier flat-out run when the voice behind the lantern yelled, "You two. Stop right there."

That decided it. For the second time that night, Bobby and I were making a grand exit, racing against discovery. It was a good thing I'd worn my calf-sculpting sneakers. Oh sure, I was supposed to stay eternally young and fit and all that, but a girl couldn't be too careful.

As I dodged around a grave that seemed to spring up out of nowhere, Bobby pulled ahead of me. No matter. I knew that with our super-speed, we'd both be out of the way before Old Mr. Haskins could catch us, but his voice seemed surprisingly close when I heard him mutter, "Not in *my* graveyard. I'll catch you this time, you fool kids."

Bobby had paused at the gate, holding it open for me like a true gentleman and waiting to make sure I got out. I blew him a kiss as I breezed past, and he slammed the gate shut behind me. We dashed together into the night, but I caught Bobby's hand and pulled him behind a nearby tree to glance back.

Apparently, I'd watched way too much *Scooby-Doo* as a kid, because "Old Man Haskins" was surprisingly young. It'd only been my own expectations that had painted the caretaker as doddering. Truly, he was more like twenty or thirty, not much older than whatever kids he was grumbling about. I couldn't tell what his face looked like, because he sported the same haircut as Johnny Rzeznik from the Goo Goo Dolls—choppy patches of hair falling in front of his eyes. It was a wonder he could even see. His breath puffed out in curling clouds, an indication that his mouth was where you'd expect to find it, but that was about the best I could do as a description besides "tall" and "lean."

There were no other lights in the cemetery, and from outside of it I could no longer sense my little girl ghost. I wondered who the *he* was that I was supposed to protect her from. Tommy Haskins? Sheriff Corwin? The Salem Strangler? (Or were the previous two one and the same?) I was going to have to find out.

"I'll be back," I whispered, a promise she probably couldn't hear.

"What's that?" Bobby asked.

"Let's get the others, and I'll tell you all about it."

A quick call around, and everyone agreed to meet up at the brew pub, where Brent and Marcy would soon be going off shift.

We arrived just half an hour before last call. The pub looked like an old warehouse or fire station that had been converted: square and brick, with newer-looking stained glass windows replacing the boring old ones. Matching stained glass lamps hung above each booth, and flickering red tea lights were set on every table, giving the room a warm, firelike glow. It was cozy, except for the industrial-grade carpet that crunched, rather than gave, beneath our feet.

We ordered beers we were too young to be served, and incapable of drinking anyway, as an excuse to take up a booth. Way back when I'd first been vamped, me and some others had tried to drink something besides blood and were forcibly introduced to our insides. It wasn't something I wanted to repeat any time soon. Or ever. Unfortunately, we weren't seated in Brent or Marcy's sections, but the blond barmaid who did wait on us (with the kicky blue streak in her hair) had a nearly empty area and seemed to appreciate our influx of business. Eric and Nelson got there about a minute after we did, and Eric tried to make up for the rest of us by ordering a burger and cheese-fries, only to be told the kitchen had closed at midnight.

Disgruntled, he followed the barmaid as she left with the drink orders and surreptitiously grabbed a bowl of mixed nuts off the bar when she turned her back. He returned to the table, mouth full, hugging the bowl to his chest as if any of us might wrestle him for it. Like even if I'd been alive I'd have gone where a thousand barflies had been before me—no telling who hadn't washed their hands before diving into the mixed nuts. Besides, all that salt made you bloaty.

The waitress gave a knowing smile but didn't say a word when she spotted Eric with the nuts on her way back with the drinks.

"Just let me know if you need anything else," she said as she set the last glass down. "My name is Olivia."

As soon as she left, Bobby asked, "*Now* will you tell me what happened back there?"

Everyone looked at me. "I think we should wait for Brent and Marcy," I said, not quite ready to tell him I was feeling all maternal about some little ghost girl I couldn't actually see. *Me.* Maternal. The two things went together like polka dots and paisley.

"We'll fill them in later. Spill."

I stared at my hands, which now that I looked were sorely in need of a new coat of polish. Or some remover, if I really wanted to get into my role at Haunts.

"Gina," Bobby prompted.

"Okay, *fine.* Our apartment isn't the only thing haunted around here."

"Well, we knew that," Eric started, but Bobby shut him up with a look.

"There's a little girl spirit in that graveyard behind the Old Jail who doesn't want me to let 'him' get her."

"Him who?" Bobby asked.

"I don't know," I moaned back. "I wish I did. She was so scared."

"You *saw* her?" Eric asked. "Talked to her?"

"Not exactly. I *sensed* her and yes, she spoke to me."

"Do you know who she was?"

"I was standing in front of the gravestone of a six-year-old girl, Jenny Coggs. It could have been her."

"But you don't know."

"No."

"Interesting."

If he said so. What mattered most to me was whatever was threatening her. She'd already grabbed me by the heartstrings, and whoever she was, I knew I'd have to find a way to help.

"What else can you tell us?" Eric asked.

I gave them everything I had, which wasn't much, and Bobby picked up the story when I switched to the part about the Old Jail. He skirted around exactly what we'd been doing up against that dryer, but then, I supposed, it wasn't any of their business.

"Now you," he said to the others when he wound down.

Eric had already finished his beer during Bobby's retelling

and had just taken his first gulp of the one we'd ordered for Nelson, so his nephew began the tale.

"While Ulric had everybody at the shop mesmerized with the flaming wallet trick, we slipped into the main part of the store and found the laptop under the counter. It turns out the coffin was bought from JC Theatrical Supplies, labeled 'authentic Victorian coffin of man buried alive.' The body was sold separately, I guess."

"Any indication of how JC got away with selling the human remains?" Bobby asked.

"It was listed as 'skeleton—medical specimen.'"

"Bull crap." Strong words, coming from Bobby.

"Yeah. But the question is, did they know it was crap?" Eric asked.

"Well, that was our question," Nelson agreed. "We searched around on the Internet." Since we'd had to leave all our smart phones, laptops, and anything else traceable through data plans, IP addresses, and GPS signals behind when we went on the run, we were reliant for the moment on public and borrowed access. "JC Supplies does everything from props and costume rentals for theatrical events to procurement of authentic clothing and artifacts for recreations and collectors. A partial list of clients includes the Secret Salem Historical Society, Boston Battle Reenactments, the Puritan Players—"

"Could this seriously be the Salem Strangler?" Bobby asked, very practically. "I mean, we're talking about the remains of a guy who died, like, two centuries ago. If the spirit was going to act up, wouldn't he have done it before now? All he's done is give Brent a scare."

"So you think it's the ghost of Sheriff Corwin, like everyone says?"

"I don't think it matters who it is. We have to stop him."

"Let's break it down," Eric cut in, like he was the dad of the group, which was about right. He turned his place mat over to use as notepaper. "Anybody got a pen?"

As we frisked ourselves for writing utensils, Brent and Marcy approached and loomed over us. "We took care of your check," Brent said. "You all ready to go?"

"Join us for a minute?" Eric asked, coming up with a pen himself. Brent and Marcy slid into the booth, squeezing us all pretty tightly together. Eric grunted, as if put out, even though he was the one who'd invited them to sit down.

Grown-ups.

"Okay," he started. "In a way, Bobby's right. It's not like we're putting together a case against the ghost. It's not so much about who-done-it as about how, and why now. A spirit should not have the kind of power we're talking about here, which means there's got to be some kind of human or inhuman force behind all this. That's what we have to track. We have to cut things off at the source. As I see it, we've got a few different things to explore: the Spectral Strangler, the Ghosty Girl, and the Very Active Artifacts."

"Whoa," Brent cut in. "How much have we missed?"

"Only everything. Don't worry, I'll fill you in later," Bobby promised.

"Well," Brent said, catching us all with a look that said whatever came out of his mouth next would be significant. "Marcy and I have news of our own. The rest of the Ghouligans crew arrived today. They came in tonight for dinner."

"Crap," I said.

"Don't these types of shows usually scout locations weeks or months in advance? Don't they need time for permissions, research, release forms, and all that jazz?" Bobby asked.

Brent shrugged. "They must have fast-tracked this one because of the murder. You vamps have to watch out. We've monitored—I mean, *the Feds* have monitored—the Ghouligans program. They've got all kinds of high-tech equipment and special monitoring devices. If they figure out you're vampires, I don't know where on earth you'll be safe ... from them, or from the fangs, or religious fanatics, goth groupies, you name it."

"Good Lord," Eric said. Then, "Do you think the Ghouligans would let me get a look at their equipment?"

But I'd stopped paying attention right around "fangs." Mine were extended, fully at attention and getting pokey with my bottom lip.

"Uh, guys," I said with a lisp, "we're going to have to stop for a bite on the way home."

Eric's eyes got wide. "Do you think that's a good idea? With the Ghouligans in town and everything going on? Maybe Brent and I should—"

"Should what? Feed all four of us?" I asked. "You'd be,

like, anemic in no time. And knocking over a blood bank would draw too much attention."

"Okay, but maybe you could hunt a town or two over, yes?"

I looked at Bobby. Now that the hunger had made itself known, I couldn't *not* be aware of it. I felt so hollow it was like I'd deflate if I couldn't find blood to fill me out again soon.

"Fine," Bobby said, looking back at me, "but I think we'd better go now." I noticed, when he spoke, that his fangs were fully extended as well, and wondered if it had just been too long for all of us, or whether the scent and the remembered taste of food all around us was making it worse.

Either way, I needed food, stat. It had been far too long since I'd eaten.

7

The next night, I came to with a start—literally *came to*. While daytime doesn't send the fangtabulous into a deep sleep so much as it sucker-punches us into unconsciousness, nighttime comes on like ice water in the face, bringing us suddenly and shockingly back to the land of the "living." It was like that every damn time, though Bobby always seemed to weather it just a little bit better than me.

But never *this* well.

The first thing I saw when my eyes burst open were his eyes... *way* the freak too close. So close that it looked like he only had one eye. One deep, dark pit of shadows. The kind that held secrets imprisoned on some trumped-up charge without the benefit of a trial. He had me trapped, his lower body resting over mine, his upper body held off of me by his arms, which pressed into the mattress to either side of my head like he was doing push-ups.

It was so … so … un-Bobby.

I tried to scuttle away from him, and when that didn't work, because I'd come to the very end of the pull-out couch, I pushed at his chest.

He didn't budge.

I was starting to freak now. I'd been claustrophobic ever since waking up in my coffin months ago and having to claw my own way out. *Also Bobby's fault*, at least the waking up part. Someone else had been responsible for my actual death, though I still wasn't sure whether to blame my evil ex, Chaz, or the car that intentionally side-swiped us.

This was *not* the boy I knew. Something had gotten into him.

"Bobby!" I called.

His head jerked back like I'd slapped him, confusion in his eyes—two of them now. But they were still dark and angry. Not his brilliant blue. Slapping him suddenly seemed like a very good idea.

So I did.

His head whipped left from the force of it, even though I'd been careful not to use my full strength and, anyway, his vamp reflexes should have let him roll with it.

When he snapped back to look at me, there was still bafflement, but it shone from his true-blue, beautiful eyes.

"Gina?" he asked uncertainly, as though he didn't even

know the question he was reaching for but figured I'd fill in the blanks. But I only had questions of my own.

"Bobby," I said. "Where did you go?"

He put his hand to his reddened cheek. "I didn't go anywhere. In fact, I was right here when you … did you *hit* me?"

I looked away. "You were"—*looking at me funny* sounded so lame—"not yourself for a minute. I woke up and you were staring at me like a creepy guy on a street corner who I'd normally hurry past."

"I was?" he asked. "But—why would I do that?"

"You don't know?"

"I don't remember."

Salem was *really* starting to flip me out.

Still without answers, Bobby and I reported for work at Haunts in History. Ulric pulled me aside as soon as we arrived. Bobby looked like he was going to protest, but he subsided at a look from me. Maybe it was trust. Or maybe he'd decided that with his super-vamp hearing, he could just listen in any old time. Which, now that I thought about it, wasn't the most comforting idea in the world.

Ulric closed the curtain behind us and looked me straight in the eye. A surprising little tingle went through me. It was a good thing I'd fed the night before. I was still a little buzzed from it, actually. We'd cruised one of the nearby bars just as it was closing down and kicking everyone out for the night. I still wasn't sure we'd taken in more blood than booze from those veins we'd tapped, but it was enough to stave off the hunger. Otherwise, Ulric might have been in danger of becoming a tasty treat.

"You're looking at me like I'm dinner," Ulric said, as if he could read my thoughts.

"Oh—sorry!"

"No, I like it," he said with his wolfish grin. "Makes me all hot and bothered. Want a taste?"

He offered up his neck, and while it was a very nice neck, and I knew exactly how tasty, I declined.

"You didn't pull me in here for necking, did you?" I asked, not nearly as impatient with him as I probably *should* have been, darnit.

"I could have."

I put my hands on my hips, which really tested the spatial limits of the dressing room.

"Okay," he said, hands up in a defensive gesture like I'd just offered him violence ... which wasn't out of the question. "Chip is sure someone got into his laptop at the gift shop. His browser history was cleared."

"So?"

"So, what do you know about that?"

I laughed. "Are you actually accusing *me* of knowing anything at all about computers?"

"Maybe you delegated."

"Your point being?"

"My point being that you need to be careful. I don't know what you're after, but Chip is now on the alert."

"How much do you know about him?"

"Chip? He's a good guy. Surly, but straight-up, you know."

"So then, not the type to, say, traffic in human remains or buy illegal grave goods?"

Ulric's eyes got bigger than Lady Gaga's boots, but he actually gave the question some thought. "I don't know," he answered slowly. "He might consider it a victimless crime. Does this have anything to do with the ghost who grabbed you?"

"Not sure yet. Do you know anything about a place called JC Theatrical Supplies?"

"I know Kari bought our costumes from them. Half the stores in Salem buy or rent gear from JC. Why?"

I debated how much to tell him, but I'd already said enough that he could probably guess the rest. "The skeleton in the Morbid Gift Shop—it's authentic."

"Well, of course. I never thought it wasn't. You can tell just by looking they're real bones."

"We're not talking about a medical specimen here. We're talking historical and probably not terribly legal."

"Seriously?"

"Yeah."

"Then there's no way he knows."

"Because he's too honest?"

"No, too smart. If he knew he had actual historical remains, he'd probably be looking for a private collector or something. He wouldn't have the skeleton caged like Madmartigan from *Willow*."

"Who from what?"

Ulric looked embarrassed, so I suspected it was something more geek than goth and should never have slipped out. I'd have to ask Bobby.

"Nevermind. Anyway, you could just *ask* Chip about it."

"Maybe I will. You got anything else for me?"

He grinned.

"Anything *not* dirty or hormonal?"

"Nothing dirty about it," he said, reaching for me.

I ducked out through the curtain, leaving him clutching air.

"You want to know more about JC Supplies?" he called after me, pushing the curtain aside. "Check in with Olivia at the brew pub. Her mom runs an antique store, and they do a lot of business back and forth."

I stopped and turned. "Olivia? Blond, about yay big"— I held up a hand to indicate—"bright blue streak through her hair?"

He looked surprised. "You know her?"

"Small town," I said.

"You should see it in the off season. Empties to half. But Olivia's a year-rounder. Her mom owns Ancient of Days over on Warren Street. I see the JC truck out in front of there sometimes."

"What does JC stand for, anyway?"

"Don't know. You'd have to ask him."

All I could think of was one of the ultimate religious

symbols (last name Christ). That didn't bode too well for any future meeting.

My footsteps slowed as we neared the front of the store, and I saw what waited for us there—Bryson Seacroft, the Ghouligans guy from that very first tour. Beside him were four other men, one holding a camera at rest...at chest rather than eye level. My heart sank. Bryson's dark eyes locked on me instantly, and there was no chance to duck back out of sight. I felt pinned like a bug on a board.

"There she is," he said.

Kari turned from them to me, that eternal smile bigger than ever. "Great!"

"Is there a back way out of here?" I asked Ulric out of the corner of my mouth.

But it was already too late. I felt someone come up behind us. Bobby, I knew instinctively, emerging from his dressing room, undoubtedly all suited up for the night.

His mental touch confirmed it. Just as Kari grabbed me by the arm and put her other hand behind my back to guide me toward the Ghouligans, Bobby asked in my head, *What should I do?*

That *was* the million-dollar question. Despite my desire to escape, if I bolted now I'd only make the Ghouligans uber-curious about me: unwillingness to be filmed, only seen at night, running at the sight of them. Guys like them, who ate the paranormal for lunch with a side order of science, tended to notice such things. If I ran now, I might as well keep on running, because I couldn't wait around for them to catch up with me.

Nothing, I said in my head. *I'll manage.*

I knew Bobby could read and influence minds. Could he make the Ghouligans forget anything iffy they might see tonight? Or *not* see, when they replayed anything recorded on their equipment? By the end of the night, we might have to find out.

I pasted a shy smile on my face and stepped forward with Kari. Bryson's gaze continued to bore into me. It made me totally uncomfortable, so I moved on to sharing my smile with the cameraman and others. All but the sound guy smiled back. But maybe he couldn't see me through his really thick lenses with their retro dark frames. Or maybe his baseball cap, on backwards as if to protect his neck from the moon's harmful rays, was too tight. I decided to call the others Clipboard Guy, Cameraman, and Sidekick. The tall, shaggy-haired guy with the blue eyes (my weakness) and dimples I knew to be one of the regular onscreen Ghouligans. Ty...something. You'd think I'd *know*. Half my high school friends had been crushing on him.

Karl introduced me to the crew:

Lloyd Bender=Clipboard Guy

Kaleb Margolin=Cameraman

Ernie Boyd=Sound (and no wonder he scowled, with a name like Ernie; I wondered how many times a day people asked after Bert).

Ty was Tyler McClellan—Ty for short. Was the "Mc" Scottish? Irish? I had no idea. Something from that neck of the woods. His eyes sparkled with mischief, a far cry from Bryson Seacroft's piercing gaze. In a game of good cop/bad cop, the casting would be no contest.

Then Rebecca came through the outer shop door behind them, already in costume but with her gorgeous red hair free-flowing behind her. Or, maybe not so free-flowing, since it seemed to be curled and shellacked into place.

"Sorry I'm late!" she said breezily, then stopped cold at the sight of everybody, as if she hadn't expected them. I was betting she had, based on the air and the entrance. Nice that Kari had given *her* a heads-up. In her possible defense, though, I hadn't even thought to check for messages on my disposable cell phone, since I already shared an apartment with everyone I knew in town. It never occurred to me that anyone else might be calling.

"Not late at all," Kari said. "I was just making introductions."

She began them all over again, which was good, because I'd already forgotten, like, half the names. She closed with, "You'd better get your bonnet out and get going. Any later," she explained to Bryson and crew, "and the Old Jail and Cemetery will be thick with other ghost tours."

"Do I *have* to wear the bonnet?" Rebecca asked, grabbing the attention back to herself. "So much more dramatic with the hair down, don't you think?" She shook her helmet head out to show it off, and, to my surprise, it actually swayed luxuriously. I'd have to ask her what she used ... right before I clubbed her over the head for stealing the spotlight.

Okay, so I'd given it up. Insult to injury.

Kari's smile dimmed, and for a second, I could see the hard business woman underneath. "You're representing Haunts in History," she said, sounding suddenly prim. "We pride ourselves on authenticity."

Rebecca looked at the Ghouligans in appeal, and Bryson shrugged. "We'll film it both ways and see what looks best. Either way, we'll do a really nice intro to Haunts and link to you on our website. Should be good coverage," he assured Kari. Then, to Rebecca, "My two cents, though ... with strangulation, we want to see the throat. Hair back or up, with bonnet, will probably be best."

Rebecca turned her disappointment into a cute pout. "Whatever you say," she responded, in a tone that clearly meant *I'm sure you'll come to see it my way; I can humor you for now.* "Just let me ditch my purse."

If a small purse meant a simple life—and it did, trust me—hers was as complicated as they came. Her purse could easily have doubled as a small suitcase. You could tell a ton about a person from the contents of her purse. A bag that size ... but I didn't suppose jealousy gave me enough cause for a search and seizure, especially with witnesses.

After stashing the behemoth bag under the counter of Haunts, Rebecca turned with a winning smile. "Shall we?"

This time even the sound guy smiled back, but it was Ty she had eyes for.

I huffed. Ulric shot me an amused grin.

Bobby stayed silent. I wondered, if I were to glance over my shoulder, which Bobby I'd see looking back at me ... the one I knew, or the stranger from earlier that evening. I shuddered just thinking about it.

Bryson motioned for Rebecca to proceed them. The Ghouligans fell in line behind her, leaving me to bring up the rear, totally ignored. It beat Bryson's previous eagle-eye scrutiny, but not by much.

Apparently, the news that the Ghouligans were in town had spread like wildfire. Already, a few fans had gathered outside of Haunts. As we paraded out, they went from staring in through the windows and talking amongst themselves to following behind us like we were the pied pipers of Salem.

Since I was at the rear and clearly the least important of the group, fingers tapped my shoulders, voices stage-whispered earnestly. "What's going on?"

"Is it about that girl?"

"Is it true it was a ghost?"

"This town is haunted. I knew it from the first."

Ty dropped back, and the voices hushed as if in awe.

"You okay?" he asked, sending me a dazzling smile that dimpled his cheeks.

"Yeah, why?"

"You look a little shell-shocked, to be honest."

"I'm ... uncomfortable with all the publicity. I mean, the focus should be on that poor girl who was killed, and on finding out who did it."

"You mean *what*."

"What?"

"Exactly. *What* did it, not who. You should know better than anyone that it wasn't anything natural."

"So you're a true believer, then?"

"Aren't you? After what you went through?"

"I ... guess so. The horror was real, but it's like all the rest of it was some kind of nightmare I woke up from."

"We get that a lot. The mind rationalizes away what it doesn't want to believe. Of course, we also get the attention-seekers, the kooks, the lovely older ladies who don't realize the things going bump in the night are the squirrels in their attics."

I laughed. "Seriously?"

"Clearly we never get to this stage with those lovely old ladies."

"What if it's ghost squirrels?"

"Now you're making fun of me," he said, but his dimples didn't disappear, so I didn't take him for mortally wounded.

"Guess I don't really have room to talk, huh?" I said. "Strangled by ghost hands."

Ty's attention was starting to make me a little nervous. Being who he was, I was terrified I'd give myself away. Did he believe in vampires as well as ghosts? I didn't know and wasn't about to find out. I remembered to breathe. I couldn't do anything about the non-existence of my heart-beat, but most humans never noticed that sort of thing.

"Come to think of it," Ty said, still amiably, "you sound great for someone who's been strangled. Do you still have the bruises? They'd make a great shot."

It was a test, and I'd walked right into it. Ty might be a lot more charming than his co-host, but he was no less observant. Or dangerous. I had to remember that and not let myself get distracted by a pretty face.

"They faded away, just like the ghost," I said truthfully. "I don't have anything left to show for it but my nightmares."

He looked at me unblinkingly. "That's unusual."

"That's me," I answered.

I thought he'd let it go at that. "Very unusual. Most people would jump at the chance to be on television, especially young women as attractive as you are. You don't have hopes of being discovered?"

"I have high hopes of *not* being discovered," I said, from the heart. Then, to cover, "I'm kind of shy. I don't want my friends back home to tease me for believing in ghosts."

"Where's home?"

"The Midwest," I hedged.

"Me too. Where specifically?"

Man, he was *not* going to let it go. "Indiana," I lied. It was close enough to Ohio. I'd been there once. I could fake it. Then I hastened my steps to catch up to Rebecca, who was busy getting tips from Bryson.

"Hey," I said as I got close.

Bryson cut off whatever he'd been saying, something about not looking right at the camera, to acknowledge me. We were almost to the Old Jail and the site of my strangulation. We'd gained rather than lost followers, and we now truly looked like a parade... or a funeral procession. Anyway, we'd be there soon enough, and then everyone would hopefully be too busy for questions I didn't want to answer.

"Hey, yourself," Bryson said. "You sure about this? No offense to Rebecca"—he flashed her a smile—"but you two are about as different as night and day. Usually when we do dramatizations, we try to choose someone who looks like the person involved."

There was a plea in Rebecca's eyes when she looked at me. She could save it—clear nail polish had more visibility on film than I did. Besides, the less similar my "double" looked, the less likely someone would connect us and come looking for me.

"I'm sure."

"It's a shame," Bryson added. "Your dark hair and pale skin, those green eyes... you'd be a natural."

Ouch. Words I'd always hoped to hear... meaningless now.

"Nah, Rebecca's got it covered," I said, swallowing the pain. "Besides, I've always wanted to be a redhead."

Although so not with my skin tone. Red highlights, now... that might be hot. Or purple lowlights. Something to consider.

Bryson shrugged. "Suit yourself. You ready, Rebecca?"

"Absolutely!"

Thank you, she mouthed to me when Bryson looked away. I gave her a nod and a smile, even though Bryson's words ate away at my soul. It so sucked to have your dreams so close you could taste them, yet too far to touch. Sucked worse than being vamped at your senior prom and waking up three days later trapped in a coffin in a hideous dress you literally wouldn't be caught dead in. If Bobby hadn't been waiting for me with two brimming Macy's bags when I fought my way out of the grave, well, eternal life might not have been worth living.

I stood back and watched the crew set up—the Old Jail in the background, the iron fence of the Howard Street Cemetery just visible beyond it.

I *did not* wallow.

People in the crowd held up cameras and cell phones, and suddenly there wasn't even any time for not-wallowing. It was tough to prove that you'd taken a picture of someone who didn't appear, but if anyone blogged, tweeted, or otherwise posted the weirdness online, we were goners. It was a sure bet that both the Feds and the fangs had some kind of Google Alert set up to monitor for such things.

I faded into the background, behind the cameraman and sound guy, behind the clipboard dude, Lloyd, who I assumed was some kind of producer or director or something. He looked over and saw what I'd seen. A look of irritation crossed his face. He started talking, and I thought at first it was to me, but then I noticed his headset and understood there was someone on the other end of it.

"I thought the police had agreed to send someone out for crowd control," he barked. "Well, check on the ETA."

"People," he called more loudly, moving toward the crowd. I could only hope the person on the other end of his signal had disconnected. Otherwise, their ears would be ringing. "You're welcome to the pictures you've snapped so far, but we're going to have to insist on no pictures, video or still, once we begin filming. The material is proprietary, and Feldspar Productions takes any leakage of our segments very seriously. I'll also have to ask you to move back, because we're going to have to take establishing shots of the area. You're welcome to stay and watch, but we'll have to ask you to turn off all cell phones and silence all conversations."

Clearly he'd given the speech before, but he didn't take it any more lightly for the repetition. Instead, he made eye contact with as many in the crowd as he could, probably trying to send home the message that he was noting faces.

If I hadn't been so totally bummed, I'd have been fascinated by the whole process.

In contrast, Rebecca was glowing, torn between listening to Kaleb-the-cameraman's last-minute instructions on how to behave, stand, look, speak, etc. and angling her best side toward the crowd, which was still snapping some last-minute photos.

Two officers approached from the direction of the Old Jail, and Lloyd left off eying the crowd to go meet them.

With my awesome vamp senses, I could hear them even over all the other conversations that hadn't yet been silenced.

"We're already getting calls in from the residents excited or worried about freaks flocking the place or plunging property values," one officer was saying.

"Chief told them you had a permit," said the other, who looked like he could bench-press his skinnier partner with ease.

"You've got crowd control?" Lloyd asked.

"Don't worry, we'll keep them in line," the stick figure cop said. He held up a fistful of thin plastic stakes with twine strung between them, and they went to work roping off a good section of ground.

The ghost tours scheduled for tonight were going to have to give the place a wide berth. At least it ought to keep everyone safe if the murderous ghost was still in the area.

Lloyd noticed me watching, and gave me a grin and a wink as he got back to the rest of us. I gave him a shy grin in return. I wasn't good at shy, but I was getting in lots of practice.

The production got underway. They tried it Rebecca's way first—without the bonnet. I thought she was doing pretty well, but Lloyd called me in to show her again where I'd stood, how it had happened, how it had felt and all the rest. I turned to show them where the woman with the crucifix had come from when she'd rushed to my aid—and went still.

The light on the camera ... it was green. I didn't know a lot about film or digital recording or whatever, but I knew what green meant. Green meant "go." It meant panic time!

"But you don't have my photo release!" I cried, stunned,

turning on the Ghouligans with my eyes blazing, as green as the go-light.

Lloyd hastened to reassure me. "Don't worry, this is just for background, so we can listen later and add our color commentary."

It wasn't the listening I was worried about—it was the *looking*. This would be a whole lot bigger than some random blogger with theories and rationalizations. This was a nationally syndicated show... *internationally* for all I knew. And if they believed, they'd pursue. There was no way to keep a lid on things. We were sunk, and it was all my fault. I'd insisted on staying in town. I'd been the one to tell Bobby I'd think of something. Well, I suddenly had—stopping the production and destroying the footage. More like, we'd have to get the hell out of Salem before they could review the recordings. Oh yes, I was a master strategist.

I don't know what I would have done right then—probably something desperate, like pretend all my grace had suddenly deserted me and crash hard into the camera, hard enough to destroy it—but a hair-raising scream went up from behind the twine barricades, cutting off into a painful gurgle. Other screams quickly rose up.

"Help!"

"He's got her!"

"The ghost!"

Out of the corner of my eye, I saw the camera swing toward the crowd. That would have been my moment. With everybody looking the other way, I could have destroyed the camera and no one would ever know it had been on purpose, but I knew what that choked-off cry meant. I'd lived it.

I'd had near-invincibility on my side, but I knew this person was fearing for her life. My first impulse was to spring forward, to save her.

8

The police officers who'd come for crowd control rushed to the fallen woman. Girl, really—zebra-print tank top way too cool for the night under a wide-open black hoodie with the standard jeans, and sneakers with Day-Glo pink laces. She couldn't have been more than fifteen. She was no longer struggling for breath . . . or at all. The skinny cop was lip-locked to her while the other was doing chest compressions, making me fear he'd crack a rib. Logically, I knew they were trying to get her breathing again, but it just looked so . . . abusive.

And camera guy had positioned himself to be sure he got it all on film. Just inside the shot, Ty and Bryson pulled out palm-sized gadgets that looked like something out of *Ghostbusters*.

"Is she okay?" I asked stupidly.

"Paramedics are on the way," said chest-compression cop, out of breath like he was doing his best to breathe for two.

"Definite paranormal activity," Bryson commented to Ty, who nodded. The latter's gadget swung left and right, then seemed to stop on the skinny officer. Ty looked up, from his gadget to the cop. The look was inscrutable, but intense.

"You know CPR, don't you?" Ty asked Bryson, his voice level ... intentionally so, I thought.

"Yeah."

"I think you should take over."

They exchanged a look over that, and Bryson immediately hid his device away in a pocket. He dropped a hand to the shoulder of the cop doing the mouth-to-mouth. "Let me try," he said.

"Too busy right now to step aside for you to play hero."

I saw Bryson squeeze the shoulder and the skinny officer's eyes go wide, then narrow. When he looked up at the Ghouligan, there was nothing of the protector in the cop's eyes. There *was* something infinitely colder. *Evil*, if it could be defined as the complete absence of good rather than something that seethed and burned hot.

The cop pulled away from the girl, then, with a *be-my-guest* gesture to Bryson, likely knowing that it was already too late and willing to cover his ass about his failure to revive her by putting Bryson's on the line.

I didn't want to draw any attention, particularly not with the cameras on, but ... one drop of my blood could mean the difference between life and death for the girl. *One drop.* How far was I willing to go to keep my own secret? Not that it was *just* mine.

I looked around for inspiration. Rebecca was nearby, clutching her bonnet in her hands. I could use that.

I grabbed it out of her hands and she cried out, more in surprise than anything. Then I jammed the nail of my index finger into my thumb under the cover of the bonnet, hard enough to draw blood. I had to act quickly, before the cut could heal. Already the white linen of the bonnet had started sucking up the little blood that flowed.

I dropped to my knees by the fallen girl's side, landing between her two would-be saviors to shield myself from the camera, and used the bonnet to fan her so any attention would be drawn to my useless efforts and not to what they were covering for. It wasn't enough. I stepped up my efforts, fanning for all I was worth, praying for some of my blood droplets to land in her mouth whenever Bryson paused in the assisted breathing. I restabbed my finger as needed. It was clumsy, but everyone had already discounted me. *Clearly*, I was acting more out of compassion than competency.

I *thought* they'd discounted me anyway. When I looked around to be sure, Ty caught my eye. And there was a glimmer in it I'd seen before. A *Gotcha.*

"You're bleeding," he said, quietly, but with everyone holding their breath over the fate of the girl, he might as well have shouted. Everybody looked at me.

Bryson stole the attention back. "It's no use," he said solemnly. "She's gone."

Someone in the crowd sobbed and tore away from the rest—another girl about the same age as the fallen girl, maybe a little older. Same coloring. Big sister? She fell on the girl, practically beating on her and insisting that she "Wake up—WAKE UP, dammit!"

In shock, Bryson and the cop doing the chest compressions momentarily froze, and I used the second of stun to reach across the girl's body toward her sister, aiming a droplet of blood for the fallen girl's lips before I grabbed her sister's hands, firmly enough to still her panic-stricken abuse.

She stopped on contact and let out one great sob. I let her go so I could circle around her sister's non-responsive body to offer a hug. Non-responsive. *Not dead.* I wouldn't accept that. By *The Princess Bride* standards—another movie Bobby had made me watch that I hadn't actually hated— the girl was only *mostly* dead. Meaning she could recover. Maybe. Probably. I had to believe.

The sister sobbed quietly into my shoulder, getting snot all over my shirt, and for a moment I was too absorbed by her grief to notice what anyone else was doing. Then there was a gasp and a cough . . . and all hell broke loose.

People screamed and pointed—one woman fell to her knees, hands clasped in prayer, proclaiming a miracle—and the dead girl sat up, gasping for air. I could practically hear her heart from where I stood, beating against her rib cage like a caged bird determined to break out.

The skinny officer rushed back in with his partner and tried to push the girl back down, telling her to relax, that the ambulance we could now hear in the distance was on the way. Her sister shoved me away to rush to her side.

Left behind, I looked around, thinking maybe now I could go for the camera, while everyone was dumbfounded with shock and awe. But the cameraman had never wavered. He was tightly focused on the recovered girl, ignoring her rescuers.

I felt eyes on me off to the right and turned to see ... Ty, closer than I remembered him being. I didn't like the look in his eyes—speculative, thoughtful. *Way* too observant.

It was totally imperative that we get rid of all evidence. And I knew just the man for the job—Eric, our resident mad scientist. What he couldn't do with machines couldn't be done. Period. He could literally do the impossible; it was his mojo. When we'd met him, he was tinkering with improbable inventions and thinking it was a conspiracy that no one would admit to being able to duplicate his results. As a man of science, a magical explanation had never occurred to him. Then we came along and rocked his world.

"Miraculous recovery," Ty said, shooting me a sidelong glance to check my reaction.

"It sure was. I've never seen anything like it."

"Oh no?"

I studied his face. Either he wasn't very good at disingenuous or he wasn't trying very hard.

Shitshitshit. Time for diversionary tactics.

"Bryson must be a miracle worker. Isn't that why you had him take over CPR from that cop?"

"No."

"Then why?" I asked.

"I'll show you mine if you'll show me yours."

"My what?" I asked, pulling back from him. He hadn't struck me as a perv.

"Your secrets."

I shrugged casually. "I'm an open book."

He snorted. Very elegant. "Yeah, right."

He waited for me to say something more, and I let him wait. And wait.

Finally, he said, "The instruments picked up some unusual activity surrounding that officer."

"Wow, could you be less specific?"

He grinned, like he had me hooked, which, okay, *maybe* he did.

"We call it a shadow. Think of it like this—all life has a certain energy, even plants. Tests have been done on exposing plants to different kinds of music and monitoring—"

"CliffsNotes version?" I asked. "Unless you're trying to tell me the cop is some kind of photosynthetic-American, in which case I'm down with diversity and all."

"No, what I'm trying to say is that people give off a measurable energy, a wavelength that can be measured. All living things do. Have you ever done a wave experiment, say sound waves? One consistent tone gets you one uniform wave. Two and there's interference, crisscrossing crests and valleys."

"Okay, so you're saying his wavelength or aura or whatever is choppy?"

"That's exactly what I'm saying."

"But what does it *mean*?" I might be getting it, but I didn't know what it was I'd got.

"A spectral presence—either hovering very near, potentially whispering in his ear, or even temporarily in control."

I stared at him. "You mean, like, in *possession*."

"Basically."

I felt a chill, but I didn't think it had anything to do with the weather. All I could think of was Bobby's eyes earlier, their usual deep blue darkened almost to black, like all the light had gone out of them. Eclipsed? Another presence taking over control?

"You said temporarily."

"Most spirits don't have the energy to maintain control for long. It takes a vast amount of power."

"Like the kind of power it would take for a ghost to physically strangle someone?"

Ty's eyes flashed. "More. Like the kind of power a spirit might *gain* by stealing a life, through strangulation or whatever."

I didn't like the sound of that. Not any part of it. "It isn't possible to keep possession, like, *permanently*, is it?" I asked.

"It isn't common. Usually it takes too much energy to fight for control with the soul already present. But sometimes a spirit might find a body very close to death, the soul already fled or on a very tenuous tether, and *snap*!"

He snapped his fingers to prove the point, and I had to keep myself from jumping. All I could think of was Bobby, and all my unanswered questions about the state of our souls. What if vampires didn't have them? Maybe they'd gone the way of our heartbeats and our ability to withstand the sun. What if one of Salem's resident spirits had found itself a hot new home in which to set up shop?

But Bobby still had a will, a consciousness, a code at the very least. He could still love—me in particular. That had to count for something.

"Let's say someone was possessed. How would you fight it?"

Ty's eyes flashed and his gaze intensified. "You know someone like that?"

"Let's say hypothetically."

"Exorcism."

The word alone nearly did me in. Crosses, holy water, casting out the devil and whatnot ... Bobby would never survive.

"You okay?" Ty asked.

"Fine. I just need to ... make a call."

He didn't look at all convinced. Given the crappiness of my performance, I wasn't surprised. I was probably paler even than usual, as I drifted off beyond the edges of the gathered group and fiddled with my cell phone, just to put on a show while I gave Bobby a mental shout-out.

There was no answer. I had to hope he was in the middle of leading a tour, that it wasn't that the lights were on but no one was home. I had a sudden fear that the Feds and fangs didn't need to track and kill us—Salem would do the job for them.

Since Bobby was unavailable, I used the phone the way it was intended—to call Eric and beg him to do something about the Ghouligans' footage. Back in Florida, he'd built the machine the vamps had used to mind-swap Nelson into his current Cro-Magnon form. He'd also built the portable electromagnetic pulse machine that had helped us take out the Feds' sick supernatural testing facility. Problem was, we couldn't exactly use it here ... at least not unless we could lure the Ghouligans and their gadgets to some deserted place. If we pulled something like that in a crowded area like this one, anyone with a pacemaker or other implanted electronics would suffer for it.

This was a hot mess. I was starting to worry about whether the team would be better off without me. I was a liability, making mistakes that could get us all killed. I thought wistfully of my old life back in Mozulla, Ohio, where the biggest thing I'd had to worry about each day was what to wear and whether Marcy and I might clash, an issue that required serious nightly discussion.

Eric didn't answer my phone call, so I left a message and thought about my next step. Bobby'd always been my go-to guy, but I was suddenly afraid to share my theories with him. How did I know which *him* I'd be talking to? Would I be tipping my hand to the enemy? Was I imagining things?

Gah, I wasn't used to so much self-doubt. It sucked worse than strawberry shakes with chunks of the fruit lodged in the straw.

9

Ulric was just returning with a group when Rebecca and I made it back to Haunts. A reed-thin girl, with wispy brown hair pulled back into a lopsided ponytail, was asking him a tell-all book's worth of questions about orbs and energies and hanging on his every word.

He shot us a look as we came through the door that said while he didn't exactly *need* saving, he'd be eternally grateful for it all the same. That fit in perfectly with my plans, as I figured we had no time to lose in solving the Case of the Supernatural Strangler and getting the hell out of town.

"Ulric, thank goodness, just the man I need to see," I said, abandoning Rebecca at the entrance. "Can we talk?" I gave the brunette an apologetic look. "Sorry, I need to steal him away."

Without giving her the chance to protest, I pulled Ulric away by the arm, tucking mine in his.

"*Thank you*," he said, letting out a huge breath. "I think she's an aspiring Ghouligan or something. She had another question for every answer."

"She wasn't interested in the answers."

"O-kay, I'll bite," he answered.

"She was interested in *you*."

"Well, that explains the really nice tip. Anyway, I couldn't just brush her off."

My eyes sparkled. "You know, for a pain in the butt, you're actually a pretty decent guy."

He looked around surreptitiously. "Don't tell anyone. You'll ruin my street cred."

"What street cred?"

He clutched his hand to his heart. "You wound me."

"Not yet, but give it time."

"Oh, promises, promises. I don't suppose you jumped in because you were crazy jealous and wanted me all to yourself?" he asked hopefully.

"Sorry."

"Figures. What can I do for you?"

Well, that was unusually direct and helpful for Ulric.

"I need to talk to Olivia," I answered. "As soon as possible."

"So talk to her."

"Since you know her, I think it might go better if you smoothed the way."

He didn't look too certain of that. "Suppose we could catch a drink afterward?"

Ah, *there* was the catch. I gave him a *look*.

"Right, you don't drink. Except, you know ... " He dangled his index and middle fingers in front of his lips, simulating fangs. I slapped his hand down before anyone could see.

"Ulric!" I hissed.

He gave me that cocky grin of his. "What? I'm not complaining. In fact, I'm volunteering. Any time you want to give me a nibble, you just let me know. But remember, turn-about is fair play."

"I'll keep it in mind," I said wryly.

"So, is that a yes for later?" he asked.

"Yes to you coming with me to talk to Olivia. No to the rest."

"Pity."

The teeniest tiniest part of me agreed with that. I loved Bobby, but somehow that didn't lessen Ulric's pull, only how I chose to respond to it. I could well imagine that without my B-boy, Ulric would be dangerous. Maybe not to my health, but definitely to my equilibrium.

I gave him another look.

"I love it when you go all disapproving school marm on me. Makes me wish you'd hold me after school."

See what I mean—I was *so* not the school marm type. The fact that Ulric brought it out of me ... completely messed with the natural order of things.

It was Kari's turn to ride to the rescue this time. Sort of, anyway. She found us and dragged me toward the front, breathlessly telling me that she had a new tour group ready to go and they'd requested "the girl who'd gotten strangled" as their guide. She was sure that if I acted it out for them, I'd make out like a bandit in tips. After seeing the zebra-striped girl fight for her life earlier, the thought of capitalizing on the killer-ghost made me sick. But a girl had to eat. Or, at least, she had to keep Brent and Eric in eats. And I did demand a roof over my head that didn't sit atop four wheels. That sleeping-in-a-coffin crap you see on TV was just that—crap. Discerning vampires preferred beds.

I didn't get back to the Haunts shop for over an hour, and when I did—strung out on nerves, wondering how many would be tweeting and blogging tonight about their photographically challenged tour guide—there was yet another group waiting for me. I barely had time to check my voicemail in between. I'd gotten one from Eric letting me know he'd received my earlier message. I'd just started to relax a bit when he added, "But if they've already uploaded the footage to some off-site backup, we're sunk."

Between that and all the pictures I'd been unable to avoid not-starring in tonight, sending Eric after the Ghouligans' equipment was starting to feel futile. Oh sure, I could disappear, quite literally. But what about the others? Yup, responsibility sucked big chunks of strawberry through teeny tiny straws.

It was late when I returned with my second tour group.

Nearly closing time. Bobby and Rebecca were nowhere to be seen. Kari was counting up the register and looking very pleased with herself, and Ulric was just emerging from the back. He'd changed out of his costume, into all black—from biker boots with silver spikes as trim to a leather jacket with spiky epaulets. In the dimness of the back hallway, his deep brown eyes were nearly lost beneath the flap of dark hair that obscured his face. For a minute, I wondered what he was hiding beneath the spikes and the hair and the humor.

"Wait right there," I ordered, heading for the changing rooms myself.

"Are you sure you don't want me in there with you?" he asked. "Then you could keep an eye on me to be sure I follow orders."

I paused to glare, fighting the smile that wanted to ruin it all. "I know that *you* know that if you don't listen, I'll hunt you down."

He grinned. "Could be fun."

"Yes, but not for you."

"Spoilsport."

"I've been called worse." Like *school marm*, but we weren't getting into that again.

I hurried in to change. If we got out of there before Bobby returned from his tour, he couldn't get on my case about not taking him along for backup. My heart ached. I felt like I was betraying him, stepping out with another guy, even if it totally wasn't like that. I wanted the trust back. I wanted my Bobby back, and he hadn't even gone anywhere.

When I emerged from the dressing room in my skinny jeans, long-sleeved scoop-neck tee, and fleecy jacket, Ulric was waiting for me with a smile and a proffered arm. "Shall we?"

I ignored the arm, since my tennies didn't require the extra stability, and Ulric didn't need any encouragement to think of this as a date.

Not to be outmaneuvered, Ulric grabbed my right hand and tucked it in his arm anyway, pressing it tightly to his body to keep me there. I shot him a look, and he raised a brow as if to ask what I was going to do about it. With or without vampirical enhancements, it wasn't exactly a hard grip to break, but I let it go. After all, Ulric was helping me out. Might was well throw him a bone.

"Fine, you win," I said, finally giving in to the smile that teased at my lips.

"I won't even ask about the prize. I think I have that right here." He patted my hand.

If I weren't taken, it would have been charming. Okay, it *was* charming. But still...

He seemed to know not to push his luck, and instead started moving us toward the door.

The sound of a returning tour bounced around the building as we hit the street, and I sped up a bit to avoid running into them and their guide. Ulric didn't say a word.

The brew pub was within walking distance, as was everything else in Salem proper, and we were there inside of five minutes. Between Haunts and Brews, we passed one cemetery, two witch museums, and a town square with a huge statue of a television witch sitting on the moon—from *Bewitched*, Ulric told me, and a huge bone of contention within the town. We also passed three restaurants, a hotel, and two magic shops, one seemingly dedicated to the darker side—based on the word "hex," a prominent part of its name—and the other—crystal something-or-other—seemingly dedicated to the lighter.

As we stepped through the doors of the brew pub, Ulric dropped my arm and strolled up to the hostess stand. The woman behind it didn't miss the move.

"She here?" Ulric asked, like there was only one person he could be referring to.

Apparently, there was. The hostess eyed him hostilely. "Why, you here to break her heart again?"

"She's the one who—" Ulric stopped, took a deep breath, and continued as I watched with interest. Oh yeah, he and whoever—Olivia, I guessed—had history. "Is she here?" he repeated.

"She'd be gone already but for the table that won't die. I ought to be calling them cabs any time now. You can go sit in her section and wait." She turned the evil eye on me. "You with him?"

"Not the way you think."

"Good." But she didn't let the approval seep into her voice.

"What was that all about?" I asked quietly as I followed Ulric around a chest-high wall into a back section of the pub.

"Olivia and I . . . had a thing. Her ex-boyfriend kept

reappearing, twisting her up and getting her all conflicted. I ended the conflict."

"You took yourself out of the running?"

"There comes a point where someone either wants you or they don't."

"Maybe she was confused."

"Clearly."

He positioned himself with his back against the wall of a booth so that he could sit more or less sidelong in the seat and watch the whole room.

Olivia, bearing a tray overloaded with coffees, pies, and brews, didn't see us at first. She was focused on her table and on blowing her bright-blue streaky hair out of her face. The tray bobbled as a shifting lock of hair revealed Ulric lounging in her section. I thought for a minute that her table was going to be wearing their food. Then she recovered and pointedly ignored us as she delivered her goods—smiling, flirting, and catching a hand as it reached for her backside, definitely up to no good. She managed to return it to its owner with a smile, which was more than I could have done.

But the smile disappeared as she hugged her now-empty tray protectively against her chest and turned to us.

"What do you want?" she asked, eyes only for Ulric.

"Some of that pie, to start. Was that chocolate pecan?"

"To go?" she asked.

He pretended to miss her message. "Olivia, this is Gia. She's a ... friend ... from back home."

Olivia gave me a sour look. "An *ex-girlfriend*, maybe?" She glanced back at Ulric.

"Matter of fact, no. Look, I'm sorry if you think I've somehow wronged you." To his credit, Ulric actually sounded sorry. "But that's not why I'm here. I need you to talk to Gia. You know that girl who was attacked the other night, almost strangled?"

"I'm her," I cut in.

Olivia's eyes widened, and she lost her petulant look as she turned on me. "That's awful! What can I do?" Then she held up a hand to stop me from answering and called out over the half-wall, "Marley, can you cover me?"

Marley popped her head over the partition, saw Ulric and me, and then skimmed right past us to focus on Olivia. "Sure thing."

Olivia plopped down beside me, making me scooch in. "How can I help? Charm of protection? Warding spell?"

"Information," I said, at the same time Ulric explained, "Olivia is a witch."

"Cool," I said. "So you can give your arch-nemesis chronic bad breath or hairy armpits or whatever?"

Olivia got a pained look on her face. "Why does everyone think the Craft is all love spells and curses?" It had to be a rhetorical question, because she kept right on. "I probably *could*, now that you mention it. Giving Ulric here a case of jock itch would be pretty satisfying." Ulric squirmed and Olivia grinned, showing nice white teeth. "But it's against our tenets."

"Like?"

"First, do no harm." Oh right, that one.

"So, you're a Wicca witch. But there are other kinds, right? I saw a hex shop on my way over. That doesn't sound like all sweetness and light."

"It isn't. That's a darker magic. We don't dabble."

"We?"

"Me and my coven. So, what kind of information do you need?"

I was going to launch into questions about JC Theatrical Supplies, but since we were on the subject of magic...

"All this stuff with the spirits getting riled up, people being attacked—could it be a spell? Not a Wiccan spell, of course," I rushed to add, "but something else?"

Olivia's pale blue eyes, emphasized by the streak in her hair, narrowed at me. I thought that if she could shoot lasers out of her eyes, like the X-Men's Cyclops—Bobby's influence again—I'd be toast. "Do you *really* want to go there?" she asked. "Given the history of this town, do you actually want to start a new witch hunt by suggesting that magic is involved?"

Ulric put a hand over Olivia's where it was clenched on the table, and she turned that laser-like gaze on him. "Move it or die," she snapped.

So much for "do no harm." But I recognized her tone for what it was ... bravado. All bark, no bite. Olivia was scared. Legitimately scared. Down to her toenails.

Ulric wasn't. He didn't draw back his hand—or a bloody

stump, since she didn't make good on her threat. Instead, he stroked a thumb gently over her hand. While Olivia's death-glare didn't lessen, I did notice an untensing of her body by degrees.

"I *don't* want to start a witch hunt," I said. "In fact, I want to prevent it. Look, the supernatural starts acting up and most people think *magic*. They don't know that there are different kinds, and that one isn't like a gateway drug to the others. I can't be the only person wondering, even if I'm the first to say it out loud. The best thing we can do is figure out what's going on and how to stop it, ASAP."

"Before the tourist trade or anyone else gets killed."

"Ulric!" I said, shocked. "How can you even be thinking about tourism at a time like this?'

The look he gave me was dead serious. He wore it well. I wasn't used to seeing this side of him, and it was kind of…impressive. "You don't understand. You don't live here. The end of September through the beginning of November—Halloween season—is when the residents make about seventy-five percent of their income. Before and after…it's a dead zone. A quiet town without a lot of traffic or attention. For most here, the tourist trade is literally a matter of life and death. Financially speaking, anyway."

I'd never even thought about it. Since I'd been vamped mere months ago, I'd been living *Fright Night* full time, playing dress-up, putting on personas. My Halloween had become a year-round thing.

"Back to stopping it," Olivia said, taking back her hand

from Ulric. "How is that your business? Like Ulric said, you don't even live here."

"I do now." If I was going to gain her trust, I'd have to give something in return. "But it's a fair question about my business. I came to Salem with a few friends. We wanted to start over and didn't exactly fit in elsewhere, if you know what I mean." And I thought she might. "We like it here. We'd like to stay. But one of my friends... he's a sensitive, and this place is making him nuts. If we can lay the spirits to rest..."

Olivia's gaze softened. "That's rough. I can build him a dampening spell, something to shield him from all the energies."

"How about answering my question?" I asked gently, not wanting to put her back on the defensive. "Could it be a spell? Should we be looking for dark magic? A dampener would be great, but it won't keep girls from getting strangled. I should know."

I raised a hand to my neck to remind her of my personal stake in all this, the *other* reason she could assume I was so interested. Luckily, my jacket covered the fact that I was all recovered from the ordeal.

She looked at me in sympathy and started to reach a hand out before drawing it back, still not clear, I guessed, on my relationship to Ulric and whether it was okay to like me.

"I want to help, but—well, my coven and I have already done a spell to search for the origin of the trouble, to try to lay the Salem Strangler to rest."

"And?"

"And whatever it is, it's stronger than us at its core. It doesn't *read* like a spell, which is bound with components, woven together, diffuse."

"What does it read like?"

"I don't know ... a beacon? A beam? Focused, intense. Ancient, I'd say, but I don't know why."

"Like an object of power?" Ulric cut in. "Like Excalibur or something like that?" He sounded like Bobby.

"Probably not Excalibur," Olivia said with an amused twist of the lips. "But something. Yes, maybe an object of power."

"An object we could track?"

"Maybe. We tried and didn't get very far. All I can tell you is that it's here, in Salem."

"Could it have come from JC Supplies?" I asked.

Her eyes narrowed again, but not to the point of arrow slits; more like she was trying to figure out what I was getting at. "They don't deal in the arcane. JC is more about antiques and theater props."

"Maybe they didn't know what they had."

"I guess it's possible. Why are you so focused on them?"

"A few of the things my friend, the sensitive, has reacted to have come from JC."

She shrugged. "You could ask. I have their number right here." She pulled her phone from a jeans pocket beneath her apron, pressed a few buttons, and handed it to me.

"It says 'Tara,'" I noted.

"That's who I always deal with."

"Not JC?"

"Never met him...her? Don't even know if there is a JC or what that stands for."

"Thanks," I said, entering the number for "Tara" into my own phone. I noticed I had two missed calls from Bobby and I felt guilty all over.

"Don't mention it," she said.

She looked at Ulric and her face was so sad, like she was looking at something she knew she'd lost. "For the record," she said, lowering her voice as if she could shut me out of this part of the conversation, "I gave Jesse the boot right after you left. You were right. It's just...he's always known the right buttons to push."

"Clearly I didn't."

Her gaze dropped at that, and I didn't know if anyone but me heard her whisper. "Yes, you did."

I looked at Ulric's face, though, and I didn't think it would matter. Something about it said that once he was done, he was done, and there was no going back. I hurt for them.

I didn't look for Marcy as we left. Or Brent. Truth was, I wasn't thinking about either one.

"You couldn't cut her a break?" I asked Ulric as we left.

"No."

"But *I'm* spoken for, and you're always trying to get between me and Bobby."

"And you always tell me 'no.' Very firmly. That's the difference."

"But still you try."

"Lady, a man would have to be dead not to try to get with you. I mean, dead-dead. Not, you know, undead."

"Thanks. That's probably the weirdest, sweetest thing anyone's ever said to me."

He groaned. "*Sweet.* Yup, that's me all over."

"I like sweet."

"Don't start throwing me a bone now. I'll just take it for pity."

"Hon, there is nothing about you that says 'pity' to me."

A couple brushed by us on the sidewalk and Ulric moved in unconsciously to shield me, as if I weren't the bigger bad, but I didn't dare call him sweet again. Not to his face. A man could only take so much.

"Does anything about me say *for a good time call?*" he asked.

I grinned. "Ah, there's the Ulric I know and ... like."

"Ah ha, nearly made you say it."

"In your dreams."

"Sadly, you don't cooperate there either."

"Go figure."

He walked me back toward Haunts, but slowed to a stop as he saw Bobby waiting out front, looking impatient, edging toward panic. Bobby froze when he saw us, his body language changing from near-panic to something a helluva lot more complex—relief, tension, hatred ... all wrapped up together. I was reminded of the scary-intense moment earlier that night, when I'd woken up to find him staring down at me, all alien and strange.

"I'll take it from here," I told Ulric.

"You sure? Your boyfriend doesn't look too happy to see us together."

"I've got this. You go. *Really*. Don't you have a show to get ready for?"

"Not on Sunday night."

"Then go home. Get some sleep."

He looked from me to Bobby and back. "Call if you need me."

"I promise."

Ulric went, like I told him. But I got the sense he didn't go far. How I knew that when I was about as sensitive as a Mack truck I had no idea, but I did.

"Hey," I said as I approached Bobby.

Whatever that crazy-complex look had been about, it was gone now, and Bobby was all concern.

"You had me worried! I couldn't reach you. You didn't leave a message about where you'd gone."

He didn't reach out to touch me, as if he wasn't sure of his reception. I wanted to touch *him*, but … okay, yes, I was a little afraid. So we stood toe to toe, both of us wanting but neither of us *doing*. I thought of Ulric and Olivia.

"Why didn't you use the mind-speak to talk to me?" I asked.

Bobby looked uncomfortable. "I … couldn't. Something about Salem is really messing with me."

"Bobby, we need to talk."

I could practically see his shield walls dropping into

place, shuttering his expression. He thought he knew what this was about: Ulric. But he was wrong. I'd decided there was no way I would hide from Bobby. He needed to know what I'd seen in him.

What I feared.

10

Bobby insisted on sharing with the class.

We didn't have too terribly much time to kill before Brent and Marcy got off duty. Without the Gothic Magic Show to observe tonight or any other job as of yet, Eric had the van idling outside the brew pub with us and Nelson already loaded in, all set to collect Brent and Marcy when they emerged.

I kept shooting glances at Bobby to make sure it *was* Bobby beside me and not his evil twin. At least, I assumed it was evil. I didn't have a whole host of experience with possession or horror flicks, but it seemed to me one didn't possess an unwilling host in the pursuit of world peace.

While we waited, Eric geeked out about the Ghouligans' tech and how he'd been able to use the cool new lockpicking skills he'd learned from Donato to break into their hotel rooms and wipe the recordings while the Ghouligans hung at the lobby bar. Turns out that even if he'd been able to use the electromagnetic pulse machine, it would only have fried the equipment, not necessarily the memory cards, etc. And all that only if the equipment was turned on. Anything currently locked and stowed, inert, would have been saved. Eric'd had to do the erasures manually. He'd even thought to screw with their clocks so they'd think some kind of space-time-spirit anomaly was responsible. There'd been only one room he couldn't get into—one member of the team who was burning the midnight oil, going over footage. That was going to be a problem.

Even still, I was only half listening. "It'll be okay," I whispered to Bobby, who I *was* focusing on. He was sitting statue-still beside me. With me, but not, his thoughts seemingly about a million miles away.

"Sure," Bobby said unconvincingly. "As long as you lock me up so that I don't murder you all in your sleep, and keep a watch on me all day everyday."

"You haven't killed anyone yet," I said, going for cheery. "For all we know, I was imagining things. Or the spirit was just passing through."

"Then what's messing with my magic?"

I didn't have an answer for that one, and I could tell he didn't really expect one.

"What's that?" Eric asked from the driver's seat.

The side panel doors of the van slid back, scaring me half out of my wits, and Brent and Marcy appeared—the former looking tired and the latter energized, like she was ready to party the night away. Humans vs. vamps. For Marcy it was like mid-day. Meanwhile, it was probably way past Brent's bedtime. Not that he'd kept bankers' hours when working for the Feds.

"What's what?" Brent asked, apparently having heard that much … or having picked it up when he touched the van, being a telemetric and all.

"Get in," I ordered. "Close the door and I'll tell you."

He followed my instructions, and once in, everyone turned to look at me. I glanced at Bobby, not necessarily for his permission to talk, but … well, it *was* his tale.

"I'm possessed," he announced without preamble.

"*Might be,*" I insisted.

"Probably am," he said firmly. "Gina says I wasn't myself when I woke up tonight, and something's been interfering with my magic all evening."

"If you're not yourself, who are you?" Marcy asked.

"We don't know."

"Then how do you know it's anything to worry about? You could be, like, the second coming of Errol Flynn or something." I gave her a look, and she hurried to add, "Usually I don't go in for those black-and-white guys, but he was seriously hot." She stared at Bobby closely, as if to see if he'd developed any Flynn-like tendencies.

Brent leaned toward her. "Uh, honey, you do realize that only the *films* were black and white, right. Not the people."

She gave him a death-glare to put Olivia's to shame. "What am I, stupid?"

Brent's face drained of all color. Oh sure, he could buck the Feds and face down the fangs, but present him with Marcy in all her fiery fury... "No, of course not. It was just the way you said it... "

"You are *so* sleeping on the couch."

"Hey," I protested. "That's ours."

"Oh yeah, like you'll be getting a whole lot of sleep with your boyfriend's head spinning a three-sixty and him spitting pea soup and all," Marcy snapped.

"I'd first have to *eat* pea soup," Bobby pointed out reasonably.

"Fine, *blood* then. Because that's tons better."

"Huh?" Eric asked.

"*The Exorcist*," Marcy replied. "Classic movie."

"Never seen it," Eric answered.

She gasped.

Wow, the things you learn about your bestie after you're dead. Back in Tampa with the steampunk vamps, she'd been all excited over her doomsday dress and poison ring, as excited as I'd ever seen her over strappy sandals or haute couture... and now I found out she had a secret thing for old films and horror flicks. What else didn't I know? Was it even possible that she could be a closet goth?

"We'll totally have to remedy that," Marcy was saying. "Like now. Tonight. Those video rental boxes outside the 7-Eleven are open all night."

"I think we've got bigger problems than Eric's classic movie education," I cut in before Hurricane Marcy could sweep us all up in her gale-force winds. Girl was a force of nature. "Eric, tell them."

"You're the one who got caught on camera," he grumbled. "Or *not* caught."

But he told them about the filming, the equipment, and his attempts to destroy the evidence.

"That's it," Brent said. "We can't stay in Salem. I don't even think we can risk going back for our things. Eric, drive."

Eric seemed prepared for this reaction, because he had the van in gear and rolling before the words were completely out of Brent's mouth.

"But—" I started.

Brent cut me right off. "Already ahead of you. I know we can't leave Salem to fend for itself. We'll call the Feds, dump the phone, and get the hell out of Dodge. If we're about to be exposed, we need to go straight to Plan B."

"Which is?"

"Develop a Plan B, and then a C, D, E, and F while on the move."

"Wait," Marcy said. "Don't we get a vote? Who died and made you boss?"

We were seeing signs for the highway junction only miles ahead. Eric was heading right for it.

"Look, I know the way the Feds think. I was one. Maximum distance away for a scrub team is, maybe, Boston.

How long do you think it would take them to get to us?" Brent asked as Nelson squeaked, "Scrub team?"

"As in scrub us off the face of the Earth," Brent said, not gently. "Sanitized for your protection."

No one was paying attention to Bobby, and we should have been. It wasn't until I looked over for his reaction that I saw that his eyes had gone dark. Not a deeper version of his blue, or even storm-cloud gray, but a brown from which no light escaped. One shade off of total abyss. Bobby had left the building.

"Uh, guys!" I called, hoping to get their attention.

Bobby—or whatever now occupied his body—was mumbling something under his breath, almost a chant, and starting to rock back and forth.

When I leaned in to catch what he was saying, he launched himself at me, hands in rigor-like claws.

"You won't take me alive!" he cried. Even his voice was different. Deeper. Scary.

Those claws lashed out for my chest rather than my throat, as if he could punch his fist right through it and yank out my unbeating heart. I fell back at the horror of seeing him so transformed, the terror blotting out all else, even self-preservation.

"Holy hell!" Eric shouted, losing control of the car for a second as he looked back to see what was going on.

Bobby was thrown on top of me, which suited him fine. His clawed hands ripped at my shirt like it was tissue paper, shredding it. Blood welled to the surface and fangs snapped into place. *His.* Mine.

I barred my fangs at him and pushed with all my might, but there was more than vamp strength driving him. There was crazy-delusional superpower backing it up, like in those cases you heard about where a man hopped up on drugs was shot, like, forty-seven times and refused to drop—the body not knowing it was impossible for it to keep going. Brent and Marcy had both thrown themselves on Bobby, pulling and tugging. Marcy had him by the hair and, to my horror, was left with a handful of it when he wrenched himself away, out of her grip, heedless of the pain.

"Bobby, stop! Come back," Brent shouted. "Bobby, you're hurting her!"

Bobby hurled his now-freed head back, crashing the back of his skull into Brent's nose. I heard bone crunch and cried out, my legs scrabbling uselessly on the floor of the van, trying to propel me away. But Bobby seemed to have gained weight and mass. He felt like a boulder, like an immovable object.

Nelson untangled from his seat belt and launched himself from the passenger's seat into the back just as Bobby screamed, "No!"

A pulse of power went out of him, flaring, lighting up my every neuron, flaying my skin. The others cried out in agony and the van seemed to buck like a bronco—then it shuddered to a stop and died.

We were rocked by cars blowing past, laying on their

horns, but I could barely hear them over the ringing in my ears, the death cry of every single one of my nerves. My body's electrical system was fried.

"Oh my God, Brent!" Marcy wailed. Her agony easily putting mine to shame. I fought my way back from the blackness that wanted to eat at me and steal me off into oblivion. I forced my eyes open, forced them to focus. Bobby had fallen across me, heavy and boneless. It took a monumental effort to move him. My arms felt like over-cooked spaghetti—soft and weak. I didn't know how to make sure he was just dead weight and not truly dead. No pulse, no breath … but apparently, Marcy was having the same problem with Brent, only *he* couldn't live without all his systems on go.

She was beating at his chest, having no idea about CPR. "Beat, damn you, BEAT!" she ordered his heart as she pounded. Blood tears streaked down her face.

"What can I do?" I asked.

"Your boyfriend killed him! Bobby killed him!"

"He wasn't himself!"

She turned away from me, continuing to pound on Brent's chest. Eric was slumped over in the driver's seat, and Nelson lay moaning where the blast of power seemed to have blown him against the far wall. I yanked out my cell phone, fearing Marcy would kill Brent accidentally with her vampire strength rather than save him, and fearing I'd do the same with Eric.

"911," the voice on the other end of the phone said as my call rang through. "What's your emergency?"

"Car accident. Highway..." I went to the windows, looking for a sign. If not for my vamp vision, I'd never have seen it. "Interstate 95. Just south of Salem. Hurry. My cousin—I think his heart's stopped."

"Miss, I'll dispatch an ambulance to your location, but I'll need some more information. Please stay on the line with me—"

I cut her off. "He's dying. Please, hurry. And my uncle—"

The 911 operator was saying something else. I knew it was protocol, but I couldn't waste time with that right now. I hit mute but left the call connected in case they needed to track the signal.

"Marcy, stop!" I yelled. "An ambulance is on the way. We have to get out of here."

"I can't leave him," she wailed.

"You have to. There's no choice. Give him a drop of your blood. If he can be saved, that will do it. The EMTs will do the rest. We can't be here when they arrive."

I threw myself across Eric's inert body, listening for his heartbeat. There—very faint, thready. He'd be okay.

"Why can't we be here?" she screamed at me, already opening a vein for Brent. "Why can't we be here for them?"

"Because with an accident the paramedics will insist on checking us out as well. They're bound to notice a little thing like the lack of heartbeat."

She froze, her face a mask of indecision, knowing I was right but unwilling to accept it. I'd have been the same about Bobby, but he was coming with us.

"Let's go!" I prompted, after she'd let her blood spill.

Already we could hear sirens in the distance. I went to Nelson and slapped him awake. He was clearly hurting, but I told him we had to get out, asked if he could take Bobby, and got a nod in return.

"Oh no you don't," Marcy said, putting herself between Nelson and Bobby. "He *caused* all this. Let him get caught."

"Let me get this straight," Nelson said, his tone reasonable. I waited to see what he would say, because there was no way I could be reasonable with Marcy right now. "You want us to leave him here—with Eric and Brent, the two most vulnerable of us. What if he wakes up?"

Marcy nearly swallowed her tongue. "Fine," she said, as if it tasted like ashes. "Bring him, but keep him away from me."

"Wasn't. His. Fault," I said through clenched teeth.

Nelson reached for Bobby before Marcy could change her mind, and I got the side door open for us in an instant. I could have carried Bobby. I *wanted* to. But with the difference in our heights, it would have been an awkward thing. So much easier for Nelson in his near-giant form.

"Marcy, out," I prompted.

She glared as she went, the blood tears now smeared across her face where she'd unsuccessfully wiped them away. It was a fierce look, but I could barely spare it the attention it deserved. Bobby still hadn't awoken, and with that immense blast of power, I had a horrible fear that he'd burned himself out until there was nothing left.

"She's not thinking straight right now," Nelson comforted

me as he jumped down after her. Like *he* was the voice of experience and not younger than us all.

"None of us are."

We ran off into the woods alongside of the road. Waist-high grasses, brambles, and branches caught at us as we raced the onrushing sirens.

11

We stopped when we were far enough away from the road to be sure we were out of sight and earshot. No doubt someone would come looking for the girl who'd reported the accident, but we had a little time. The first responders would be too focused on helping those who needed them.

I'd purposely left my cell phone back at the van. There was nothing incriminating in the call history. Not much at all beyond the call to Eric, who they'd already have, and Bobby's calls to me. His phone would have to go as well.

Marcy's cell was our best bet to call for help. She'd been with Brent practically non-stop. They'd have had no reason to call back and forth.

"Marcy, give me your phone," I ordered. She didn't ask why. "Nelson, frisk Bobby for his. Separate the battery from the body and toss them as far as they'll go in different directions."

Bobby moaned, as if in weak protest at being frisked, and my heart nearly restarted at the evidence that he was alive ... or at least, undead.

"He's waking up," Nelson said unnecessarily.

"If you need someone to punch his lights out again," Marcy said, "I volunteer."

"*Marcy*—"

"*Gina,*" she countered.

I had no answer for that. Or anything else. I fell back on the one thing I did have an answer for—our stranded state. That answer could be summed up in a word: Ulric. I dialed, and he picked up on the second ring. "Everything all right?"

I was baffled, until I remembered that he'd been worried about Bobby's reaction to seeing the two of us together. It was just to question Olivia, but still ...

"Did I wake you?" I asked.

"No, and you didn't answer my question."

"Everything's not all right, but it has nothing to do with Bobby." Marcy gave me a *look*. "Well, it does, but not what you're thinking. Can you pick us up? We've had an accident out on I-95 and had to leave the van behind."

"Where are you exactly?"

I told him as best I could.

"Find a mile marker," he ordered, "and call me back. I'm leaving now."

"Thanks, Ulric, I owe you."

"Yeah, yeah, I'll put it on your tab."

He hung up and I looked at the others, a little afraid to

leave Marcy alone with Bobby while I went searching for a mile marker. But she wouldn't really be alone with him. Maybe it was best, anyway, for us all to stick together.

"We've got to hike down the road," I told them. "Figure out where we are so that Ulric can come for us."

"W'as goin' on?" Bobby slurred from his sack-of-potatoes perch on Nelson's shoulder.

It *sounded* like Bobby. I rounded Nelson to check his eyes. Blue. Awesomely, blissfully blue.

Marcy hip-checked me out of the way to get right into his face. "I'll tell you what's going on. You went all psycho, tried to kill Gina, and maybe did kill Brent. His heart stopped. It *stopped…*" Marcy ended on a sob.

Bobby's eyes met mine, as if he was hoping I'd say it wasn't so, but I couldn't. Instead, heart breaking again, I looked away and put an arm around Marcy. "It wasn't him. You know that."

She shook me off. "I don't know anything but that we're trapped. We can't leave. We can't stay. If Eric and Brent didn't dump their IDs, the cops or the scrubs are going to find out who they are when they go looking for info to fill out their paperwork. You think the Feds don't have us flagged in every database known to man? You think we didn't all just sign our own death warrants?"

"*I think*," Nelson cut in, "that we need to get a grip. Freaking out won't do us any good."

He started off at an angle toward the highway, so that we wouldn't end up too close to the stalled van. He put Bobby down after a few feet. Apparently, an unconscious guy bumping against his back was one thing. A fully conscious Bobby, nose smooshed to his spine, was another matter entirely.

"*Behave*," Nelson warned. "Or I let Marcy at you."

Bobby looked back at me in appeal. "I still don't know what you're talking about. I don't remember any of it," he said.

"We do," Marcy answered coldly.

I let Marcy stomp and Nelson trudge ahead of us, and I stayed back with Bobby—only partially to keep an eye on him.

"How do you feel?" I asked, all caution.

"Like I've been tasered."

"Yeah, that was you."

"Me?"

"You let out a huge burst of power that hit us all."

"That's what made Brent's heart stop?"

I nodded.

"I really tried to kill you?"

I looked up into those beautiful blue eyes and ached for him. "Yes."

He took my hand—gently, tentatively. First just brushing me with his fingertips to see if I'd flinch away, and then sliding his palm against mine, twining our fingers together. "You know I would never, right? Not in my right mind ... " He raked his free hand through his hair, leaving it sticking up and out at crazy angles. Those shaggy brown locks did haphazard really well. Luckily, disheveled worked for him. "What's happening to me?"

"That's what we have to find out. We can't leave town without the answers, but the others ... we may lose them."

He used our linked hands to haul me up short and look at me. Desperately. Like a starving man might look at a burger and fries. "You said 'we.' You're with me? Even after I tried to kill you?"

"Wouldn't you stand by me?" I asked.

"Of course."

"Well then—"

He kissed me. A sudden, hard kiss that turned sweet. I didn't let myself tense up, even though I flashed for a second on him coming for me back in the van, murder in his dark eyes. No, not his eyes. Someone else's.

I drew back at that, unable to stop myself, and covered with, "We'd better catch up to the others. We're not out of the woods yet."

"Literally," Bobby said with a smile, but it was bitter-sweet. He knew I'd pulled back, sensed that no matter what I'd said, we weren't quite okay. Not really. But he wasn't going to call me on it.

I wanted us to be okay. I really did. But until it was just him in there ... until I knew that the person who leaned in for the kiss would be the same person involved in the follow through ...

Oh, Bobby.

I grabbed his hand again. That much I could do. I pulled him along with me. Marcy was already on the phone to Ulric when we burst out of the bushes and onto the side of the road. I hoped that all the vegetation would spring back into place before too long—it'd been way too easy for me to follow the path Nelson had bulldozed. Of course, our trail would dead-end at the road.

"He'll be here in two," Marcy reported. "He's only a mile or so down the road."

She'd barely finished speaking when Ulric rolled up in a really retro Crown Vic in powder blue. It was so not him that I could only gawk.

"It's my aunt's," he said defensively as he leaned across the passenger seat to get a look at us. "Get in."

He didn't have to tell us twice. I put Bobby next to Ulric in the shotgun seat, since I didn't trust Marcy with him in the back.

Ulric had never taken the car out of gear. We rolled forward as soon as the final door was shut and pulled a U-turn the first chance we got, nearly bottoming out the car when the median wasn't as low as it looked.

We were just getting up to speed as we passed the ambulance, with an EMT slamming the doors shut and a police car right behind it.

Marcy rolled down her half-frosted window, but I didn't know what she hoped to see. "Is there any way to find out how they are?" she asked. "Maybe a radio station will have something?"

"So soon?" Ulric asked.

"Try traffic," Bobby suggested. "Morning commute is

only a few hours away. They'll say if an accident or police investigation will slow things up."

"How will that help? We already know there's a stalled vehicle. We were *in* it," Nelson said.

"They'll say if it's a *fatal* accident," Bobby answered.

Marcy made a small sound and Bobby shut up, fiddling instead with the radio knobs. *Knobs*, not buttons … and the windows had been crank. Just some of the totally unimportant details the brain noted to avoid fixating on the really big stuff.

The traffic advisory channel was silent, so Ulric suggested a local station and Bobby dialed it in.

"How did it happen?" Ulric asked, nodding at the scene in the rearview mirror, which now showed the ambulance and police unit pulling out onto the road. Lights flared and whirled, but there were no sirens. I didn't know if that was good, meaning Eric and Brent weren't in imminent danger, or bad, meaning they were beyond help. The fast food commercial playing on the radio wasn't any help. Rather than making a U-turn over the median, the ambulance rushed ahead to the next exit.

"I didn't see any damage to the van," Ulric commented. "Wait—before we get to that, where am I taking you? Home?"

"Not safe," I answered. "Take us … " Take us where?

"What about your place?" Marcy asked.

Ulric glanced at her. "I'm staying with the aunt I borrowed this car from. All I've got is a room. You'd be welcome to it but my aunt cleans like a fiend, leaving tread marks like

Zen garden patterns when she vacuums. She'd be bound to notice the passing of so many feet." He got a sudden evil grin on his face. "I'll take you to Donato's. You'll fit right in."

"What's that supposed to mean?" Nelson asked.

"Oh, you'll see." The expression on Ulric's face said he was looking forward to it.

"Shh, everyone. Listen." Bobby reached for the radio and turned it up.

"*—found strangled in her room at North Shore Medical Center, where she'd been taken after surviving an earlier attack. Until tonight, no one had been assaulted in any place other than the Old Town section of Salem. However, sources say that given the strange serial nature of the crimes, the girl, who was being held for observation at the Medical Center, was left with a police guard outside her door. Where this guard was at the time of the attack is unclear. An investigation is underway . . .* "

I cried out. Zebra-stripe girl! But—but I'd *saved* her. She should have been fine. I couldn't imagine what she needed observation for, unless it was hysteria or an abundance of caution on the part of the police. I wondered whose idea it had been to take her to the hospital. Hers? Her sister's? Did she feel safer at the hospital with an officer on the other side of the door?

And who was that officer?

"Follow that ambulance!" I called.

"Is that where they'd take Brent and Eric?" Marcy asked, already knowing the answer.

"It would have to be," Ulric said. "It's the closest hospital."

"Then step on it," Marcy ordered.

If the Salem Strangler had taken possession of the cop back at the Old Jail, as Ty-the-Ghouligan had implied, at least we'd have a physical enemy to fight. But what if the cop was as innocent as Bobby? Would he do jail time for a crime he didn't commit, just as Nelson would have if he'd ever gotten his own body back? And what was with this sudden rash of possessions, anyway?

I glanced over at Nelson and he looked sick, even paler than his usual white-bread vampire self. He had to be thinking about the parallels with what had happened to him. And did the cop's compatriots know that he'd committed the murder? If so, they'd never believe he hadn't been himself at the time. At best they might settle on temporary insanity. But if they didn't know ... if he hadn't been caught in the act ... then we had a killer cop on the loose with a badge, a gun, and the drive to use it.

So we had no plan, a life-sized liability in Bobby, a cop to corner, and a rescue to mount. Oh yeah, piece of cake. Moldy, maggot-infested sewage soufflé.

"What are we going to do about Bobby?" Marcy asked, echoing my thoughts.

We all looked at him.

"Knock me out," he said.

"How?" Nelson asked. "You're a vampire. You know us—super-fast healing and all. Plus, who's to say your psycho side won't wake up before you do?"

"The trunk," I said, shooting an apologetic glance at

Bobby. "I'm so sorry. I don't see what else we can do. You're too big a risk. We've got to secure you until we can figure out and fix the problem, and that's all we've got."

Bobby wanted to argue; I could see it in his face. It was on the tip of his tongue. Then he shut his mouth on whatever he was about to say and his face went all-over hard. I had a terrible feeling I was losing him, and that it was all my fault. "You do what you have to do," he said, his voice just as hard as his face, which could have been set in stone.

"Bobby, I—"

"Later," he barked. Then, softly, like he wasn't sure he meant me to hear it, he added. "I'd never lock *you* in the trunk."

"And I'd never try to kill you," I said, quicker than thought. Because if I'd given it even a moment, I'd have known better than to let it come out of my mouth. Bobby was hurting. Bashing him upside the head with reality was only going to make it worse.

So what if part of me thought that if Bobby truly loved me, he'd have been strong enough to throw off the compulsion to kill me? That was just romantic drivel anyway, right? Who knew how strong possession could be? Who was to say he hadn't fought his damnedest and it hadn't been enough? But deep inside, I realized that the very fact that I *couldn't* know, that I had doubts, might be the first nail in our coffin.

The fact that Bobby had doubts about me—putting him in the trunk, going off with Ulric earlier in the night—created more nails or wedges or whatever kind of construction metaphor worked. I didn't know. Maybe a relationship was like a house of cards. You knock out the trust base and it all came tumbling down.

But none of that was going to get dealt with in a sentence or two ... with witnesses.

I blinked first and looked away. His blue eyes were like an ice ray with all the warmth gone out of them. If I kept looking, I'd freeze up. Brent and Eric didn't have time for that.

So we hatched a plan, though not without a lot of back-and-forth over who was going to do what, and Bobby growing more remote with every passing second. Given his amazing powers, he was used to being a linchpin in any plan. Now he was a liability, sidelined through no fault of his own ... and by his own girlfriend. I couldn't even imagine what he was going through.

•　　•　　•

The plan started with Marcy stabbing herself in the parking lot. There was blood everywhere. She made sure of it.

Ulric lifted her almost like he had vampire strength, or she weighed no more than a feather. He waited for Nelson and me to go through the emergency room doors ahead of him so that we could be in place to slip unnoticed into the treatment area at the moment of maximum distraction. Then, just as the doors were sliding closed behind us, he strode onto the pressure plate with Marcy, bouncing the doors open again and stepping dramatically through the entrance.

"Help me!" he yelled. "Somebody help me! My girl-friend—she's been stabbed. I don't think she's going to make it."

Heads swiveled around, in the waiting room, from the reception area. Someone came running—a nurse in scrubs far too cheerful for the situation. She took one look at Marcy and the extreme pallor of her face and radioed for someone to "bring a gurney, stat!"

"Hurry!" Ulric shouted, reinforcing the urgency. "She's so still. I think she's stopped breathing!"

As the door to the inner treatment areas opened for the gurney to rush through, Nelson and I were in the perfect position to slip inside after it. No one paid us any attention. We hurried to the first curtained area and whipped the curtain back, hoping to find Eric or Brent. What we saw instead was a little boy on a breathing machine, his whole body shuddering with each breath, like every one was a struggle. The tech administering the treatment gave us a hard look at the disturbance. We apologized and quickly backed out, making noises like we'd gotten the wrong room. The curtain on the next cubicle was open with no one inside, so we moved on to the one after that...

"What do you think you're doing?" a nurse asked, clip-board clutched like a shield over her chest. "Unless you're with someone, you can't be back here."

Nelson turned, his thick Cro-Mag brows smooshing together in concern. "My uncle was brought here," he said, "in an ambulance."

She didn't look convinced. "You checked in at the front desk?"

"Yes. They said he's here."

"No one escorted you back?"

"She got called off for a stabbing victim."

The nurse looked at us for another moment, then the door behind us was flung open again—the crash team coming through with Marcy, a worried-looking Ulric trailing them. One of the team looked over at the nurse. "Is Surgery One open?"

The nurse's eyes went wide, and she nodded. To us she called, "Other side of the nurses' station, last room," and she hurried off.

Score! Now it was up to Marcy to make a miraculous recovery and Ulric to get her out of there before anyone could take so much as a blood sample. Eric and Brent were our responsibility.

We hit that last curtain with no further challenges, and Nelson peeked behind it.

"They're alone," he said.

We slipped inside. Eric and Brent were on adjoining beds, the former awake, the latter looking vampire-pale.

"Brent's alive," Eric said, his voice still a little thready, like his pulse had been back at the van. "Doctors think he had a minor heart attack. They want to run some tests."

Nelson rushed to his side and began pulling out tubes as his uncle talked. "Do they know who you are?" he asked. "Did they find any ID on you?"

Eric was shaking his head. "We're too smart for that," he said, tapping a hand, still trailing tape, to his forehead. "But it made them very suspicious. Police want to talk to me about driving without a license and all. I claimed amnesia, a concussion when the car's electrical system seized up." He grinned. "I blamed an ungrounded power line and said something about suing the city. Kicked up quite the fuss. Medical guys finally shooed the police out because I was getting too worked up, but I don't think they're finished with me."

"They are now," Nelson said, helping him out of bed.

I checked Brent over. He hadn't so much as moved, and I was getting really concerned. "What did the doctors say about Brent? Is he okay?"

"He was snoring a little bit ago," Eric said. "Almost dying will take a lot out of you. He's got a goose egg on the back of his head, but swelling out rather than in is a good sign."

People were calling back and forth to each other in the hallway—orders, observations, in some cases just friendly chatter—but one voice caught my attention and lit up my *holy crap* o-meter.

" ... called down, said something about a stabbing."

It was the killer cop. I knew from the chill that settled into my heart. We were out of time.

"Eric, can you walk?" I asked quickly. He nodded. "Nelson, can you carry Brent?" He nodded as well, baffled at my sudden urgency.

"In about ten seconds, there ought to be so much commotion that you can walk right on out of here."

"But—"

"*That* was the possessed cop. I'm sure of it. He's heading toward Marcy, and she's his favorite type of victim—female."

"Crap," Nelson spat. I thought it warranted a whole lot more than that, but it would do for now.

12

I raced down the hall, circled the central station, and vaulted a crash cart that was wheeled out in front of me. Someone yelled, someone else grabbed, but I was already gone. I burst through the closed curtains of the cubicle I'd seen Marcy wheeled into and found Ulric and an orderly unconscious on the floor, and Marcy fighting for her life.

I knew the strangling couldn't do her in, since she didn't need air, but the killer inside the cop had some preternatural strength behind his grip. If it was enough to decapitate her, that would be true death. Even just a snapped neck would incapacitate her long enough for a killing blow if he figured out her secret. The cop's eyes were bugging out from the effort it took to choke the life out of my friend. The frustration of failure was clearly starting to get to him, and I knew any second he'd change his tactics.

I launched myself onto him before that could happen. He tried to buck me off, like a dog shaking himself after a bath, but I hung on, giving as good as I got or better. I didn't dare give him the chance to call for help, but dug into his neck for all I was worth, trying to cut off *his* air. Human form meant human foibles.

But he didn't let go of Marcy. Instead, he dragged her from the bed, his hands gripping her neck. Then he whirled with me on his back, slamming me against the counter that ran along the one actual wall of the cubicle and cracking my back. I fought not to let go. As she struggled, Marcy's legs belled out the curtain into the adjoining cubicle, but if anyone squawked it was drowned out by the roaring in my ears. With my hands around the cop's neck, still choking off his air, his pounding heart and rushing blood were so close to me that they sounded like a storm raging.

My fangs nicked my lips as they dropped into place and instinct took over. I shifted my grip for better access and sank my teeth into his neck, close to the jugular. Instantly, he went rigid beneath me.

Marcy hit his forehead with her own, and his grip on her relaxed. She hit him again and he released. She dodged before he could grab her back, and he went down hard onto his knees—from concussion or blood loss, I didn't care. His blood raced through my system. Powerful, potent, spiked with adrenaline and all kinds of other craziness that made me want to howl at the moon.

Something else seemed to transfer with that blood. Someone, or ones, else burst into the room, but I couldn't spare them any attention—something was moving within me. Something alien. In panic, I let my fangs slip from the cop's neck and he crashed to the floor. I tore at my hair as something rifled through my brain, as if I could tear it out by the roots—not my hair, the *thing*.

It was putrefaction. Vile, evil, rot and ruin, poison. Hatred, disgust, lust ... more than my vampire bloodlust. The lust for pain and suffering.

"What's going on here?" the new arrival demanded.

I turned, and the thing inside ... saw. It saw the newcomer—the killer cop's beefy partner. It leapt. There was no other word. There was a tearing—as if it took some of me with it—and then it was gone, leaving chaos behind.

I staggered, disoriented. The killer cop was down, but ... was he really? I looked from his collapsed form up into the now-crazed eyes of his partner and knew the true killer was still with us. He'd just changed vehicles.

Apparently, though, he was going easier on his new host than he had me, because the only pain in those eyes was promised to others.

I aimed a blow for the new cop's nose, pulling my punch just enough, I hoped, not to drive the nasal arch up into his brain like we'd been taught in spy training. Luckily, the killer hadn't yet figured out all the bells and whistles on his new toy, and he didn't react quickly enough to stop me.

"Run!" I said to Marcy as he went down. I grabbed Ulric off the floor and ran with him, back the way we'd come, heading for the exit.

The newly possessed officer bellowed for backup. Medical staff dodged into or out of our way as we made our mad dash for the doors. It was like running an obstacle course, though with ninja-vamp reflexes.

The universe seemed to be on the side of us fallen angels. As we spilled out into the reception area, a man was coming through the sliding glass doors from the outside. They hadn't yet closed behind him. We were able to slip right through.

Nelson had Ulric's Crown Vic idling just outside the doors. The trunk—where we'd left Bobby—looked bashed and battered, half ripped away. The car doors flung open for us as we approached. I threw Ulric into the back seat with Brent, and Marcy and I dove on top of him. Nelson peeled away as the door closed on my foot and sprang open again, air whooshing through the car and trying to suck me out with it. Eric leaned over from the front seat, shoved at my foot, and grabbed the door shut.

Fear roared through me. "Where's Bobby?" I asked, looking around like I could have missed him somehow. Like the battered trunk didn't mean what I thought it did.

"Gone," Nelson said, his tone dripping apology. "When I got to the car he was already gone."

"We have to find him! What if whatever's driving him doesn't know to get out of the sun before it rises? He'll be vaporized."

I could just hear Bobby in my head: *that would mean turned into vapor, but actually the reverse would be true*...he'd be turned into ash. I wished he was there to correct me in person. I never thought I'd miss his lectures, but...I did. Terribly.

"So far he's been Bobby more than he's been ... whoever. I don't think the spirit can keep control for too long," Brent said. Probably he meant it to be soothing.

"I don't like that 'so far.'"

The car hit a pothole and we all jumped. My teeth clacked together on top of it, and sent a ringing through my head.

"I guess I'll be the first to bring up the eight-hundred-pound gorilla in the room," Eric said into the sudden silence.

Nelson groaned. "I think you mean elephant."

"But that makes no sense," his uncle said. "Elephants weight far more than eight hundred pounds—"

"No, it's eight-hundred-pound gorilla, *or* the elephant in the room," Nelson corrected his uncle. "Not both. We've talked about this. Stop trying to use vernacular. You're no good at it."

"Well, of course, they wouldn't *both* fit in the room," Eric answered, completely missing the point.

I rolled my eyes. "Guys, can we focus?"

"My point *is*," Eric said, "that we have to call the Feds and get out of town, just like Brent said. We may not like their methods, and Nelson and I are still committed to bringing down their detention centers, but this case is getting too much attention. The news, the Ghouligans, the cops. *Killer* cops."

"You think the Feds aren't already on their way?" Brent asked. "With all this attention, they may not be coming for *us*. They may not know we're here. But I can almost guarantee you that they're at least coming to search out new supernatural assets, and maybe even to solve the mystery."

"See," Eric said, raking us all with his gaze. "If they're in, we've *got* to get *out*."

"No," I said. "We are *not* leaving Bobby behind."

I caught Nelson's gaze in the rearview mirror. If anyone could talk sense into his uncle, he could. "Tell them, Nelson," I insisted.

He looked away, and my heart sank. "I'm sorry, Gina. As you say, we're already a man down. If the Feds are coming... there's no way I'm getting sent to one of their hellholes. I signed on for destroying those places. We're not doing that here. We're not doing anything here but busywork—day jobs and all that. This was just supposed to be a short stop to replenish our finances but instead we're getting attacked, sidetracked."

"You don't think whatever's stalking Salem needs to be taken down every bit as much as those hellholes?"

"This is for the greater good," Eric said for him. "We can't save anyone if we're locked up. But free—"

I cut him off. It sounded like an excuse. Like good-bye. "Brent?" I asked.

He was crushed in against the far wall, Ulric half on top of him. He looked at Marcy before looking back at me. "I'm not leaving a man behind. I'm still all for destroying the detention centers, but right now we don't have any leads. If the Feds do send a team, maybe we can track them back to a center."

"If you don't get caught and sent there yourself," Eric mumbled.

"Then we'll take it down from the inside," Brent argued.

If Marcy wouldn't kill me for it, I'd have kissed him right then. I finally drew my gaze to hers, but she only had eyes for Brent, and they were shining with love.

"Marcy?" I asked.

"What he said," she answered. Then, realizing that it sounded a little follow-y, she added, "I mean, it's Best Friends Forever, right? Not BFFN."

"BFFN?" Brent asked.

"*Best Friends For Now.* You didn't leave Brent when he was in the hospital. I'm not leaving Bobby."

The world took on a rosy haze, and I realized I had blood tears in my eyes.

"Thank you." My voice cracked embarrassingly.

"I never thought I'd say this," came a muffled voice from beneath me, "but please get off of me. And unless you've suddenly become sunproof, you might want to pull over and let me drive you all to safety before dawn."

Marcy and I shifted to let Ulric sit up. Nelson pulled the car to the side of the road and we all had the least-fun-ever Chinese fire drill.

"Sure you're okay to drive?" I asked Ulric. "You were just out cold."

"Not like it's the first time," he answered.

We were silent the rest of the ride to Donato's place.

Ulric soon pulled into the driveway of a dark, wood-shingled house, its front entryway nearly overgrown with ivy. We piled out of the car and approached the door, Ulric in the lead. I realized that the ivy wasn't the only thing overgrown—the front lawn looked like it'd been given over to the weeds, and they'd thrown a party and invited friends. The only statuary was a store-bought zombie that looked like it was trying to pull itself up out of the ground.

"A little early for Halloween, isn't it?" Eric asked.

"Oh, he's got that out year-round. You should see what he does for Halloween."

Ulric rang the bell, which played five deep tones that sounded like "Do-De-Doom-Dum-Doom."

"Cheery," I said.

Ulric gave me a grin.

I wasn't prepared for Donato to look so ... normal ... after all that. I'd only ever seen him all done up for the Gothic Magic Show, but he met us at the door in bare feet, jeans, and a long-sleeved gray henley.

"Welcome," he said, stepping aside to let us pass. "Good thing you called ahead. I'm usually dead to the world by now." If he noted our bedraggled and bloodied state—and how could he not?—he didn't say a word.

The foyer inside was lined with bookshelves of the old floor-to-ceiling library variety, only there were few actual books involved. Instead, there were skulls, things I didn't want to examine too closely floating in jars of fluid, spiders and scorpions encased in glass, and what looked like a taxidermied, two-headed turtle. I kept my gaze straight ahead, not wanting to see any more. I wondered what Ulric meant when he'd said we'd fit right in. Did he mean "with all the other dead things"?

Of course, Eric was fascinated. He started asking questions immediately, and Donato, proud of his collection, began showing it off with a spiel for each object, like a museum guide. Nelson cleared his throat and reminded his uncle that it'd been a long day and many of us needed our sleep. Like right now. Donato looked disappointed until Eric indicated that he'd love to continue the tour as soon as everyone else was settled.

Settled was apparently a relative term, since there was nothing at all settling about the basement where he intended for us to bed down. Only a couple of small, high, blacked-out windows provided any access to the outside world. The cement floor and old-fashioned wood paneling made it look like someone had hastily refinished what was basically an oversized root cellar, used to store jam and canned beets in the olden days. The blacked-out windows made me wonder if, perhaps, we weren't the first vamps to visit in modern days.

My first thought... fear... was *spiders*.

I must have said it out loud, because Donato said, "Don't worry, I sprayed last week."

"Great—*dead* spiders," I answered. But I smiled to show that despite the comment I really was grateful to have a spider-infested basement in which to stay.

Donato smiled back, almost as if he bought it.

Ulric pulled him aside to talk, and the rest of us got

comfy ... ish. Last night, Bobby had been beside me. Tonight I didn't know where he was. Or even who.

I chose a sleeping bag from a pile Donato had dumped in the middle of the floor and carried it away from the others, trying to see well enough through my blood tears not to stumble.

13

Eric and Nelson were gone when we awoke at sunset, but they'd left us a note and a clue.

Sorry we had to go suddenly, it began.

It was thin, hurried handwriting, like that of a doctor who'd written way too many prescriptions. Eric's handwriting, if I'd had to guess. Brent had to decipher the meaning of the note as much through telemetry as sight.

> *After I woke, I just couldn't sit around waiting to get caught. I bundled Nelson up and took him away with me. Tell Donato his neighbor's truck can be found at the train station, and tell him I'm sorry. Oh, and I owe him a sleeping bag.*
>
> *As a parting gift, I've got a name for you: Rebecca Simms. JC Supplies says she was the one who sold them*

the coffin and remains. Happy hunting. Thanks for all you've done and ... I'm sorry.

Please find us if I can ever be of service and you're not followed. Burn after reading.

Rebecca. So *she* was involved in all of this.

As for Eric and Nelson, I wondered how they planned to fund their fugitive flight. If leaving the truck at the station wasn't merely a smokescreen and they really did take the train, it posed a bunch of risks. A regular seat would have too much exposure to the sun for Nelson. They'd probably have to spring for a sleeper, and I understood those were pricey. Maybe Eric's machine mojo let him speak with ATMs, or maybe he'd bought one of those card-scanners thieves used in malls and such to pick a man's pocket without ever touching it, reading and recording card numbers electronically. It didn't sound like him, but I was starting to wonder whether I was quite the judge of character I'd always thought.

Besides, there wasn't anything people wouldn't do for family. Just look at me, staying behind in somber Salem to save Bobby. He'd become my family. And Marcy, my soul sister, was still with me despite the dangers, along with her plus one.

Speaking of whom ...

"I found it when I woke around mid-afternoon," Brent was saying. "It's been killing me not to follow up, but I didn't want to leave you alone and unguarded, in case ... " There were so many ways to finish that sentence: in case the

Feds find us; in case the killer cop comes to finish you off; in case … It could go on and on.

"Ulric called," Brent continued. "Seems that Haunts doesn't run tours on Monday nights, or at least not until the October rush. He's on his way over here to pick us up. Donato's already gone out."

"Has there been any sign of Bobby?" I asked.

"Not that Ulric said. Nothing on the news, either. I'm hoping all the restless spirits have wiped themselves out, at least temporarily. What they're doing should be exhausting."

I chewed on a thumbnail. It was something I rarely did anymore. The manicures I'd gotten since the age of ten had been my mother's bribe for me to kick the habit. She and Dad both had been big proponents of parenting by throwing money—or manicures—at a problem.

Marcy slapped my hand away from my mouth with a maternal glare. I glared back until smiles started to overcome us. Until I felt guilty about smiling with Bobby in trouble.

"Okay," I said, refocusing. "When Ulric and I talked to Olivia at the pub, she said something about an ancient force, an object of power, being responsible for all the restless spirits. And now we find out Rebecca's been digging up old artifacts … people, even! I think there's a good chance she's found a lot more than she can handle."

"Something she's dug up causing the problems … " Marcy mused. "The coffin or something else, do you think? You said Olivia mentioned JC doesn't deal with the arcane, so maybe whatever else she found she kept for herself?"

I thought about the pendant Rebecca wore, the one she hadn't wanted me to see. She'd never answered me about its significance.

I went out on a limb. "I can't be sure until I can get a good look at it, but Rebecca wears a necklace she keeps tucked away under her clothes. Jewelry is mostly meant to be seen, you know? Hiding it away doesn't make sense, unless—"

The doorbell rang, and Brent, being the only one of us who didn't look like he'd just rolled out of bed, went to answer it.

I ran my tongue along my teeth. Peeps, let me tell you— onion, morning, and garlic breath are *nothing* compared to blood breath. I'd left my toothbrush back at our Danvers apartment, so I still tasted like cop and copper gone horribly wrong...like a bad penny. I'd swear my tongue had a film. *Yuck.*

I met the guys, Brent and Ulric, at the top of the stairs and waved them out of my way as I made a mad dash to the main part of Donato's house to loot it for toiletries.

"I think I might know where Bobby's gone," Ulric called after me.

That was the one statement that could stop my quest for clean. I whirled around. "What?"

"Your apartment. I swung by there before coming to get you, and someone's inside. Unless you left the lights on."

"We didn't," I said.

"I didn't think so."

I was torn. The bathroom and cleanliness called to me.

Not just for selfish reasons—I was literally afraid that stealth would have no meaning for me in my current condition. Anyone with vamp senses could smell me before they saw me. But a minute, give or take, could be all Bobby would need to vanish into the night.

"Two secs," I said. "Tell Marcy the same. Tell her *Code Red*."

Ulric looked at me funny, but Brent laughed. "Will do."

I bolted for the bathroom, finding it easily. I finger-brushed my teeth, cringing at the overly sweet, overpowering taste of mint. I way preferred the natural pastes to the brightly colored brands that hit you over the head with their flavor, but beggars couldn't be choosers. I splashed soap and water on my face to wash away the tracks of yesterday's blood tears... not that I could see them in the mirror that refused to "like" me back. I grabbed a hairbrush and raced back to the others. I could brush in the car.

We were out of time.

Four seconds later, we were outside by the Crown Vic, its smashed trunk reminding us why.

"And then there were four," Brent murmured as we got in.

Unlike last night's escape, no one had to lap-sit to fit, and it was stupid sad. I never thought I'd object to having a seat to myself. I hoped Eric and Nelson had gotten away good on that sleeper car. I hoped they would find what they were looking for—Federal facilities to destroy. An unworthy little part of me hoped they'd draw off any pursuit with them. Not that I wanted them to get *caught*, of course, but if any of the Feds who might have been after us caught wind of them instead and got led astray, all the better for us.

The Ravenswood Apartments weren't far, and the building looked just as stark and depressingly institutional as it had when we'd left. Sure enough, when Ulric drove around the back, we could see that there was a light on in our basement unit. But whoever was there was smart enough not to move around in front of the windows. If there was any action, we couldn't see it.

Ulric parked at the far end of the lot, the part that was always empty because it fairly screamed "carjack me."

"I'll go," Brent announced. "If someone's in there, all I'll have to do is touch the handle to know."

"*I'll* go," I said. "That might be my boyfriend in there. I could mist in and bypass the door entirely."

"You're too emotionally involved," Marcy said. "You might not do what needs to be done."

"Like what?" I asked, trying not to screech or panic.

"The very fact that you have to ask means you're not ready to do it," Marcy said. "Don't worry, we'll get him out safely. We need *you* on the outside to keep an eye out for the Feds, in case Brent is right and they're already on their way to investigate. Or the police."

If my heart could beat, it would be pounding. I tried to take deep breaths even though they weren't strictly necessary. Marcy was my BFF. I trusted her with my life.

But it was Bobby's I was worried about. She'd been

ready to kill him herself when he caused the accident that put Brent in the hospital.

"I still don't see—"

"Neither will the authorities," Marcy cut in, anticipating me. "If someone comes, you're the only one who can literally disappear. You can ghost inside and get word to us. There's no way they can catch you."

"Why can't Ulric play look-out? He can honk if he spots anyone snooping."

"And who's going to back him up if they take him out first?"

I didn't like it. I was fairly sure that if I'd been thinking straight I could find a flaw in her reasoning, but that was the whole point, I guess... that I *wasn't* thinking straight.

"Fine. But if you break him—"

"We bought him. Yeah, I get it."

"Here." Brent tossed me his phone. "Marcy has hers. If you see anything, call. If we need help, we'll do the same. We won't be out of touch for a second."

I made sure the phone was set on vibrate and tucked it into my bra.

"Stay," I told Ulric. "If anything goes wrong, we need you as our getaway driver."

"Your wish is my command."

"Cute," I told him.

"About time you noticed."

I smiled, but I'm not sure it reached my eyes... not with Bobby running amok.

Ulric grabbed my hand as I moved to get out of the car, and even though I had strength on my side, it held me still.

"Hey, it'll be okay," he said. He gave my hand a squeeze and released it before I could even think it was any kind of come-on.

"Thank you," I tried to say, but I was all choked up. I got out of the car with the words still stuck in my throat.

I knew Brent and Marcy would call the second they found anything, but even so I had to stifle the urge to contact them for a status report. Instead, I prowled away from the car—less stealthy in physical form than mist, but way better able to use my senses. In ghosty form, I could sense things pretty well—heat, noise, commotion, any atmospheric anomalies—but I couldn't actually *see* per se. It was a little freaky. I much preferred to rock the bod.

So I paced the night, all the while keeping watch on the building, my surroundings, everything. Just in case the past should come back to us in the form of Feds, fangs, or killer cops . . . in case the current menace should be in a playful mood . . . or in case anything should get past Brent and Marcy.

All was quiet, except for one of our neighbors blasting Bon Jovi's "It's My Life" and jumping around her apartment like a loon, backlit by all the lights she had blazing.

Then something thumped off to my right, and I turned instinctively to look for the source. I swung back a millisecond later, when I sensed movement coming from the opposite direction, but it was too late. The onrushing action was vampire-fast, and something hit me upside the head before I could react.

Pain exploded my vision and dropped me where I stood. I fell to the ground, trying to control my fall, to land in a position to sweep my attacker's legs out from under him, but he'd had the same training I'd had. He leapt back out of the way as I kicked, and I caught sight of his beloved face, twisted almost beyond all recognition.

"Bobby!" I cried out, hoping to call him forth, that somehow the sound of my voice would penetrate through the crazy.

But he swung again, and I could see that his weapon was some kind of metal bar with a forked end—a crowbar? No wonder my ears were ringing.

I rolled to the side, to avoid the blow, then rolled back into it as it landed. I tried to wrap my body around the bar—to gain control or at least make *him* lose control. Anticipating me, he yanked it back as soon as he saw that it had missed, and it ripped through my side like ... well, like a crowbar. My whole body screamed, but I tuned it out. If I could live, I could heal. First things first.

I had to stop thinking of him as Bobby. He wasn't. Not at that moment. I rocked back onto my shoulders and hands and flipped up to standing, a move they'd taught us in spy training.

Bobby had a wicked-creepy grin on his face as he lifted the bloodied crowbar like a bat. "Master says bring you," he said, showing fully-forward fangs. "Why would you fight it?"

Master? Okay, that was new.

I didn't waste breath on an answer. Instead, I flew at him, hoping to get inside his arc before he could swing. I dove straight for his neck, fangs aimed at his jugular. The bar caught a glancing blow to my back. I heard something crack, but then I was in. My fangs sank deeply into his flesh and even the pain receded in the euphoric rush of his blood. It was like New Year's and prom, the hottest dress ever, a miracle makeover, a full-fat mochachino with the calories of a skinny latte, and the rush of a first kiss all rolled into one. It was hot, tasty, decadent, amazing, and sinful. My brain shut down on the comparisons then and I just *felt*.

If I'd still been fully functional, I probably would have sensed the stake coming at my back in time to avoid it—

• • •

I awoke to voices. Not that I indicated that I was conscious by so much as a twitch.

"I said bring me the *guy*, the telemetric you told me about. Not ... *her.*"

Rebecca?

We'd found out she was trafficking in dead bodies and grave goods, but kidnapping? Assault? I hadn't pegged her for a criminal mastermind.

"He went inside," not-Bobby was saying. "And he had backup. *She* was alone. I thought we could use her as bait." It broke my heart to hear that voice. Bobby's, but not. A little too high and ... crazy. Because, yeah, a voice could totally be crazy, and his was it.

"You're obsessed," Rebecca spat. "You'd have gone after her regardless."

I cracked open my eyelids just a touch. I had to see where I was and start looking for escape. I didn't know what they needed Brent for. He had to be the telemetric they were talking about.

I still didn't know who Bobby was when he wasn't himself, though I was starting to get an inkling. The first time he'd acted possessed, we were inside our apartment . . . and despite all the rumors about the hauntings there, the place had been mysteriously quiet ever since we'd moved in. Possibly because our resident ghost had found a new home in Bobby.

"Obsessed?" not-Bobby asked. "Maybe. Could be. *Get the girl—get the girl—get the girl.* It runs through my head like little spiders creepy-crawling."

"Ick, another obsession of yours—spiders!" Rebecca screeched. "How hard is it to get good help these days? Stupid amulet. I call for Tituba and I get Renfield. It's like it's defective or something."

Tituba? Renfield? Wait, I knew both those names. I couldn't remember how I knew them, but I was pretty sure they didn't go together.

My head was pounding and with my eyes barely slit open, all I could see was stained off-white carpet and feet encased in squared-toed boots. Pointy toes were at least direct and, well, to the point. Squared-off shoes weren't to be trusted, especially when they were coming closer and all my sensitive spots sat at their level. I closed my eyes again so that Rebecca wouldn't see that I was awake. I wondered if she'd realized that I wasn't breathing. I couldn't very well have faked it while unconscious, so I had no idea whether I should start now. I decided to try to hedge my bets with slow shallow breaths, barely noticeable.

"You're not fooling anyone, Sleeping Beauty. Wakey-wakey."

When I didn't respond right away, she hauled back one of those snub-nosed boots and swung it my way. I flinched, trying to bring my arms forward to block the kick, but they were trapped behind my back, which protested the movement rather vehemently. *That* was when I remembered the stake that had struck me down. I tried to strike out with my legs, and found them tied as well. I was lashed like an old-time heroine left on the train tracks. I could ghost out of the way, of course, but I wasn't ready to go just yet. I didn't have a plan for getting Bobby away, and even after he'd poked me with his pointy stick, I wasn't prepared to leave him behind. Or go without learning whatever I could about what this was all about.

Rebecca's boot connected with my ribs, whooshing out the air I'd pretended to breathe in. I winced and curled protectively around my stomach. Too late.

"Bitch," I spat. Ghosting out and knocking her on her butt was starting to look better and better.

"Oh, honey, is that all you've got?" She laughed, and I could have killed her. Twice. Once for each of us, Bobby and me.

She held her hand out to not-Bobby, and he looked at it in confusion. Impatient, she waggled her fingers. "Hand it over."

"The walkie-talkie?"

"The *phone*, yes."

Bobby pulled my borrowed cell out of a pocket and dropped it into her hand like it was a hot potato. She slid it open, flipped through one of the directories, and pressed a button.

"Sit up," she ordered me.

I did, but only because it was way more dignified than lying down. She watched me, but I refused to watch her back. Instead, I looked at Bobby.

"Bobby," I said softly. "Come back to me."

He looked smaller now. It was like he'd caved in on himself. His shoulders—Renfield's shoulders, apparently—were all hunched, and he was doing his best to gnaw his fingernails right off. I hoped his fangs weren't extended or it could get downright painful.

But Rebecca was talking into the phone now, and I had to focus back on her to see if I could pick up both sides of the conversation.

"I've got the girl. Gia or whatever her name is. If you want her, you come by yourself. *Just* you. If I see anyone else, she dies." She paused to listen for a second and then asked, "Proof? Here's your proof."

Rebecca reached down to hold the phone to my ear, probably the whole reason I'd been allowed to sit in the first place.

"Don't listen to her," I started.

"Are you al—" Brent began.

Rebecca ripped the phone away from my ear.

"So noble," she said into the receiver. "You don't want someone like that to die just because you wouldn't follow instructions, do you? Good. Derby Wharf, the schooner pier. Ten o'clock."

"Not the witching hour?" Bobby asked, spitting out his latest nail-biting success.

"Ten o'clock gives us plenty of time for it to get dark and deserted down at the pier."

She looked meaningfully in my direction, as if some part of that was meant to be a threat, which implied to me that she had no idea that nighttime-without-witnesses played right to my strengths. That hope was dashed a second later when she squatted before me, the pendant I'd wondered about swinging free of her shirt.

"So vampires really exist?" she asked, studying me.

I made myself turn away to glare at Bobby in betrayal, rather than stare at the pendant and reveal just how interested in it I was. Bobby surely hadn't been able to help himself. It was probably impossible to keep secrets from someone—some*thing*—that shared your body and brain, but still ... I hoped there were some things that he'd held back. For instance, I did *not* need this Renfield guy knowing what I looked like in my skivvies.

"Answer me," she ordered.

I skimmed past the pendant on my way to give her the

death glare of doom. The piece wasn't much to look at, at least not at first glance—just a pure black stone, like obsidian, ringed by a twisted wire setting and strung on a leather cord. But the longer I looked, the harder it was to look away, like the stone was some black hole, sucking me in. Rebecca caught my stare and tucked the pendant quickly away with a glare all her own.

"Answer me," she snarled, again.

I met her gaze. "We're not like genies. You can't compel us to answer."

Her eyes went wide. "Djinn exist too? How do I get one?"

"Have you tried digging up Aladdin's lamp? Seems like you've dug up everything else."

Those eyes narrowed again, and she flipped her long auburn hair over her shoulder. "I'm no grave robber. I was looking for something."

"Tell that to the guy whose grave you robbed, the one whose skeleton is sitting in the Morbid Gift Shop looking for hand-outs." She'd probably never expected that JC Supplies would resell it so close to home.

She hissed. "How much do you know?"

"Everything," I lied.

Except what she was looking for. And why? What did she want with Brent? Or this Tituba person? Had she found what she was looking for? Was it the pendant?

"Then you know about the Book of Shadows," she said, studying me.

Oh crapcakes, that didn't bode well. "Of course." *Not.*

She leaned in, practically salivating. "Do you have it? I would ransom you for the book."

"I thought you were planning to trade me for Brent."

"If I have the book, I don't need *him*."

Ah, so that's how things stood. "I'm sorry to disappoint you, then. We don't have it."

"Fine," she spat. "Let's go." She looked at Bobby, who stopped gnawing the last of his nails to dip his head in a mini-bow.

"Master?" he asked.

"It's *mistress*, I keep telling you. Bring her."

He crouched next to me to grab my arms and haul me to my feet. He was so close I was tempted to go for the vein again, but I could barely even smell the blood beneath his skin. He was still low from my earlier feeding and hadn't replenished. That might even the playing field, with me all tied up, but I just couldn't do it. For once, I had an entourage, and I was determined to use it. Brent, I was sure, would not come alone, no matter what Rebecca said. Marcy would never let him.

The ride to Derby Wharf was nearly silent but for me trying to get more information out of Rebecca about this Book of Shadows and how it all tied in to Salem's troubles. Apparently, though, she'd read the Evil Overlord rules and knew you didn't monologue about your plans to the good guys, giving them a chance to escape and foil everything. You also didn't arrange ridiculously convoluted and slow deaths for them or set explosives to actually go off at zero as opposed to, say, ten. But I was hoping that last one wouldn't become relevant.

Rebecca drove, and Bobby sat in the back with me, staring eerily and stroking my hair, saying creepy things like "smooth as spider silk" and something about how they made sweaters out of alpaca but my hair was so much softer. He gave me the chills, and not at all in the way I was used to them from Bobby. I didn't like it.

Renfield! I suddenly remembered. The insane henchman from all the Dracula movies. He'd never lived in Salem—or at all—but Renfield Syndrome, with its craving for blood and all, *that* I thought was a real thing. This made it more and more likely that we were dealing with our asylum ghost.

When I leaned away, Bobby aka Renfield came with me. So I gave up, rather than risk him falling right into my lap.

By the time we parked at the wharf, I was ready to crawl out of my own skin to escape. There was a commercial side to the wharf, complete with a little loop of stores and restaurants featuring anything from knickknacks and incense to steamed clams, but we weren't there. We were at the actual piers, past the Maritime Museum, where an antique-looking ship rocked—the schooner Rebecca had mentioned, I guessed. It appeared ready for another voyage at any second. The museum was, of course, closed, and the pier was dark except for a few low lights at foot level. Faces would be in shadow.

Only one person stood on that pier, halfway to the end. With my vamp sight, I could see it was Brent. I knew he wouldn't have come alone, but scanning the area, I couldn't spot Marcy or any other backup. Now that it was no longer an option, I realized what a huge advantage Bobby's mind-speak ability had always been for coordinating attacks. I couldn't read Brent's mind, and he couldn't read mine. We were going to have to wing it.

"Is it him?" Rebecca asked her Renfield.

He nodded.

"Good. When we get to the pier, you stay on the shore with Gia while I go out to meet the telemetric. Once I've got him, you can free her."

Renfield-Bobby did that head bob again. "Yes, Master." But there was a sly tone to his voice, like the whole master/mistress thing was intentional. Or maybe he knew the bit about letting me go was just for show and there was no way it was really gonna happen.

With my legs bound together, I had to take tiny, mincing steps toward the dock. Rebecca soon outpaced Renfield and me, leaving us behind, as planned, when she walked out onto the pier. Renfield held my bound arms in one hand and had the other wrapped around my neck. It reminded me chillingly of the ghostly hands choking me on my first night at Haunts. I broke out in a blood sweat, not because I had anything to fear from strangulation, but because I was afraid of *Bobby*. I didn't know where the night would take us or what I'd be forced to do.

We watched as Rebecca stopped, face-to-face with Brent.

"You came alone?" she asked, as if Brent would tell her otherwise.

He nodded.

"As soon as you let me bind you, we'll let your friend go. I have no use for her."

I could hear the lie as clear as a bell from where I was standing. I wondered if it sounded any more convincing at close range.

"Let her go first," he demanded.

"Not on your life."

Brent looked at me, and I wished I knew what he was trying to tell me. Renfield pointedly tightened his grip on my throat.

"It doesn't seem I have any choice," Brent said.

His shoulders slumped in defeat, and he held his hands out to her for cuffing. A look of triumph flashed across Rebecca's face.

As she made a move toward him, something burst out of the water right behind her and tore her feet out from under her. Rebecca hit the pier hard, barely catching herself with her hands and banging her chin with a smack that should have her seeing stars. She flopped like a landed fish and clawed at the wooden planking for dear life as Marcy pulled her by the ankles toward the freezing cold waters.

I didn't wait for the splashdown, but ghosted out of my bonds and Renfield's grip. I rematerialized as soon as I felt both fall away, close enough to Renfield to head-butt him in the nose. If I'd been any shorter or he hadn't bent to grab me, I might have failed. But he yelped, blood spouted, and I whirled out of the way of a counterstrike, ending up behind him where I launched a kidney-kick to take him down. It hurt me, I think, more than it hurt him. The boy was made of solid iron, but I staggered him.

He landed on hands and knees, immediately sweeping a leg out to knock me down. I jumped it like a rope and aimed another kick at his head, but he reared up and caught my foot in mid-air. He twisted, and it knocked me off balance. I started to topple and turned it into a shoulder roll at the last second to keep from face-planting into the pier.

Renfield was up again.

"Master!" he called.

I looked at where I'd last seen Rebecca, but she'd vanished. Brent was staring down at the water, so Marcy must have succeeded in pulling her in, but from the way the water was churning, the fight was far from over.

I took advantage of Renfield's distraction to jump him, grab his head in my hands, and *twist* for all I was worth. Breaking his neck broke my heart. I felt it snap along with his vertebra.

He lay still. So still. Dead. That his condition was temporary didn't do much for my state of mind. He'd heal, but it would take time, especially without the benefit of new blood.

Marcy popped up from the depths, dripping wet and spitting water out of her mouth. "Do you see her?" she asked urgently. "The girl is like an eel. She got away from me."

Brent, who'd been studying the water, shook his head. "No sign of her. She didn't ... drown, did she?"

"I wish. She kicked off my chest and I lost her."

"There," Brent shouted suddenly, pointing.

"Hold this," Marcy ordered, tossing something up onto the pier.

It was Rebecca's obsidian pendant. It must have come off in their struggle.

Marcy struck out in the direction Brent had pointed. But after an initial burst of speed, she got slower and slower until she started to sink instead of swim. She bobbed to the surface, gasping, "Help!"

Before I could even process the SOS, Brent had his shoes off and was diving in after her. I was torn between guarding Bobby and doing the same, but Brent had Marcy in no time. He hugged her to him with one arm and stroked back to the pier with the other as I waited anxiously topside. I knew she couldn't drown—she didn't need to *breathe*—but that didn't do anything to calm my fear for my friend.

He pushed her up out of the water to me, and I took her under the arms, drawing her out and laying her down. Brent pulled himself up after her, panting as he stood above us.

"What do we do for her?" he asked. "CPR won't work."

"Feed her a bit of your blood," I told him. "That'll do better than CPR."

He bent down beside her, grabbed a knife out of his back pocket, flicked it open, and cut himself. He opened her mouth gently and let the blood fall in.

"What happened?" I asked him. "What went wrong?"

"If I had to guess..." Brent paused. "Well, mythology has it that vampires can't cross running water, which we've always thought was hokum. Clearly, they got from the old world to the new, so they've crossed oceans. Must be, though, that it takes a lot out of them. I don't know the scientific explanation. I'm not even sure there is one."

"Well, damn, let's get her away from the water then. Let's *all* get away. We have Rebecca's pendant, at least. We don't want to risk her coming back for it."

Brent lifted Marcy into his arms in one of those heroic carries with her head cradled against his chest. Me? I went, as always, for the bling. Rebecca's necklace lay abandoned on the pier, its dark stone sucking light. Marcy had touched it, so I knew it had to be safe, but there was something about it I didn't like. I pulled my fleecy sleeve down over my hand to pick it up, careful not to touch it with my bare skin. I tucked it quickly away in a pocket and we walked to where I'd left Bobby, who was still unconscious. My beautiful, brilliant boy, all beaten to a pulp. *I'd* done it to him. Me.

"Do you need a hand with him?" Brent asked, nodding at Bobby.

He had his hands full, and I had my vampire strength. And my guilt. "No, I've got this."

Brent watched me, just to be sure. "Do you think we should call someone about Rebecca?" he asked, pretending not to see me struggling to get all of Bobby's limbs where I needed them to be after declining his help.

"As soon as we get back to the car. Where is it?"

"Ulric drove us here, but we left him back on the other wharf. We couldn't let Rebecca see him or the car—it wasn't safe."

"He didn't put up a fight?"

Brent's lips twisted. "We told him it was for *your* safety. That seemed to convince him. Gina, the boy's got it bad. You're going to have to tell him if he doesn't have a shot."

I looked over my shoulder at Bobby's upside-down face where it bumped my butt. He looked so ... *him*. So handsome and non-homicidal. So peaceful, like a fallen angel. I looked back up at Brent. Whatever he saw on my face, he didn't push it.

"I'll call for pick-up," he said, gently lowering Marcy's legs to the ground.

"No need," came a voice out of the darkness. Ulric. "I parked way back at the seafood shack, but I couldn't stay away. Guess you didn't need my backup, though." He was looking at me when he said it, his eyes all intense. "I'm so glad you're okay. Can I take that from you?"

That being Bobby. "Nah, I've got this, thanks."

This. That. As if Bobby was nothing more than my own personal baggage.

"Let's get out of here," I said.

"My aunt's out tonight with her bunco group. We can go back to her place."

"What about our footprints on her rug?"

He shrugged. "So maybe I'll vacuum."

Ulric, being domestic. The mind boggled.

Marcy was coming around, and she was able to walk with Brent's support. "Wha' 'appened?" she asked, her head lolling against his shoulder as he supported her, their arms wrapped tightly around each other.

"You don't know? You were swimming after Rebecca when you just seemed to run out of steam."

It took her eyes a second to focus on Brent's face.

"I 'member now. I felt so heavy."

I didn't like the sound of that at all. I thought of the old witch test. If you floated, you were a witch. If you drowned … well, I guess maybe you were a vampire. Either way, the test seemed like a lose-lose proposition.

"Do you think Rebecca's a witch?" I asked, not realizing that I was the only one riding my train of thought.

"Why, because of her pendant?" Brent asked.

"No, the Book of Shadows."

14

Everyone looked at me blankly, and I realized that no one had a clue what I was talking about. I was so used to sharing mind-speak with Bobby, to having someone know what I was thinking, that even with everyone around, I suddenly felt totally alone.

Then I heard a *snap* and my gaze riveted on the boy in my arms. Bobby was adjusting his neck like he was working out kinks rather than totally realigning his spine.

I felt the piercing stab of guilt with every crack. Then his heart-stopping blue eyes focused on me and the most amazing smile lit his face. "Hey, beautiful."

My knees gave out, and Bobby would have toppled to the ground if Ulric hadn't steadied me and then helped lower him to the ground.

"It's you!" I said stupidly.

Then I dropped beside Bobby and kissed his face—his cheeks, his eyes, his chin, finally his mouth. Such a flood of warmth washed over me that I thought I might spontaneously combust. He looked a little confused until I got to his mouth, and then he held onto me for dear life. You know those crazy-awesome film kisses after the hero and heroine have just survived a killer virus or mondo explosion or, like, Doctor Doom. Well, it was like that, with tongue.

Then there was the throat-clearing in the background, but we ignored that. It was the hooting and hollering from the drunk people just stumbling out of one of the bars over on the wharf that did the trick, especially when two of the guys started offering suggestions about what should come next.

We moved on to Ulric's Crown Vic. He grabbed a towel out of the trunk for Marcy to slosh on. The rest of us piled in—Bobby riding shotgun, since he was the tallest of us.

"So what now?" he asked. No one suggested he get into the battered trunk. We knew there was no point.

Shooting sidelong glances at Bobby all the while, I told them about the Book of Shadows Rebecca was searching for. It took all of one second, since I didn't really know much.

"And she thought I could help?" Brent asked.

"She knew you were a telemetric. She must have had something related to the book that she thought you could read."

We both looked to the pocket where I'd stashed the pendant.

"You think?" he asked.

I reached into my pocket, but hesitated to pull it out.

Rebecca had summoned spirits with an object of power. I had the overwhelming sense that this was it. The amulet was making Salem's spirits strong. What if it had some kind of control over Bobby ... or rather, his ride-along? We could lose him again. Or he could go nuts and fry the Crown Vic like he had the van.

"Only one way to find out," Brent said, as if he could read my mind. I knew he couldn't, but ... maybe I was just that obvious.

Reluctantly, I brought out the amulet, watching Bobby the whole time, looking for the first sign that he was going to go all Renfield again. But for the moment he just looked curious, and tired. Almost human.

"Wait!" Marcy said as Brent reached to take it from me.

She grabbed his ears and gave him a scorching kiss first. Everyone else looked away.

"*There*. Now you won't get lost in it or anything. You'll remember what you have to come back for."

"Always," Brent said, heart in his eyes. Okay, ewww, bad visual.

I passed the amulet off to him before there could be any more mushy stuff that didn't involve me and Bobby.

Brent's eyes almost immediately rolled up into his head.

"Brent!" Marcy called, but I grabbed her before she could rip the amulet from him.

"Give him a sec," I said. "We need to learn what we can."

"But—"

Brent spasmed and dropped the amulet like a hot potato.

"That's definitely what's powering the spirits," he said, gasping for breath. "It's like some sort of energy cell with no off switch."

"Any connection to a Book of Shadows?" I asked, pulling my sleeve over my hand again to rescue the dangerous amulet from where it had fallen.

"Could be. I got a pretty good sense of the original owner. You'll never believe this."

"What? Who?" I mean, on a previous mission we'd met Rasputin. *The* Rasputin. The Mad Monk, advisor to the doomed Romanov royal family killed during the Russian Revolution. Next to Elvis, Jesus, and Dracula, how much crazier could it get?

"Tituba," he answered.

There was that name again, and I still couldn't remember what it meant. Marcy's face crinkled up in confusion.

"The name sounds familiar," I started. "But—"

"The witch!" Bobby exclaimed, and suddenly I remembered it from all the times he'd read us Salem history snippets until we wanted to brain him. "The slave who taught those Salem girls the 'spells' that they felt so guilty about, they started acting out."

"Wait, I remember this!" I said, excited. "She and her husband John Indian were accused of witchcraft."

"He turned on her to save himself, just like the girls," Bobby jumped in again.

"That so sucks," Marcy said, totally recovered now.

"Not so much," Bobby responded. "Unlike so many others, she wasn't put to death. Someone bought her way out of prison."

"So, what's this amulet?" I asked Brent.

"Something she brought with her from her homeland. When Tituba sensed that the authorities were coming for her, she knew everything she had would be confiscated—the accused basically funded their own trials. Tituba hid the pendant and her Book of Shadows to save them for her daughter, and also so they couldn't be used against her. She foresaw her own imprisonment."

"Harsh," Marcy commented.

"But she didn't hide the pendant and book together," I cut in, "or they'd have been found together."

"I didn't get all that from the amulet. Imprints are only left when strong emotions are involved—I got Tituba's fear that witch hunters would come for her, and her acceptance of an almost-certain death, which turns out wasn't so certain after all. I don't have much more than that. Her daughter did get the pendant somehow, because I feel her here as well, overlying the memories, obscuring the hiding places. I have images, but not much else … nothing that means anything to me. The necklace was in a secret spot, a hidey-hole within the household where she served. The book … wasn't," Brent answered helpfully.

His gaze shot suddenly to Bobby, as if something had just occurred to him. "Should he be hearing all this?"

We *all* looked at Bobby, whose eyes were, mercifully, still baby blue.

"Brent, it's *Bobby*," I said, even though I had the same doubts.

"For now. But you said Rebecca knew I was a telemetric. I know Bobby wouldn't have intentionally told her about me, but he doesn't seem to have any control over himself, and I don't see how else she could have known."

"I'm right *here*," Bobby said.

"That's exactly my point. Until we break this . . . spell or whatever, you can't be trusted. What if this is plan B? What if you're still somehow bound to her and she meant for you to come along and turn on us once we solve her mystery and find the book?"

"Paranoid much?" I asked.

"Occupational hazard," Brent answered.

"What occupation? You wait tables."

"Enough," Ulric said, cutting across us all. "You can't start turning on each other. If you want the amulet destroyed or deactivated or whatever, I know who to call." He didn't sound happy about it.

"Olivia?" I asked.

He nodded.

"But the coven's already tried to lay the spirits to rest. They couldn't do anything."

"They didn't have the source of the problem to study, though."

"You'll make the call?" I asked.

"Um, yeah, hold that thought."

Ulric had slowed the car to a crawl and was staring hard out the window ahead of us.

There was a patrol unit about a block away on the right, along with another car, both parked on the street. Since all other cars on the block were tucked away in driveways or garages, this seemed pretty significant.

"Your aunt's place?" Marcy asked, jumping to the same conclusion I had.

Ulric nodded. "But why?"

He pulled over to the side of the road and started to get out of the car. Brent reached over from the back seat to stop him. "What are you doing? It's probably you they're after. They probably have the Crown Vic on tape at the hospital driving away after the incident there. You can't go in."

Ulric shook him off. "I have to! What if something's happened to her?"

"Wait!" I said urgently. "Think about this for a second. I'm not saying don't go. Just, if you do, if you're questioned, remember that the police don't have anything on you. If there's footage from the parking lot, they'll know you weren't the one driving getaway. You weren't even conscious."

"Whatever. I'm not worried about me. What if the killer cop's the one in there interrogating my aunt?"

We all went silent.

"You all go," he said. "I'll handle this on my own. But I have to go in there."

"No," I said. "I mean yes, you go. But you won't be alone."

"But they can't see you..."

"They won't," I said. "And neither will you."

He gave me a funny look, but I didn't explain and he didn't wait around for it. He was already out before I turned to the others. "You all bug out, in case they search the car."

But don't go far, I mind-spoke to Bobby, forgetting for a second that his abilities were on the blink. *You stay you until I get back. I love you.* I wished... I slipped out of the car, pushing aside the pain of the wishes I couldn't make come true. Instead, I focused on going insubstantial. Almost in an instant I was as light as air. The sounds and smells of the night lost their clarity. The ground was no longer beneath my feet. Even my sorrow seemed a distant thing. It took all my concentration to move myself after Ulric. I wondered if this was how actual ghosts felt. If so, it was no wonder they took possession of a body, to recover the immediacy of life when they could.

I floated, past the police car and the other cars, toward the house. I sensed rather than saw Ulric let himself in, mostly by the change in the air as the heat from the house met and mingled with the cold air outside, creating a swirly pattern of contrast. I aimed for that turbulence, but he must have shut the door right behind him, because as I hit the entrance, I smacked up against something dense. Only my momentum pushed me on through... or rather, it felt like pieces of me squeezed through, like spaghetti through a press. Panic that all my parts might not get sorted out again on the other side overtook me. This happened every time

I went through something solid. I hated it. *Hated.* With a fiery passion rivaled only by my feelings toward my old arch-nemesis, Tina Carstairs.

Then I was *in*, past the door, all together again. Or so I hoped. I tried to get a sense of where *in* put me. A big open space that I'd be caught out in at any second? The safety of a coat closet?

I sensed the air, stretched out my awareness, and tried to let the impressions come. It definitely wasn't a closet, or I'd have subtle pressure from the contents on all sides, but it wasn't a big space either. Air currents were swirling just beyond—people talking or moving around. I *had* to know what was going on.

The more solid I became the better spy I'd make, but also the more discoverable. I floated behind some big object—like one of those typical New England pieces that combined a wooden bench for pulling on your boots with a mirrored back for seeing how you looked in them, and a wide back-splash with hooks on either side for hanging jackets and scarves. Aside from that, the area felt almost entirely taken up by boots, lined up all the way to the door like soldiers standing at attention, reporting for duty.

Luckily, the behemoth piece of furniture was big enough to hide me, which was a good thing, because I had to go at least semi-solid to hear. I peeked out from behind the jackets and could see straight into the sunken living room, in which Ulric's aunt, I guessed, was serving two uniformed officers—luckily *not* the killer cops—tea and cookies. I craned my neck to see farther into the room, and nearly knocked all the coats aside in shock. My heart wanted to beat just so it could stop all over again.

There, right in Ulric's living room, were our former Federal handlers: Agents Sid and Maya, aka Stuffed Shirt and Stick-up-her-butt.

Brent had been right that the Feds would be on top of the goings-on in Salem, and wrong to think that they wouldn't be instantly connected to us. It couldn't be mere coincidence that it was these two agents who'd showed up. Here. Now. We were so screwed.

Seeing Ulric, his aunt—a militantly trim woman in a lavender sweater set, her gunmetal gray hair like a helmet on her head—straightened. A teacup with hand-painted cherry blossoms dancing across it was clasped in one hand and a matching kettle in the other. She trapped him with her steely gaze and demanded, "Ulric, what have you done?"

I was both relieved and offended on his behalf. Family should give you the benefit of the doubt. On the other hand, at least she was safe.

"Now, ma'am," Agent Sid said soothingly, "we don't know for certain that he did anything. But your car was caught on camera at North Shore Medical Center, where an officer was wounded last night, and you say he borrowed it, so, of course, we have to follow up."

Sid's gaze transferred from the aunt to Ulric, and there was a *don't-screw-with-me* look to it. Given his aunt, though,

I was guessing Ulric had experience handling himself under that kind of scrutiny.

In fact, Ulric answered all the questions with claims of amnesia. He was knocked out at the hospital and came to in the car—all the absolute truth, if only a fraction of it. Nobody trained to read cues, as I knew Sid and Maya were, could possibly cry foul, though Sid clearly wanted to. The interesting part came next, when Agent Maya pulled out pictures to show Ulric and his aunt.

"Have you seen any of these people before?" Maya asked, fanning the stack out on the table. Bobby's pic, Marcy's, and mine must have been from our pre-vamp days when our images could still be captured. I so hoped mine wasn't from junior year, when my mother forgot to check the airbrushing option to cover up the fat lip I'd gotten from a stray volleyball in gym class.

She and Sid studied Ulric closely as he looked at the pictures. They knew very well that Ulric had met Bobby and me back in New York when I'd infiltrated the goth gang. They were hoping to draw him into a trap.

"Yeah, that's Geneva ... Belton? Bison? Belfry, that was it. I knew her back in New York. Strange girl. And I might have seen him around." I was guessing he'd indicated Bobby. I wasn't at the right angle to see. "We didn't hang. He was a brain."

"You were smart enough," his aunt started in on him. "You just didn't apply—"

"Ma'am," Sid cut her off, "we've got this. So," he said to

Ulric as she huffed her indignation, "you haven't seen them *recently?*"

Oh crap on a crispy, crumbly cracker. Haunts in History—they'd find out, if they didn't already know, that we all worked together. They'd assume he was in league with us. Which, of course, he sort of was. We'd put him right in their crosshairs.

I didn't know exactly what that meant anymore. Back when we'd worked for the Feds and I thought we were on the side of good, I'd have assumed they'd merely put him under surveillance. That was before I'd seen their secret "medical" facilities, with vampires being bled for goth-knew what use of their blood, kept barely alive. Ulric didn't have any special powers. He could be of no possible use to them. What if they decided he was a liability? What then? We had to hope they viewed him as someone who could lead them to us Federal fugitives—someone worth keeping alive.

I was torn between staying behind to watch Ulric and ghosting out to give the others the bad news. We were going to have to ditch even the phones we had left and buy a bunch of burners. If the Feds knew about Ulric, they'd be tracking all calls to or from his phone. We might as well be carrying around our own personal Bat-signals.

Suddenly, the hip radios on both of the uniformed officers went off simultaneously. Everyone in the room stopped cold, eyes riveted on the radios like they'd suddenly display 3-D video or something. Instead, someone snapped out code, cross-streets, and shock. Definitely shock. Whatever the code meant, it was no run-of-the-mill drunk and disorderly.

"Officer-involved shooting?" one cop said to the other. "What the *hell* is going on in this town?"

"Can we ride along?" Sid asked.

"Knock yourselves out. Just stay out of the way."

Sid looked like he'd like to spit nails as he ground out, "Sure thing."

That was my cue. I ghosted out again before anyone could discover me and floated through the night. A weird vibration brought me crashing back into my body across the street from where everyone was exiting Ulric's house. I stumbled with my sudden materialization, and ducked between two houses, out of sight. The strange vibration continued, and I realized it was Brent's cell phone in my pocket. I answered quickly before it could go to voicemail.

"Gina, thank God!" Marcy said immediately in my ear. "Everything okay?"

"If you consider an officer down okay."

"What?" she screeched. "What went on in there?"

"Oh no, not at Ulric's. The police got a call while I was inside. We'd better follow."

"Crapcakes with suck sauce."

My thoughts exactly. I walked until the phone was no longer necessary and I had the others in my sight. Bobby was the first one I looked at, of course. Eyes … still blue. A good sign.

"So, any ideas for playing follow that car?" Brent asked.

As if I'd summoned it, there was a honk out on the street. I smiled. "I think that's our ride."

"Shouldn't we leave him out of it, given the official interest in him?"

"You convince him. I'll watch. Anyway, I think it's a little late for that."

Ulric popped the locks as we approached.

"How'd you convince your aunt to let you take the car again after all that?" I asked as I got in.

"Who says I asked?"

"You mean you stole it?" Bobby asked, horrified. Yup, still *sounded* like Bobby.

Ulric pulled out, barely sparing him a glance. "*No*, stealing is the intent to keep. This is more like borrowing."

"Without permission," Bobby pushed.

"Easier to ask forgiveness than permission." Ulric spared a look away from the street to flash us a wolfish grin.

"You're not worried about the police and the questioning?" Marcy asked.

"Been there, done that. Have the rap sheet to prove it," Ulric answered.

"Really?" Marcy sounded impressed. Everyone looked at her in shock.

"Driving without a license," he offered.

"Oh."

"I was fourteen."

"*Oh.*"

"Down girl," Brent said, putting a hand possessively on her leg.

"Rebel without a clue," Bobby added.

Jealous, both of them. Stupid boys.

Clearly, all the numbers spouted off on the radio had meant something to Ulric, because he didn't need to follow the long-gone cops to the scene.

It was chaotic enough that I thought we might not be noticed if we stayed far enough off. Unless Bobby went mental again. We didn't have any choice but to bring him along and keep watch. We already knew the trunk wouldn't hold him. I had no idea what would. Since shots had been fired, the scene was attracting a *lot* of attention ... including from the Ghouligans, who were standing by. The cameraman held his piece at hip level—not filming, but ready to start at a moment's notice. They were behind the crime scene tape with the rest of the hoi polloi, but just barely. I was fairly sure I could get the full story out of Ty if I could get close enough, but I didn't dare risk it.

Ulric tapped someone at the back of the gathered crowd, one of the few who wasn't talking on his cell phone or holding it above his head hoping to get good and gruesome pics. "What happened?" he asked.

"*Dude*, these guys—cops—stopped a girl for reckless driving and they got into it with her. What I heard, one tried to strangle her and the other had to shoot him to save her. Crazy, right?"

"Is the girl okay?" I asked.

He turned to me and the fumes from his breath nearly knocked me back. I was guessing a bloomin' onion and some kind of garlic dipping sauce. My eyes watered.

"They took her out in an ambulance instead of a body bag, so yeah, I'm guessing. Medics are still working on the cop."

I shot a glance at Bobby. He was sniffing, but not in the direction of the onion breath. He was sniffing high. Something in the air, then. I stepped away from the guy, with a mumbled "thanks," to scent the night myself.

Blood and fire.

Literally. The air smelled of cordite and death. I hoped it wouldn't trigger bad-Bobby.

"Bobby," I said gently, "that's still you in there, right? Stay with us."

He looked at me, and his eyes were still blue, but deeper, darker ... stormier. The *other* was fighting for control. I could see it.

So could Ulric. "We've *got* to get all this under control," he said.

"Thank you, Captain Obvious," Marcy said.

"Bobby, look at me," I said.

He did, but not with recognition. I stood up on my tip-toes to grab him around the neck and draw him down to my level so that I could rest his forehead on mine, look him in the eyes. "Bobby, it's Gina. Your *girlfriend* Gina. I—" I'd said it before in mind-speak, but ... but what? If it could save him, keep him whole, what was pride compared to that? "I *love* you. Stay with me. You're not going anywhere, dammit. Don't you dare cross me on this."

"Gina," someone said. I was so focused on Bobby that I almost missed it. "*Gina*," Marcy said, more insistently.

I looked up and spotted Ty making his way toward us. Of course. The man missed nothing.

"What do we do?" I asked.

I looked to each one for an answer. Bobby, still fighting his demon, didn't look back.

The last thing I wanted was for Ty to catch on and call an exorcist.

"We need allies," Marcy said quietly.

I made a decision. "You all hang back. Watch Bobby. I'll see what he wants."

I headed Ty off before he could get to the rest of the group. The others faded back into the crowd.

"There's a BOLO out for you," Ty said as he approached.

It took me a second to realize he wasn't talking about the stringy western tie, but something official, a *Be On The Look-out*.

I shrugged. "Whatever they want me for, I'm innocent. Something weird is going on, so I'm dodging the police just now, but trust me, there's another side to the story."

Ty smiled, but his eyes were full of secrets. "You mean the story about how those puncture wounds appeared on the officer's neck after a commotion at the medical center last night?"

Well, crap.

He waited, like he was looking forward to hearing whatever I came up with that he was fully prepared not to believe. Knowing that, I didn't even try.

Instead, I lifted my chin in defiance. "You didn't rat me out. You were standing right over by the cops, right up to the tape line. You could have put them onto the fact that I was here. You didn't. What is it you want?"

"An exclusive."

"Come again?"

"Look, I figured you out. I can't be the only one. It's only a matter of time before some modern-day Van Helsing comes hunting you. But think about it—vampires are *hot* right now. There's never been a better time to come out of the closet."

We'd tried that once. Back in Ohio, where the gang and I had first been vamped, we'd tried to expose the whole thing to the press. The Feds had come in and swept it all under the rug. They were already here in Salem, hot on our trail. Why should I believe that this time would be any different? I asked Ty the same question.

"Because *we* believe, and we won't cave."

Sure, until the Feds initiated some kind of search and seizure on the Ghouligan's equipment or audit on their finances, or pulled out any of the other big guns in their arsenal.

"What would be in it for us?"

I didn't know what made me ask that. I'd been standing out here for too long already. The cops could notice me at any moment.

"We could help you."

"How?"

"You tell me."

I thought about it for a second. "A set of wheels and enough money to disappear."

"After we get what we want."

"Of course."

"I'll have to talk to my producers. How do I get in touch?"

"I'll find you." *Allies.* I tried to focus on that. If Ty really could do what he said ... if he could shine a light on supernats and do an exposé on the Federal facilities that exploited them ... would things actually get any better, or just go farther underground? Would vamps be the next superstars or would we be hunted like the witches of Salem? Or both?

Ty nodded. "Okay, for now."

"Did you record the killer cop on your equipment? I mean ... do the police know he was possessed?"

"They don't believe us."

"Stupid-heads."

That surprised a laugh out of him.

"One more thing," I said. "Maybe two." I was still debating how much to say, but things were moving too quickly for caution. "Do you recognize this?"

I pulled the amulet from my pocket and dangled it before his face. He grabbed for it, and I snatched it away, back into my pocket.

"No. What is it?" he asked.

"Maybe the cause of all the trouble. We're going to find

out, and stop it. If you learn anything or hear about a special Book of Shadows ... "

"I'll, what, call you? You said *you'd* find *me*."

Oh, right.

"Leave a message with someone at the Gothic Magic Show. I'll get it."

"If you need an expert to take a look at that"—he nodded to my pocket—"you let me know."

"Thanks, we've got our own expert." I hoped.

I walked away. After about a dozen paces, the others fell in beside me.

"What did he want?" Brent asked.

"He wants to tell our story."

"You trust him?"

"To tell the story? Yes." But was that what we wanted, or would it just send us from the frying pan into the fire?

"Okay, so we'll call that plan H," Brent said.

"Why H?" Marcy asked.

"For Hell in a Handbasket."

Bobby was standing quietly ... too quietly, one hand raised to gnaw again at his non-existent nails.

"Come on, we've got to get him out of here." I put an arm through one of his to pull him with me, but he dug his heels in and refused to budge. His eyes were brown, and his whole body radiated leashed tension. Holding his arm was like holding a live wire.

"Where?" he asked. "Can't go far. Can't leave. There be sea monsters."

So much for sanity.

Ulric grabbed his other arm, and together we managed to propel him along with us and get him into the front seat of the car.

"Where are we going?" I whispered to Ulric, which was just silly, because Bobby's vamp hearing would pick it up anyway. But human habits died hard.

"I talked to Olivia. She'll meet us at the brew pub after closing, and she's calling in reinforcements."

"Huh?"

"Her coven."

"Oh—cool."

We all rode in silence the rest of the way to the pub, except for the silly song Bobby sang to himself as he began to rock:

"... That wiggled and jiggled and tickled inside her
She swallowed the spider to catch the fly
But I don't know why she swallowed the fly
Perhaps she'll die."

I shared a glance with Ulric in the rearview mirror, like parents might share about their five-year-old's imaginary friend. It made me feel old. And scared.

"What do we do with Bobby when we get to the pub?" Marcy hissed to me.

"Well, we can't leave him alone," I hissed back.

Which meant we'd be bringing him along. Babysitting had so never been my gig.

Bobby suddenly started to get agitated. Like ... *really.* He went from gentle rocking to flinging his body into the backrest and kicking the dash. He tore at his hair with nubby nails and beat at his head.

"Stop. Stop, STOP!" he cried. "Stop thinking so loud. I CAN HEAR YOU, YOU KNOW!"

We all stared at Bobby. Was he talking to himself? Renfield telling Bobby to just stop fighting? Or was Bobby somehow coming through, warning us that his alter-ego could hear our thoughts? Bobby had said he couldn't access his powers any more. But what if his counterpart could? What if our spoken words weren't the only things he could overhear? Spooky.

"Shh-shh-shh!" I tried to soothe him. "No one's saying a thing." I turned to the others. "Blank your minds."

Bobby gave me a suspicious look, but he paused from spazzing out long enough to listen. A second later, he sank bonelessly into the seat, no longer fighting *or* humming. I'd have thought him asleep if he didn't flinch with every bump in the road. My heart hurt for my boy.

We had to finish this. Now. Tonight. Before the Feds found us or anyone else died.

We had to coax Bobby out of the car, toward the closed and locked doors of the nearly deserted pub. He dragged his feet the whole way until something caught his attention and his head suddenly shot up. Like a predator, his eyes became laser-focused. Following his gaze, I barely caught sight of a creepy, crawly movement before he pounced, slapped a hand over a shadow with too many legs, and swept it into his mouth. I heard the crunch of exoskeleton and nearly threw up all over the evergreens flanking the entrance.

"*But I don't know why he swallowed the fly,*" Bobby sang, smacking his lips. "*Perhaps he'll die.*"

I was never kissing that mouth again.

When Olivia answered our knock and let us in, her face was all concern. "Are you okay?" she asked. "You look like you've seen a ghost."

"Close enough," I answered, unable even to look at Bobby. I knew it wasn't actually *him*, but at the same time … "Let's hurry."

I shooed her inside, and held the door open for the others before yanking it closed and locked behind us.

Olivia led the way to a table at the back—or really, three tables pulled together, where her friends already sat. I don't know what I'd expected—pointy hats, green faces, or just more blue hair like Olivia's—but it wasn't what I got. Around the table sat five perfectly normal-looking people … and Chip from the Morbid Gift Shop.

Olivia introduced us all, first names only. The coven was like a study in contrasts. Beside Chip was a gorgeous African-American lady with thick braids every variant of color from blond to black, twisted into a complicated updo, and skin that would make cosmetic companies weep because it needed no enhancement. She was so thoroughly occupied with the knitting in her lap—a baby-blue blanket—that she barely looked up at her name, Pru. Next to her was a pierced princess: eyebrow, nose, lip, and five studs marching up her right ear, the first with a chain connecting it to the last, and just two studs in the other ear, each with a blood-red little gem. Her hair, lips, and brows were black, but her blond roots were showing.

At the end of the table was a handsome man with sandy, close-cut hair wearing a heather-gray cable knit sweater like he'd just stepped off an Irish fishing boat. Then there was a businessy blond wearing her ponytail so tight that she looked surprised into an instant face-lift, and finally a hippy chick in a way-colorful dashiki and feathered earrings. If I'd been a pollster looking for a random sampling in a mall somewhere, I'd totally pull these people together, never suspecting they had anything in common. Certainly not witchcraft.

Through it all, Bobby rocked and sang to himself and the others shot him worried looks until Chip asked, "What's his deal?"

"Actually," I answered, "he's part of the problem. The reason Olivia called you here is that we think we might have found the source of the sudden insanity plaguing the town. We thought that if we brought it here for you to examine, you might be able to help us stop it."

We had everyone's attention. I took the pendant from my pocket, touching it with my bare hand for the first time. I felt the tingle of power it possessed, but nothing else happened as I let it drop to the end of its cord and dangle for all to see. "We think this is what's been riling up the spirits, fueling them to the point where they can possess and even kill."

"So this guy is … *possessed*?" the pierced princess asked, like she was fascinated rather than repelled.

"Yes."

"And you brought him *here*?" Chip asked, just as Pru gasped, "Tituba's necklace!"

Chip froze mid-rise from his seat at the table, halfway to getting all up in my grill. "Say what?" he asked, turning on Pru.

She didn't take her eyes from the amulet as she spoke. "At the Historical Society we have this sketch of Tituba—the only one, as far as anyone knows—wearing *that* pendant. There's no record of what happened to it after she was arrested. See, the officials used to confiscate all an accused's belongings, but since she was a slave, everything she had was considered her master's, so it wasn't overly strange that it never made it into the record. Where did you find it?"

I looked to the others and Brent gave me a shrug, spreading his hands in invitation, like it was my show.

"We got it tonight, from a girl named Rebecca Simms."

The pierced princess gasped, and all the coven members exchanged a glance.

"What?" Brent asked sharply.

All gazes settled on Irish, who I assumed to be their leader. "She was one of us, once," he said. "But we weren't … edgy enough for her. She didn't want balance. She wanted *power*."

"I'd say she found it," I commented, glancing at the amulet.

"But how did she get it?" Pru asked. "And where? Tituba escaped the gallows. That's what's fanned the continuing belief that she was the one true witch in the whole hunt. The histories say someone was allowed to buy Tituba's way out and she left town, never to be heard from again. I'd have thought she'd take the necklace with her."

"Unless it was sold to raise her ransom," Irish suggested.

"Or passed on to her daughter," I said.

"Violet?" Pru looked contemplative. "It's possible. That would explain how it stayed in the area. By all accounts, Violet was left behind, stuck with the Reverend Parris until his death."

"What happened at Violet's death?" Ulric asked, leaning in.

Pru shrugged. "I could try to find out, but unless they were getting sold or persecuted, no one thought slaves' lives much worth recording back then."

"Ancient history," Chip said, impatiently. "Correct me if I'm wrong, but we're interested in the here and now."

"*Those who cannot remember the past are condemned to repeat it,*" Pru quoted to him.

"You sound like my eighth-grade history teacher." Chip nodded to the necklace. "Shall we?"

Everyone looked at the amulet. Then Olivia looked at us. "We'll need you outside of the circle," she said gently. "We're not attuned to your energies, and they'll interfere with our reading."

I had no idea at all what that meant, but I took Bobby by the arms. He flinched and started to lash out a hand, but then stopped to stroke and sniff at my hair instead. It was beyond weird to feel revulsion rather than attraction at his touch. I stifled the urge to pull back and led him to another table, along with Brent and Marcy. We watched from there. At the table we'd left, the coven reseated themselves around the amulet and began chanting, eyes closed.

I'd never seen magic before—which sounded odd when I thought about the fact that I was facing eternal youth with a boyfriend (assuming I ever got him back) who could move things with his mind, and that I could go ghosty. But I meant the external, power-to-the-people kind of magic. The kind that, apparently, glowed . . . just like the amulet.

True story—the amulet hovered there as we watched, about an inch or two off the table, and shone red. It was the kind of red an overactive imagination might assign the eyes of a demon staring into the house from the bushes outside, waiting to ambush you. It was a good thing I didn't have an overactive imagination. Still, it gave me the creeps.

Finally, I couldn't take the silence or the eerie glow a second longer. "So, the enchantment . . . you can break it?

The amulet dropped to the table with a clatter, but it took longer for its light to ebb.

"The user has bound it by blood," Irish said. "We could, perhaps, shield it, isolate its power, but to stop it . . . if you sever a force like that rather than put it to rest, there's backlash. There's no telling what it might be. It could kill those who are possessed, or lock in the spirits. It could drive them mad."

"So that would be a 'no'?" Marcy asked wryly.

"A 'no,'" Irish agreed. "Perhaps if we had time to study it."

"What if you were able to study the spell book of the original owner?" Brent asked. "Would that tell you what you need to know?"

The man's eyes lit up like a jack-o'-lantern caught in a flamethrower. "Tituba's Book of Shadows? You have it?"

"We were hoping you could help us find it," Brent responded.

The light in his eyes dimmed. "How?" he asked.

"Some kind of spell," Brent answered. "Like a locator."

But already Irish was shaking his head. "That spell book is legendary—people have been looking for decades. It might work if we had a connection. But if I've read it right, this amulet has had at least two owners since Tituba: her daughter, and then Rebecca, to whom it's blood-bound."

"Then any lore you might know," Brent pushed. "Where Tituba lived, where she might have hidden the book."

Irish thought about that. "The only surviving house dating back to that time and associated with the trials is the Witch House. At least according to their promo. It was the home of Judge Jonathan Corwin, who used to interrogate witches there. They run tours now, but not at this time of night. Anyway, Tituba would hardly have hidden it there."

Renfield-Bobby cackled suddenly and slammed a foot down on the ground. He reached down to pick up whatever he'd stomped and popped it into his mouth. My stomach fought to reverse itself. I wondered when his would do the same. Back when we'd first been vamped, a few of us had been silly enough to try real food and drink—and almost got to see ourselves from the inside out.

He saw me looking, and probably turning several shades of green, and grinned.

"Crunchy!" he said, like it was an endorsement. There was a wire-thin leg sticking out from between his teeth. Blood flooded my mouth like bile.

I had to choke it down again before I could rejoin the conversation. "So, what you're saying is that we have to figure out what the town was like back then—what was standing and where she lived."

Daunting didn't begin to cover it.

"I can check the hall of records or the historical society archives in the morning," Brent said.

"I can help," Pru offered.

But I didn't think we had that kind of time. Inspiration struck.

"I know someone who might help," I said suddenly. "But she's a little shy."

All eyes were on me. I mean, not *on* me. That would just be gross. Looking my way, let's say.

I explained.

"You know a ghost?" Irish asked, awed.

"So do you." I cut a glance at Ren-Bobby. He was back to rocking and chanting, but now instead of the "There Was an Old Lady," it was a twisted little childhood song. I knew it well:

"The worms crawl in
The worms crawl out

The worms play pinochle on your snout…"

A sound from outside cut across his song.

Marcy and I exchanged a *look*. She'd heard it too—a car, maybe two, pulling up outside the closed pub … at this time of night.

"We'd better get out of here," I said.

She nodded. The rest looked at us in confusion.

"We have company. Out front," I explained.

Olivia got up to go look and came back a few seconds later. "The police. But why are they here?"

"At a guess," I said, "because of *us*. I have to go, and I don't think my ghost is going to want company."

"You're not going alone to see her," Brent said firmly.

I rolled my eyes at him. "Fine, I'll take Marcy."

"We need someone with"—*vampire strength,* he didn't say—"someone *very strong* here to deal with Bobby, in case—"

"Then I'll go alone. Somehow I don't get the sense that my ghost girl would be comfortable with a guy."

"I'll go!" Olivia said immediately. "I've always wanted to see a ghost."

"This isn't exactly a meet and greet," I said, exasperated.

"I promise I'll be good. You'll barely know I'm there."

"Fine." I took the amulet and stuffed it into my pocket as a knock sounded at the door. To the rest, I said, "I'll call when I have a location or the book." I shot a glance at Bobby. "Take care of him."

"We will," Marcy promised.

It would have to be good enough. The only way to save him was to go. Snoop. Find. Foil.

"Come on, then," I said to Olivia.

She didn't have to be told twice. She showed me the back way out—through the kitchen, all spic and span, shut down for the evening. Brent, Marcy, and Ulric followed behind, ushering Bobby along with them, and disappeared into the night.

15

The cold air slapped us in the face on the way out, a touch of moisture to it, like rain or unseasonable snow might be lurking. But it was only late September; snow would have been *really* unseasonable.

"Brrr," Olivia said, to emphasize the point.

I agreed. Just because the cold didn't particularly bother me didn't mean I didn't feel it. "Which way to the Howard Street Cemetery from here?" I asked.

She looked at me funny. "You do know that cemetery is from, like, a hundred years after the witch trials, right?"

"It's still a couple centuries older than we are, and only a few generations removed from the trials. Didn't generations tend to live and die in the same houses back then?" I'd learned something from listening to Bobby after all.

Olivia thought about that. "I guess."

She led the way, and I picked her brain about magic and what she knew of the mysterious Book of Shadows while we walked.

"A Book of Shadows is the sum total of a witch's knowledge, gained throughout her life," she told me. "At the beginning are spells learned from others, maybe copied down from a mother or grandmother. Then later there'll be things the witch developed herself—potions, spells, castings. It's priceless. A witch would as soon lose her life as her spell book."

"Yet she left it behind."

Olivia stopped suddenly, as if she'd just thought of something. "Wait. Tituba was from the West Indies somewhere... or was it Africa? Her Book of Shadows might not even be in English. We might not be able to read it."

"We'll cross that bridge when we come to it," I said.

Someone had to have a smart phone with an app or *something* that would let us read the book.

I didn't have Bobby's mental mojo to manipulate locks, and ghosting through the cemetery gates wouldn't get Olivia in, but I'd aced my class on lock-picking back at spy school. I was all set to go to work, only Olivia didn't lead us to the gates but around the side of the wrought-iron cemetery fence, where two bars bowed out in different directions like some strongman had gone to town on them.

Someone—the cemetery people, probably—had planted honeysuckle along the fence to climb the bars and cover the gap, but the vines weren't quite thick enough yet for that.

"How long has this been here?" I asked.

She shrugged. "A few months. The locals know about it. Kids like to dare each other to sneak in. Drives Terrible Tommy nuts."

Speaking of the devil, I didn't see his light anywhere, so either he was off duty or occupied elsewhere.

"You sure he had to be driven?"

"Okay, *more* nuts, then," she said, ducking through the gap ahead of me.

I led the way once we were through. I didn't see or sense anything tonight, but I signaled Olivia to stay behind as we got closer to little Jenny's grave. It occurred to me at that moment that I couldn't make contact without revealing myself to Olivia. But I didn't see an alternative. Anyway, the gang and I would be blowing town again and taking on new identities as soon as this was put to rest. I ignored the pang this caused me once again. I'd never thought I was a "putting down roots" kind of gal, but this constant running and hiding wasn't my style either. I wanted a place, I realized, where everybody knew my name. The real one.

I stifled a sigh and focused on my ghost hunt.

"Close your eyes," I whispered to Olivia.

She did, but I couldn't tell if she *kept* them closed, because in that second I vanished, going as insubstantial as a ghost. All I could do was sense the differences and densities of the air around me—including one small, human-shaped form huddled at the base of a stone. I couldn't call out to Jenny in this form, but I drifted close, and the form seemed to startle. Something swept through me—a questing hand?

It felt weird, like butterfly kisses. I backed off just a bit and went solid again.

"Jenny?" I said quietly.

She flickered in front of me, and I caught sight of her for just a second. Big brown eyes, a fly-away corona of red-gold curls, freckles.

I pulled the amulet out of my pocket, not wanting to compel her, not sure I even *could* with it still bound to Rebecca, but hoping it might lend her strength.

"Jenny, can you talk with me?"

I watched the spot where she'd flickered, and slowly she reappeared again, her arms wrapped protectively around her knees, which were drawn up under her long colonial skirts. She looked like she belonged to the era of Betsy Ross, but I was totally no expert.

"Just with you?" she asked, her voice no more than a sigh. "What about your friend?"

She cocked her head Olivia's way, but those big brown doe eyes stayed on me, studying me for any kind of threat or trickery. I wondered what she'd been through in her life, or death, to make her so distrustful.

I debated how to handle it, and decided the truth was the way to go.

"She'd love to meet you as well, but only if you're comfortable with it."

Her gaze flicked to Olivia and back quickly to me.

"Is she like us?" Jenny asked.

"Like us?"

"Dead."

My heart kicked ... or wanted to. I was *not* dead. Or, anyway, not truly. I died every time I left a new self behind. Every time I had to turn away from people and places I'd come to love. Okay, and yeah, I supposed medical examiners might declare me dead if they ever got their hands on me, but—

Focus.

"No." I leaned in to whisper and counted it a victory when she didn't lean away or wink out. "She's a witch," I confided.

Those big eyes widened. "A real one?"

"Why don't you ask her?"

She worried her ghostly lips between her teeth. From the look of them, she did that a lot. Her brows drew together as she thought. It was a really serious look for someone so young. Although, if the dates on her gravestone were right, truly she was older than me.

"Okay."

I motioned to Olivia, who had long since opened her eyes even though I'd forgotten to give her the go-ahead, and she smiled excitedly, stepping carefully toward us. Seeing that I was squatted down in front of a grave, she crouched beside me.

"Can you see her?" I asked.

"I see ... something." She squinted like she was trying really, really hard.

"Olivia, this is Jenny. Jenny, my friend Olivia, the witch."

"The *good* witch," Olivia added.

"The *good* witch," I confirmed. "We're hoping you can

help us with something. If you can, we may be able to find a way that you can rest without having to worry about anyone 'getting' you ever again."

"You mean you want to help me move on?" she asked, but not with anything like enthusiasm.

Olivia more than made up for it. "Was that her? I think I heard her voice!"

I ignored her, afraid to lose my connection with Jenny. "Wouldn't you like that?" I asked her.

Jenny shook her head vehemently.

"Why not?"

"I'm ... scared of heights." Translucent tears started to form in the corners of her eyes.

I don't know what I'd expected, but that hadn't been it.

"Huh?" I asked brilliantly.

But Olivia seemed to get it. "Oh, honey, you think heaven is *up there*," she said, looking where she thought Jenny was, but pointing toward the stars in the sky, which were out in full force.

Jenny nodded, afraid even to look where Olivia pointed. "That's why I hid when the white light came for me. Been hidin' ever since." Her full lip quivering. "Sleeping, mostly, until now."

Olivia glanced at me, as if to see whether I wanted to take this one, but I was at a loss. What did I know about heaven other than that I probably wasn't getting in? Not based on the burn of the crucifix. I was going to have to make the most of this world.

"Honey, heaven isn't a place." Olivia jumped in again, seeing that I wouldn't. "At least, not one we can get to from here. Heaven is about being one with the universe, being linked to God and everyone who has come before."

"So it's like a daisy chain?" Jenny asked, her eyes glowing just a bit brighter.

"Something like that," Olivia said.

Jenny thought, her lips still again as she bit at them like Renfield-Bobby and his nubby nails. "And I get to see Ma, again, and Da and ... God?"

Those unfallen tears in her eyes made them shine with hope. I prayed Olivia was right. I hoped there was a heaven and that it was a beautiful place full of love and lollipops.

"Wait, how do you *know*?" Jenny asked, suspicion suddenly flashing across her translucent face.

"Because," Olivia answered, "in heaven there's no fear or pain. Only peace."

She spoke like she believed it. I didn't know there was a Wiccan concept of heaven. Of course, what I didn't know about Wicca was approximately everything.

"That's what CeCe always said." Jenny brightened. "That's my gran." She hesitated another second. "I'm not sure I'm going to go, you know, into the light. But I'll help you. What can I do?"

Olivia smiled, and I knew from the direction of it that she still wasn't quite seeing Jenny, but they'd made a connection all the same.

"You know the oldest parts of town," I said, jumping

back into the conversation. "The parts that were old when you, uh, lived? We need you to show them to us."

"But . . . why?"

"We're looking for a book—a really old book that someone who lived long ago hid away. She lived in the Parris house."

Jenny's whole face lit up. "You mean it's like a treasure hunt? My sisters and me used to play that. The best place for hiding anything is the tunnels. Everybody knows that. It's where I—" Her eyes got all unfocused and she looked suddenly confused. "Where I . . ." She winked out momentarily. When she flickered back into being, she asked, "What were we saying?"

I bit my own lip, worried about the little ghost girl.

"You're going to take us to the tunnels," Olivia answered, unaware of what had happened.

"Yes," Jenny said, confusion clearing and a smile starting on her face. "My sisters and I used to play there."

I was afraid from her reaction that she might have died there as well. I remembered my "death," but I understood that this was a rarity. Traumatic events tended to wipe the memory, which could account for Jenny's confusion. I hoped bringing her back to the tunnels wouldn't kick-start any painful remembrances. I hated to put her through it, but I didn't see that we had a choice, unless we wanted to lose another day in researching records. It was too late to save Jenny, but not girls like her—older girls who might be targeted by the Salem Strangler. We had to lay him, and

Renfield, and any other spirits to rest, once and for all. I needed my Bobby back.

As Olivia and I stood there, a light hit us square in the eyes. I hissed. My fangs snapped down into place, immediately reacting to the threat.

The light was followed with, "Stop right there. Stay where you are." It was Sid's voice.

Oh *hell* to the no.

I immediately dropped to the ground and scissored Olivia's legs out from under her, bringing her down as well. A shot fired, but it was too late. It zinged harmlessly over our heads, far quieter than it should have been. Silenced?

"Stay down," I ordered Olivia, probably unnecessarily.

I ghosted out, the better to sneak up behind Sid and whoever he had with him. A disturbance pointed me his way, but it was *huge*, way bigger than he and a few compatriots good ghost hunting. There was a fight going on.

I materialized close to the disturbance, in time to catch Agent Sid in my arms as he reeled from a snap kick to the chin by Marcy.

I didn't have time to celebrate the fact that the gang had followed me before a gun was pressed up under my ribs. Sid had managed to keep control of it somehow.

"Stop or I'll blow her heart apart. She might recover … or not," Sid said in his usual no-nonsense way.

Unaware, Brent and Maya continued to battle it out beyond our frozen tableau. Brent went down on his ass when Maya lashed out with a powerful blow to the ribs. He tried to take her feet out from under her as he went down. I wondered who was watching Bobby, then saw him there, eying it all with a bloodthirsty smile as if waiting for the winner to tag him in, or to feast on the loser.

I ghosted again, coming back to myself behind Sid—I hoped. He wasn't ready for the move. I'd gone rogue before the Feds could even guess at my ability. It left him off-balance, grabbing air, and Marcy seized the moment to kick the gun out of his hand.

Sid whirled away and reached into his pocket, coming out with something that looked like a grenade.

"Watch out!" Olivia said unnecessarily from the sidelines.

I hurled myself into him, ready to throw myself on the grenade before he could launch it. I hit Sid with the force of Hurricane Gina. Small but mighty, that was me, especially with the vamp speed. The momentum sent us both crashing to the ground, rolling chest over chassis across the hard earth. We ran up against a grave, the grenade trapped between us. Sid spat in my face, which seemed a girly move, but then Marcy was standing over both of us with Sid's lost weapon pointed at his head. "You can get up now, I've got him," she told me.

Beneath me, Sid cursed and went limp. I was able to take the grenade with me as I rose. To my surprise, it sloshed, as though filled with holy water rather than explosives.

But then Brent and Maya's ongoing battle crashed right into me and the grenade went flying out of my hands. It burst against the gravestone by Sid's head, and Marcy and I shrieked in concert as it splattered us with liquid that burned like the fires of hell.

My instinct was to reach for the burns, to claw away at the skin before the poison could burn me down to bones, but the distraction would get me killed. I whirled on Maya, just in time to meet her fist with my face. I stumbled to the ground, catching myself on one burning hand.

I heard a terrified gasp and had a second to regret that Jenny was seeing all this before a foot connected with my throat and sent me sprawling.

A gunshot went off then, and suddenly, Maya was on the ground beside me clutching her shoulder.

"I've got more where that came from," Brent announced, leveling a gun on the downed agents. "A full clip, I'd guess."

Maya glared but didn't try to take him, and Sid froze as well, knowing he could never get the gun away from Brent before he could fire. And Brent would ... I was pretty certain of that. He'd been one of them before he'd become one of us.

"See to her," he ordered Sid. Sid crawled toward Maya.

Then Brent looked at Marcy. "Find the other gun and stay out of the crossfire."

She did as he said.

"How did you know to come?" I asked him.

Brent didn't risk a glance away from the agents. "Bobby started getting *really* agitated right after you left. I think he sensed something."

Either that or he just wanted to get in some more hair sniffing. "Bobby!" I looked quickly where I'd last seen him, afraid he might have run off, but he just stood there licking his lips, eyes fixed on the blood seeping from Maya's wound. "Down boy," I said, nearly cutting my lip on my own fangs, which were out in full force. The pain of the holy-water grenade was only now settling down to a dull roar.

"The more important question," Marcy asked, "is what do we do with them?"

"It's a through-and-through," Sid announced, after checking Maya's wound as Brent had ordered. "She'll be okay but she needs a hospital. She's lost a lot of blood."

"Cuff them," Brent said to Marcy. "We'll send help once we're safely away."

"They'll be sitting ducks for the spirits, Maya especially," I said. I didn't exactly have a lot of love for the two, but I couldn't see trussing them up and leaving them to die defenseless if the Salem Strangler or some other disgruntled ghost should wander by.

"Well … crap," Brent answered.

In my peripheral vision, I could see ghost-Jenny flinch at the language, but, really, that summed it all up.

"Maybe they'll both fit in the trunk?" I said.

"You mean the one with the big hole in it?" Brent asked.

"Oh, right."

16

We left Sid and Maya their phones, their clothes, and little else. We'd confiscated all weapons and lashed 'em up with duct tape. It had a lot more give than zip ties, and we figured they'd have themselves out in an hour or so. It would have to be good enough. We couldn't either leave them to die or let them free to organize a state-wide manhunt. We'd have to throw it open to fate. It was more of a chance than they'd give us.

It meant we didn't have a lot of time.

We crowded into the Crown Vic—Ulric driving, my boy Bobby mashed in the back between me and Olivia so he wouldn't be anywhere near the door handles and there'd be instant bail-out should he pump up the crazy. Marcy and Brent were up front, sharing the passenger's side of the bucket seat, and the ghost girl was doing a ride-along in the amulet.

I could feel her warmth in my pocket, almost like a kitten curled up to sleep. Olivia phoned her people, who told us that they'd "let" the authorities squeeze some rumors out of them—about something strange going on at the wharf earlier—and sent them to investigate. With any luck, the cops would find Rebecca passed out on shore, exhausted from her swim. But luck, good luck anyway, hadn't put in an appearance since we'd hit the haunted city.

If only Sid and Maya had joined the cops on that wild goose chase, they wouldn't be cluttering up my list of concerns.

"You think they'll be all right, right?" I asked anyone who cared to answer.

"Right," said Marcy.

"Any agent who can't get out of those bonds isn't worth their salt," Brent added.

"Still, I wish we could have cast some kind of protection or no-see-um spell over them, just to be sure."

"If only it worked that way," Olivia said. "I can't just cast spells with no prep or supplies."

"So you need stuff to cast spells?" Marcy asked, fascinated. "Like ingredients—*'Double, double, toil and trouble'* and all that?"

Renfield-Bobby took the lines and ran with them, turning them into a sing-song. "Double, double, toil and trouble, take the world and make it rubble." Then he cackled to himself like he'd made a wonderful joke.

"I didn't know you knew Shakespeare," Brent said to Marcy, ignoring Bobby's insanity.

Marcy gave him a blank look. "Shakespeare? That's Looney Tunes."

It was Brent's turn with the clueless look.

"Witch Hazel," she explained, exasperation in her voice.

"Oh, uh, right."

Olivia looked at them *both* like they were nuts. "Witches call the power that exists in all things and focus it toward whatever they want to accomplish—healing, change, whatever. That's how we work. Different 'ingredients,' as you call them, help achieve different results, call different energies."

"So when you say the amulet is bound to Rebecca by blood, what kind of result is she going for?" I asked.

"That's some way-darker magic than I mess with, but based on what's happening, I'd guess there was probably some kind of power stored in that amulet. You can do that, you know—store up power for later. Rebecca probably used her blood to unlock it."

"To call spirits?"

Olivia shrugged. "She might have been going for one in particular. I have no way to know."

"Tituba," Brent said. "Or maybe Tituba's daughter. She wanted that Book of Shadows pretty badly."

"*Wants*," I corrected, because I just couldn't see Rebecca going peacefully. She was too much the drama queen. And it took one to know one.

"Whatever. But Tituba didn't die in Salem. Rebecca wouldn't have had any luck calling her spirit."

"Maybe she put out a kind of magical APB," Ulric

suggested. "*Calling all spirits, calling all spirits: Be on the look-out for a Book of Shadows.*"

We all stared at Ulric. He shrugged. "Hey, it's a theory."

I yelped as my pocket started to burn. Jenny was no longer a warm fuzzy kitten but a hot coal ... or maybe that was the amulet itself, trying to tell me something. I fried my fingers as I grabbed it, but as soon as I touched it, I knew what to do.

"Stop!" I called.

Ulric stopped short, throwing us all forward, making Renfield bang his knees on the seat in front of him and me almost slide off onto the floor at his feet.

We were in front of Red's Sandwich Shop. A plaque on the outside wall announced:

The London Coffee House
ca. 1698
Meeting place of Patriots
before the American Revolution

"What was *that* all about?" Ulric asked, as a car horn blasted displeasure behind us. The driver flipped us off as he went around us.

"The amulet's nearly burning a hole in my pocket. I think we must be close to the Book of Shadows."

"But look at the plaque—the shop was founded too late in time," Brent protested. "The witch trials were in 1692."

Jenny materialized outside the car, a very faint wisp in the glow of the streetlights, as if formed from the mist of the amulet's heat hitting the icy air. She beckoned me.

"I don't know what to tell you," I said to Brent. "Apparently, we're here."

Jenny put a hand on her hip, impatient with the delay, every bit like a modern-day child.

Renfield was the only one of us who didn't have to be told twice. He scrambled right over Olivia and let himself out. On the street, he did an odd sort of hop-skip-pirouette, like a demented court jester. Everyone else skirted around him as they got out, leaving Ulric to park.

Marcy looked ready to suggest, again, that we leave Bobby behind, but with the big gaping hole in the trunk, we had nowhere else to put him. Besides, they said to keep your friends close and your enemies closer. When your enemies and friends were one and the same...

"Come on," I said.

Jenny beckoned again and disappeared behind Red's Sandwich Shop. If we didn't hurry, we'd lose her.

"I'll wait for Ulric," Olivia offered.

I chased after Jenny and found her floating beside the back entrance to a nearby cedar-shingled building. The others caught up to us in no time.

"In there?" I asked, following her ghostly finger pointing the way.

She nodded.

"Is there a tunnel entrance inside?" I asked again.

She gave me a *wow, adults sure are dense* look. I tried not to crack a smile. "Why did you ask for my help if you didn't think I knew anything?" she asked reasonably, her voice like the wind—there and then gone.

"Sorry!"

Brent stepped up to the wall and put a finger to it, as though afraid to commit a whole hand. Instantly, he drew back, looking at it almost in awe.

"A lot of history here," he said. "Plus, it's hollow."

Jenny's glow got a little brighter. "Well, *of course*. It's a bolt hole. Ma and Da said they were built way back when people were afraid of religious per-suh ... per-suh ... per-specution. There were tunnels and secret entrances between some of the houses. People even sometimes used them in bad weather. Then later, the patriots used them to ... patriate."

"Was that her?" Brent whispered. "I think I heard her."

"Me too," said Marcy. "She's like a walking history book. Bobby would love her."

We all looked at Renfield, who'd gone and pressed his ear to the wall as if he could hear inside ... or as if he was trying to hug it. "Yes, oh yes!" he said excitedly. "It calls to me!"

"Uh, guys," I said, "we may want to get out of this alley before someone sees us and thinks we're trying to rob the place or something."

"Ah ha!" Renfield cried. He leapt toward the door and grabbed the handle, which turned miraculously in his hand. It didn't seem very likely that the door had just been unlocked the whole time.

Which meant that Bobby's ride-along had found a way to access his powers.

We were all in serious doo-doo if... *when*... Renfield turned on us.

We all stepped inside, cautiously waiting for our eyes to adjust. Jenny showed up more brightly in the total darkness of the store, especially once Brent, who took up the rear, closed the door behind us.

Renfield clapped his hands together in glee. "Tyger, Tyger, burning bright, grant this wish I wish tonight..."

Jenny stepped back from him like he might hurt her, her eyes wide and her light flickering.

"Stay with us," I begged her. "*Please*. Show us how to get into the tunnels."

"Keep him away from me," she ordered. "He—he's got bedlam eyes. Like before."

"Before what?" Olivia asked.

I'd almost forgotten Olivia was there, just like she'd promised way back at the pub. Jenny's eyes shot to me, as if afraid I'd make her answer... afraid she'd have to remember. Something bad had happened to her down in the tunnels, I was almost sure of it. Someone had hurt her.

She flickered out for a second and I panicked, suddenly afraid that she was gone, but not to peace—hidden away in a huddle of misery instead.

But then she flickered back again, her eyes all confusion. "Where did I go?"

Olivia's eyes welled with tears. "Nowhere, honey. You just blinked and came back to us."

I hated myself in that moment, because I knew I had

to get us back on track, and that might mean causing Jenny pain. I squatted at eye level with the little ghost. "Jenny, you don't have to stay if you don't want to, but I promise I won't let anything hurt you ever, ever again. You don't have to go down into the tunnels with us. Just point the way."

She looked around, as if she could see perfectly in the pitch-dark store. I tried, but her dim glow didn't do much to illuminate anything around her, and even vamp eyes needed *some* light to work.

Brent solved this a second later by turning on a flashlight app on his phone.

I was no expert, but with the books on the shelves closest to me labeled things like *A Moon for Me* and *Everyday Witch A to Z*, it seemed pretty clear to me we were in a magic shop.

"Ah, Solstice," Olivia said, "I love this place. Didn't recognize it from the back."

Jenny faded a bit in the light, but the confusion on her face was still clear enough. "So much has changed!" she gasped. "This is … my mother wouldn't like me to be here."

"Has it changed *too* much?" I asked.

Brent went to the wall and risked touching it again, waiting for it to give up its secrets.

Jenny bit her lip and her gaze went unfocused, as though she were looking straight through the bookshelves and racks and doodads, back to another time. She also approached the back wall, skirting wide around Brent.

"When Missy Farraday lived here, there was a catch,

right . . . " She reached a hand into a cubby full of colorful scarves and rooted around for a minute, her face a study in frustration. "I can't get the catch."

"Can you feel it?" I asked.

She nodded. "But I'm too short. Missy always had to trip it. Or Sarah."

"Can you show me?"

She nodded again and took my hand when I offered it, as tenuous as spider silk. The small, wispy fingers guided my hand past the scarves and slid back to my wrist when she couldn't reach any farther, showing my fingers where to go. I felt around a tiny crevice, like a gouge in a section of mortar.

There was a click, and I held my unused breath, but nothing happened. No wall slid dramatically out of the way. No Batcave suddenly appeared.

"Everything's in the way!" Brent said. "Even if this is the original wall, the display spaces have been built over it. The passage probably can't open."

"Bam!" Renfield said, making me jump. Before we could react, he'd launched himself at the shelves like he had at the outer wall, but this time he acted as a one-man wrecking crew. Scarves flew everywhere. Sweaters fell to the floor. Books and brightly colored jars, crystals, and worry stones, even a beautiful mortar and pestle made from a stone that looked like alabaster, went flying past my head.

"Stop, Bobby!" Marcy cried. "Stop!"

Amazingly, he did, breathing hard as if he needed the air. A human mindset in a vampire body.

"Done!" he said cheerfully. Then, under his breath, "Master will be so pleased. No, *Mistress*, she says. Always Mistress. Dumb. *Dumbdumbdumb.*"

He started to beat his head on the wall, and it gave way beneath the pressure to reveal a narrow little door. Window, really, because it was about chest-height, like a cosmetics counter.

Brent broke the stunned silence. "Probably used to be a dumbwaiter." He pushed Bobby out of the way so that he could check it out, taking his light with him.

"That's not a waiter, it's a window," Marcy said, echoing my thoughts exactly.

Brent peeked back into the room, with just enough light for us to see him roll his eyes. "A dumbwaiter was like a rope and pulley system, to deliver food and drink to another floor without having to carry it up the stairs."

The light went on in Marcy's eyes, "Oh, like a food elevator. I've seen those."

"Right, but it's gone now, and we're here. Can we get a move on?"

"Wow, it's like Maya passed the stick. I thought it was permanently implanted up *her* butt," Marcy said as she passed me to follow Brent into the tunnel. She pushed Bobby-Renfield ahead of her as she went so she could keep an eye on him.

Ulric and Olivia watched each other, not wanting to dive for the opening at the same time. "After you," he said, sweeping her a bow.

She smiled at him tentatively. "Thank you."

Wow, feel the love.

I held back for a second with Jenny.

"Thank you for taking us this far. But really, we can take it from here if you want to rest."

She gave me another one of those *you crazy adult* looks. "I want to find the treasure!"

"Uh, okay."

I climbed through the hole in the wall and Jenny drifted along behind me. Then she reached up to tap a section of wall to close the gap. She looked like she'd been given a gift when it worked.

"I'm getting stronger!" she cried, clapping her hands together and whirling around. There probably wouldn't have been room for all that spinning if she were actually constrained by the physical walls, but as it was . . .

She did seem to be sharper around the edges, but I couldn't tell how much of that had to do with the darkness of the small space and how much was due to the proximity to the amulet. But if the amulet was the cause, wouldn't she have been a lot clearer sooner? Could it be . . . ?

"Lead the way," I said, keeping an eye on her as she moved ahead of us. Everyone flattened themselves against the walls of the narrow bolthole as if she needed the space. Or maybe they did—I remembered the coldness of her hand and could only imagine what that would feel like, passing right through my physical form . . . like the chill of the grave.

It might have been my imagination, but I thought she got brighter and brighter as she went along.

I reached up to tap Marcy on the shoulder. She whirled with a stifled shriek.

"Watch this. Tell me what you see," I whispered in her ear, pulling her aside. Then, "Jenny, come back here a second."

It was subtle, like the difference between eggshell and off-white, but it was there.

"What am I supposed to see?" Marcy asked.

"Did you notice how she grew fainter as she came back toward us?"

"Oh, yeah, *that*. So what?"

"Well, the amulet grew hot when we first got near the tunnels, and presumably closer to the book. Now Jenny seems to be getting stronger and clearer, the closer we get. It's like that game we all played when we were kids—hot and cold. Jenny, do you feel any difference between here and over there?" I pointed down the corridor.

Her brows drew together. "Should I?"

"Nevermind. You just lead on. Take us to any passage-ways you know."

"Okay."

Renfield tried and failed to tug Jenny's ghostly flowing hair as she went past. "Sugar and spice, parsnips and mice, that's what little girls are made of," he cackled.

Nobody corrected him.

We all followed, and after a while, I heard Ulric whisper to Brent, "Is it just me or is she getting brighter?"

If it was clear enough now that even human vision was picking it up, then there was definitely something to my theory. Jenny glowed more strongly with every step until we no longer needed the light from Brent's phone. She tapped out a little beat on the walls as she went, with more enthusiasm than rhythm.

There were way too many people between us now for me to see more than her glow, but I could imagine her glee. For a minute I considered the fact that stealing away the Book of Shadows, and breaking the enchantment on the amulet or draining it of its power—whatever we had to do to keep the town safe—would also kill our girl. Okay, not *kill*, because she was already dead, but steal her spark, sap her strength again. To be able to influence the physical world—play a rhythm, flip a switch—and then suddenly have that stolen away...

I could only imagine it would be like living in hell on earth. Worse even than an eternity without tanning or photo ops.

Renfield continued to slap at the wall, pinching whatever he'd flattened between two fingers and pitching it into his mouth. I tried not to think about kissing those lips again. Ever. The thought broke my heart in two. I wanted my Bobby back. I missed talking with him mind-to-mind, holding him, even being lectured. Without him I felt...incomplete.

The tunnel was littered here and there with abandoned toys, looking infinitely sad graying in the corners. I wondered if the passages had ever been used again after...whatever had happened to Jenny. I prayed she wouldn't remember.

When we hit a bend in the tunnel, Jenny didn't take the turn, but tapped at the wall across from it with her foot until she spun a stone inward. "The other way is a dead end," she explained. "Help me?"

Ulric and Brent rushed to push against the wall where she stood, and it began to slide back and back until it opened into a bigger space. I had no idea where we were anymore, relative to the town above. Definitely not still under the magic shop where we'd started out. Jenny was now glowing brightly enough that we could see into the room revealed. And it *was* a room, rather than another passage. It looked to have been carved straight out of bedrock.

Brent glanced at Renfield, as if he expected him to spout more bad poetry or some historical facts, but he was far too busy using his non-existent nails to pick insect legs out of his teeth. I cringed.

Jenny skipped right into the room and whirled around happily. "Missy and Sarah and me used to play here. Sarah said this was a shelter, like whole families would come down here to 'scape...whatever, but..." Her light dimmed. "But..."

"But it didn't work," Brent finished for her, quietly.

It seemed like a strange thing to say, until I remembered that with his hand on the "door," he'd know what had happened in this room. From the look on his face, it hadn't been a happy thing.

"Jenny," I said quietly, respecting, I guess, the solemnity

of things, but also afraid to scare her. If this place had the memories I thought it did, she might bolt at any moment. None of us could blame her ... or stop her. "Can you show us any hidey-holes? Were there places you and Missy and Sarah secreted things away?"

She turned her face toward me, but very, very slowly. "Huh?"

It sounded weirdly modern coming out of her mouth, but the befuddlement on her face made it poignant as well.

"Hiding places?" I asked.

"Hssst—he's coming," she said, backing up until she hit a wall and faded halfway into it. Then she sank down onto the floor as if she'd forgotten she could go straight through and escape. She balled herself up into the smallest package she could manage, trembling and flickering in fear.

"Who's coming?" I asked, at the same time Brent said, "I know."

"You know what?" I asked quietly. "Who's here?"

"I know where to find the book."

He staggered to the wall farthest from the entrance, like a puppet not in control of his own strings, and started pawing at the wall.

I ignored him.

"Who's coming?" I repeated to Jenny. "The one who hurt you?"

She shook her head as if she could shake off the thought. "Yes," she said, her voice shaking, "the man with the bedlam eyes." She buried her head in her knees with a sob.

Crap. She didn't mean Bobby. His crazy was already among us. Which meant we had company, and it was all my fault that Jenny was going to come face-to-face again with her darkest fears.

"Hurry!" I hissed at Brent, who was squatting on the ground, a section of the hardpacked floor dug up.

"I've got it!" Brent answered, rising with a dingy old book clutched in his hand. It was bound with string—or something stringy, anyway. I didn't even want to think about what it might really be. Maybe sinew from whatever animal had given its hide for the front and back covers. The book was smaller than I'd expected, but there was no mistaking the immensity of the power coming off it.

Behind me came a sharp cry, and I turned to see such a look of avarice on Bobby's—*Renfield's*—face. He wanted the book, with a truly terrifying intensity.

"Watch out!" Ulric cried, as Renfield suddenly charged Brent. Ulric swung Olivia behind him, out of harm's way, and then dashed to intercept. Renfield swatted him away like he was nothing, crashing him into the wall where he went down like a marionette with his strings cut. Olivia rushed to him and began chanting something under her breath.

I had to trust that they'd be okay. Renfield could *not* get control of that book.

I launched myself at him, but was grabbed straight out of the air by an arm that wrapped around my waist and hauled me back to the ground. I landed roughly, and rolled with the impact to come up facing my attacker—only to stare, stunned, into the face Ty McClellan, Ghouligan extraordinaire.

"*Ty*, what are you doing?" I gasped, not getting it at first. Maybe the impact had rattled my brain. Maybe it was on overload.

But he wasn't looking at me. And his eyes ... bedlam eyes, Jenny had called them. They were no longer their own crystalline color, but something infinitely darker, glittering like spider venom. Then I remembered how, back at the officer-involved shooting, he'd been as close to the crime scene as was physically possible. Close enough to catch the ghost fleeing the cooling body of its last host? *Hellfire!*

Ty was staring avidly at the fight Marcy and Brent were putting up with Renfield over the Book of Shadows, as if deciding whether to join in or wait to take on the victor. Marcy was pounding on Renfield's back as he tried to wrestle the book out of Brent's hands, but he might have been a brick wall for all he noticed. She needed help.

I flung myself in that direction, but fast as lightning, Ty grabbed my foot, yanking me back to the ground. I fell hard on my stomach and immediately flipped, twisting the ankle still gripped in his hand, but catching his jaw with my other foot.

His grip loosened and I kicked free, using my good leg to propel myself toward Renfield and the book. The amulet in my pocket flared suddenly, and pain burned its way straight through my side like I'd been branded. The agony dropped me to my knees.

"Enough!" A voice rang through the small room, bouncing around until I thought it might shatter my head. "The book is *mine*. I'll take it."

I looked up through the red haze of pain to see Rebecca entering from the tunnel, her hair tangled and still wet, her clothes clinging to her like eelskin as if she was some sea hag newly risen from the deep.

"Mistress!" Renfield cried, finally remembering. The sight of her gave him an extra burst of strength. He wrenched the book out of Brent's arms and slammed him against the wall for good measure, as if he'd merely been playing with him all along. Then he used the book like a club to hit Marcy upside the head.

"*Never!*" Ty said, blocking her way. "*I'll* take the book. "Little girls like you oughtn't play with power."

Then two things happened at once—Renfield took a step toward Rebecca, ready to present her with the book, and Ty's hand shot out again with preternatural speed, gripping Rebecca by the neck before she could receive it.

Renfield howled, looking ready to club Ty with the book, when Marcy shook off the blow he'd dealt her and tackled him around the legs. Renfield might not have been in a condition to feel her blows, but he didn't have any control over velocity and balance. He started to topple. The book was on a path to slam right through Jenny where she sat shaking against the wall, but Olivia dashed in with a cry and grabbed the book out of Renfield's outstretched hands, spiriting it away.

The near-miss snapped Jenny's head up and her gaze into focus. She saw Rebecca struggling and Ty's hands wrapped around her neck, and her eyes began to blaze.

"No!" she shouted, suddenly growing rock-solid and as present as any one of us, as if something had given her strength. "I won't let you. Nonononononono—NO!" She seemed to grow louder and bigger with each repetition until she was the size of a Bengal tiger. "You won't hurt anyone else *ever*."

She burst out of her crouch, her anger giving her wings. She went for the fighters like a Fury, hands out like claws, fear and determination strengthening her until she was more solid now than ever. Her nails pierced Ty as she punched straight through him at chest level. His eyes rolled up into his head and he convulsed, collapsing even as she flew out again, her momentum slamming her into Rebecca, who clutched at her heart like she was having an attack. She fell on top of Ty, in a crumpled and barely breathing heap.

"Master?" Renfield asked, trying to crawl to Rebecca's side. Marcy still clung to his legs, and he kicked at her viciously, trying to dislodge her.

"Stop, Bobby. Stop! Fight this!" I cried with my head as well as my heart, hoping some part of me could reach him. "Bobby!" I shrieked at the top of my lungs, when he didn't so much as pause.

Then I did the one thing I never thought I'd do again—I leapt forward, over downed bodies and all, to kiss those lips. Even without the benefit of industrial-grade cleansers.

He froze in shock. A statue.

I didn't know who I was kissing, but he wasn't going for the kill, and that was a good thing. I pressed myself to him and breathed against his lips, "*Remember.*"

Slowly, achingly slowly, his arms came up around me, and I knew then. I *knew* this hold, this body, this kiss.

Bobby! my heart cried, and as if he heard me, his arms tightened.

I knew we had company, and that this wasn't really over yet ... but none of it mattered right then. I was afraid to stop for fear of losing him again.

"Uh, guys ... "

It was Olivia. "Uh, can we get out of here before everybody comes around?"

I laughed. It was one of those stress-relief laughs where nothing's actually funny, but you just can't hold in the joy. I had Bobby back, at least for now. *I'd* brought him back. He came back because of *me*. I took Bobby's hand in mine and hung onto it for all I was worth. If he reverted, at least I'd have him held fast.

"Let's go," I said.

Olivia hugged the Book of Shadows to her like it was the most precious thing in the world. Ulric got Marcy and Brent to their feet. Brent swayed a little as he rose, but he managed to stay upright as he limped toward the door. We left Rebecca and Ty where they'd fallen. No, Rebecca and the Salem Strangler, whoever he'd been in life. I hoped they wouldn't wake up and kill each other before we could put all the spirits to rest.

"Get her blood," Olivia ordered me, "and hair. I don't know what we'll need to break the spell, but the amulet's bound to her, so we'll need something of hers for the unbinding."

I could go her one better. Rather than just collect Rebecca's blood, I could take some of it into me. If we couldn't break the enchantment on the amulet, maybe her blood bond with it would transfer to me. At the least, perhaps I could divide its loyalties. I would never let Rebecca use it against us again.

And I *would* find a way to give Jenny peace. She'd more than earned it. I was so proud of her for fighting her demon and making her own justice, all these years later. I hoped it would bring her peace as well.

I pulled Rebecca's jacket aside. My fangs were already fully onboard with the plan, and I sank them deep into her neck. All the action had made me hungry, but even so I could only take so much of her. There was something sour about her blood. Rebecca was rotten, bitter ... but whether it was in body or spirit, I couldn't tell. I pulled back well before I'd drunk my fill and used a strip I'd torn from her jacket lining to catch some of her leftover blood before it congealed. I pulled a few strands of her hair out by the roots and wrapped them in the lining, tucking them into my jacket pocket—the one *not* the one holding the pendant, which no longer burned me like the sun.

Ghost-Jenny followed us out, small and unassuming again. A six-year-old child in form, a tigress at heart. She tripped the secret latch to close the door behind us.

17

As soon as we got into the car, the pendant started to vibrate just a little ... or maybe had been vibrating all along, but I'd missed it in the midst of all the action. I realized after a second that it was more like a purr, a melodic rumble, like it was somehow aware and happy to be reunited with the book. Like there was some kind of resonance between them. Since rising from the dead, I'd come to terms with vampires and telepaths and witches—oh my! Now I had to accustom myself to self-aware objects? A girl could only take so much.

"Is someone ... humming?" Olivia asked.

Then a funny look came over her face. "Wait, I think it's the book."

"Or the amulet," I said.

"Weird."

I laughed. *That* was weird. For a witch, she had a pretty low bar for weird.

"Shut it," I told the pendant. It stopped just like that. Rebecca's blood had to be working through me.

"Where are we going?" Ulric asked, not that the lack of direction had stopped him from putting distance between us and Old Town. Already we were blocks away.

"The Morbid Gift Shop," Olivia said. "It's closed for the night, and the theater's dark. Chip said he'd set up the circle and have it all ready for us."

Ulric didn't say anything in response, but he seemed extra focused on the rearview mirror.

"Everything okay?" I asked him.

"Ye-ah. I thought I saw a car following us, but it turned off at the last cross street and hasn't reappeared."

"What made you think it was following?"

He shrugged. "Too many cop shows?"

"Let us know if you see it again."

The amulet had stayed silent, and the car was now so quiet we could actually hear the chirping of the cicadas or frogs or whatever Salem had that made night noises. It would have been peaceful if it weren't so tense. I didn't trust the quiet.

"Hey," Bobby said into it, his voice warm and deep and totally his ... just like me.

"Hey, yourself," I said huskily.

I leaned into him, resting my head on his shoulder and breathing him in.

"Why does my mouth taste all foul?" he asked.

Ulric laughed and Marcy made a choking sound.

"You don't want to know," I answered. "Trust me."

"With my life," he said.

It was Ulric's turn to gag, but he stopped quickly as we came to the mall and he found a place to park around back, where the Crown Vic might not be quite so visible.

Olivia pulled out her phone to call Chip to let us into the locked mall.

"How long do these spells usually take?" I asked her.

"As long as they take," she answered helpfully. She patted the book. "Let's just hope there's something helpful in here that'll break or block the amulet's power and that we don't have to come up with a spell from scratch. *That* would take a lot longer."

Chip unlocked the doors for us and let us precede him so that he could lock up again. The Morbid Gift Shop exhibited an unearthly glow as we approached. I realized how on edge I was when I saw that the glow I was getting all worked up about was only candlelight, flickering behind the curtains and screens that set off the theater area. I didn't know what had me so edgy, but I had the sense of something pending, unfinished, oncoming. For the life or death of me, I couldn't think what it was. Rebecca and Ty were out cold; Sid and Maya were hopefully still tied up . . .

Brent studiously avoided touching the cage, the coffin, or any of the other antique-looking doodads decorating the gift shop. Based on the tension in his shoulders as he and Marcy preceded Bobby and me, he was feeling the energies anyway. If I had to guess, the proximity of the pendant was making the vibes all that much stronger.

We followed Chip through the curtains into the theater area, where we got to see the candles up close and personal. The chairs that were usually set out for the Gothic Magic Show had been folded up and pushed back to the outer edge of the space, to make room for a huge chalk circle in the midst of which was a pentagram. Olivia's fellow witches were standing around it.

Irish came forward. He looked a lot more... mystical now that he'd ditched the cable-knit sweater for some midnight-blue robes tied with a silver cord.

"May I see the book?" he asked.

Olivia moved out from behind Bobby and me to present it to him, holding it in both hands like an offering and giving it over with a little bow.

"The amulet?" he asked.

I withdrew it from my pocket and let the obsidian stone dangle where it could be seen.

"Place it in the center of the circle," he ordered. No please or thank you. Just do.

I shot a look at Olivia for reassurance that this was what she'd expected, and she gave me the nod.

I expected to feel something when I stepped over the chalk outline of the circle, but there was nothing. Maybe it hadn't yet been activated, or whatever it was they did. I laid the pendant down in the center and backed away as Irish thumbed through the book. His eyes got bigger with every page turned, and I could see Bobby watching him avidly. I wondered if he could read upside-down and then realized that this was *Bobby*. He could probably read upside-down, backwards, in Morse code and even Swahili. The thought gave me the chills. I was fine with him having the information, but not his brain-buddy. And with his memory...

"Blood," Irish said.

I handed the bit I'd collected, along with the hair, to Olivia, since he didn't have any more hands for holding.

"Maybe we should step into the other room," I said to Bobby once everything was out of my hands. "Someone needs to stand guard."

"You trying to get me alone?" he asked, teasing.

"You know it," I answered.

I meant it... as soon as I could be sure we'd be *truly* alone. The smile I gave him was bittersweet.

The pendant seemed to call to me as we walked away. It was like a tug, as from an elastic tether that would pull tighter and tighter with each step I took. But we stopped long before it could become a problem.

Bobby and I stopped outside of the theater area, where he sank to the floor and put his back to the partition wall, signaling for me to join him. I so wanted to just sink into his arms, but more than that, I wanted to be able to see his face, spot the second he changed, if he changed. I was standing guard for internal threats as much as external. If he went ballistic again, I didn't want him breaking up the circle and my chance at getting him back for good.

But I didn't want to be the one to bust him up again, either. I could still feel the snap of his neck beneath my hands and hear his vertebrae breaking. I wondered if it would ever leave me.

Bobby looked sad when I didn't join him. He drew up his legs, ready to get to his feet again at any moment, but then stayed low, beneath any casual surveillance of the store by, say, a security guard on rounds. I paced, too agitated to sit.

On the one hand, I really, *really* wanted to know what was going on behind those curtains. On the other, I could almost feel it. Chanting started, and the power of the amulet began to pulse in time... and me with it. I felt it like a heartbeat. I hadn't realized I'd missed it. Who would miss something they were rarely ever aware of to begin with? But now it filled my chest and reverberated through my body. Every cell vibrated with it. It was as though I'd truly been dead— empty—and now I was full, alive, restless, and sad... so, so sad, because I was going to lose it again. They were going to neutralize the amulet, and it felt like I would go with it.

Jenny floated over to us, skirting the cage and coffin as if she too felt something of their history.

"I feel... strange," she said softly, meeting my gaze. She was solid enough that I could read the fearful wonder shining in her eyes.

"Alive?" I asked, still feeling that phantom heartbeat.

Instead of responding, Jenny froze. "Someone comes."

Bobby suddenly sat ramrod straight, head cocked to the side, listening as though he felt it too.

I dropped to a squat beside him, out of the casual sight line, but I knew that wasn't going to do it. I'd just known things had been too easy. That feeling I'd had, of something unfinished, rushed back at me full force. My fashion senses were sharply honed, but my Spidey-senses... those were still a work in progress.

I saw the problem about two seconds later: two figures converging on the shop from different directions. One tall and one not-so. One male, one female. I *knew* those figures. I'd dated one of them back in Mozulla, Ohio. We'd "died" together on prom night when he'd wrapped his shiny red convertible around a tree with the two of us inside. The girl was my arch-nemesis, Tina Carstairs. I'd recognize the blond bimbo anywhere, even with a black scarf tied over her hair and muting the salon shine. My two least favorite members of my former team of fanged Federal flunkies. I should have known that Sid and Maya wouldn't be working alone. They were the public face of things. Tina and Chaz, being vamps, were a field team. But if they were here, their handlers couldn't be far behind.

"Incoming," I whispered.

I signaled Bobby to go right. I'd go left, and we'd ambush them from behind displays when they broke in. I hoped he'd hold it together that long, but even as I was thinking it, something rose to a crescendo behind the curtain, and I felt it like a fist to my heart. I cried out silently and clutched at my chest, like I could fight off the heart-attack. I couldn't catch a breath, and felt suddenly like I needed one. Desperately.

Which was absurd—unless, with Rebecca's blood coursing through me and with that blood tied to the amulet, we were somehow linked. Was I feeling *her* heartbeat? Her panic? Her gasping pain?

I didn't have time for this! I lurched toward the theater, frantic to stop the spell, forgetting about the incoming agents. Then the shop door burst open behind me and a bolt of screaming agony shot through me, piercing my chest just to the right of my heart, impaling me against the semipermanent wall like a bug to a board. A wooden stake.

"Stop right there!" Tina commanded, maliciously gleeful about it.

I didn't see that I had any choice. I craned my neck around to glare, to face death head-on, and saw Bobby hurl himself at Tina, knocking the crossbow out of her hands and throwing her backward into Chaz, who was coming through behind her. Tina tore at his hair as they went down.

Brent, Marcy, and Ulric poured out of the back, alerted by Tina's oh-so-subtle entrance and my impact on the wall. Using that wall as leverage, I tried to tear myself free of the stake to go to Bobby's aid. The pain blackened my vision and nearly made me pass out. I tried to ghost, but with the wood stuck through me, nothing happened except crippling, rippling agony, shooting through my body so that all my nerves screamed as one.

My heart squeezed one last time as the chant ended, and I shattered. My knees gave out and I collapsed, the stake ripping through me as I went down before catching on bone, keeping me half-upright, sagging like a scarecrow. I could feel the blood, the life seeping out of me, the wood like poison killing the flesh around it.

A white light beamed down from above, blasting through the darkness stealing my vision. I thought at first I was fainting. The cold stopped; the pain stopped. Time froze. But I was still aware, and the light...so beautiful, only it wasn't coming for me.

The beam fell on the face of the little ghost girl—Jenny—lighting her up like the Christmas tree of an overzealous suburbanite. So lovely. So angelic I checked her for wings. Was this the white light people talked about, summoning her to heaven or whatever lay beyond?

All I wanted to do was go toward that light, to find out, but Jenny shrank back from it—fear and longing battling it out on her face.

"Go. What are you waiting for?" I said...or tried to, anyway. I didn't seem to have lips any more. Or if I did, I couldn't get them to move.

But somehow she heard me. "I can't leave you," she said.

"You have to." I didn't know if the light would wait or if it was a limited-time offer, but I knew she had to take it. There was something about that light...glorious, warm, pure. Longing ripped through me like the stake. I wanted to go. But it wasn't there for me. It never would be.

I closed my eyes against the loss until a distant pain forced them open again. Jenny's hands, quickly going ghostly again, were grabbing at the stake, trying to pull it out, but we'd taken that away from her. She could no longer grip strongly enough to finish the job.

Gently, a pair of hands waved her aside, and I looked up into the face of an angel. My angel. My Bobby. He grabbed the stake in both hands and yanked it out in one great heave.

My body finished its aborted slide to the floor and the light started to fade from the room. Or maybe from my consciousness. I sought out Jenny's gaze. "Go!" I demanded.

"I'm afraid."

I reached out a hand, and her wispy fingers closed on it. "You are the bravest little girl I know. You're a tigress. Remember that."

She gave me a tremulous smile and turned her face to the light, taking a step away from me, then another, still holding my hand, letting it slide from hers until we barely touched fingertips.

"What do you see?" I asked past a lump in my throat.

But nothing else existed for her any more. She was being pulled into the light, a smile growing on her face that it hurt to look on. Rapture. Something I'd never get to experience. As even her fingertips left mine, the light exploded into a golden-white supernova of sparks and then she was gone. Just... gone.

I blinked away blood tears and saw Bobby gazing down at me with so much love and concern that it was like my very own slice of heaven.

"Bobby?" I asked, sounding like I'd been gargling acid. "Is it... just you in there?"

He let his head drop to mine, going nose to nose with me and saying a little prayer of thanks before raising his head again to smile.

"Just me. I think the spell worked. I'm alone in here. The spirits seem to be at rest. But we need to get you some help."

I looked around—at Brent with an oncoming black eye and a bloody arm where a crossbow bolt must have grazed him, then at Chaz and Tina, crumpled like linen on the floor, downed by my new team. I took in the stunned coven who'd filed out of the theater, Ulric and Olivia standing unconsciously close to each other, and my own blood decorating the wall behind and floor beneath me. I wondered what on earth we were going to do about it all. How did we clean up this mess?

Chip echoed that thought. "You trashed my store!"

"Very authentic," Irish said, "Decorating with real blood."

Chip didn't look charmed, but it gave me an idea.

"How do you feel about coming out of the closet?" I asked them all.

"What closet?" Chip asked.

"Obscurity," I answered. "Look, you might have noticed that we're a little ... different ... from the rest of you. Just like you're different than we are, with what you can do. Special. People are going to fear that, or want to use it or whatever. Our secrecy means they can do it without scrutiny; no watchdogs, no one to tell them they can't. We tried to come out once to the media back when we were first ... vamped." It was surprisingly hard to say, after trying to keep it under wraps for so long. "But the Feds swept it under the rug. Now, though, if we provide witnesses and proof—if people know about us—maybe the authorities will come to us next time something like this happens, and the threat can be put down before anyone gets hurt."

Bobby put an arm around me. "Look at you, speechifying." It was said with pride.

"Who is with me?" I asked, knowing I had at least one on my side. Always. "I think it's time to tell the world. With any luck, the Feds'll be too busy with damage control to worry about coming after us."

"You're crazy," Chip said. "And anyway, the world knows about witches. We're not exactly undercover. People *know*. They just don't believe."

"Maybe it's time to change all that," I answered.

"Count me out," the hippy chick said, surprising me. She stepped away from the coven and flashed us an apologetic smile as she headed for the door. "The school I work for isn't that open-minded. I'm sorry."

Irish looked at the rest of his people, lingering on Chip, who was also surveying the coven, getting nods or shrugs or whatever passed for agreement.

"We're in," Chip answered for them all.

I smiled, for the first time since the white light had come and gone without me. "Good. Because as far as I'm concerned, *you're* the heroes of this piece. You laid the ghosts to rest, saved the town, et cetera and so forth. There won't be any witch hunt *this* time."

"Until they find out that magic started the whole thing," Olivia said.

"People need to know it all—the good, the bad, and the ugly," I declared. "No more secrets. It's up to you to make sure people know the difference between what Rebecca's done and what you do."

In the end, we made the call.

And, more importantly, Bobby, Brent, Marcy, and I stayed for the interview.

The End.

© Olan Mills

About the Author

Lucienne Diver writes humorous vamps, because it's hard to take life seriously when your puppy sits under your desk licking your toes as you type. Her heroine, Gina, got her start in *Vamped* and, as will come as no surprise to those who've read it, subsequently decided she wanted more, more, MORE! Thus, one book became two and two became four. Next, Gina'd love an appearance on the big screen, if only she can find someone fabulous enough to play herself. You can learn more about the author on her website, www.luciennediver.com.